BENEDICT BROWN

A CORPSE IN THE
COUNTRY

IZZY PALMER BOOK TWO

Copyright

To my wife Marion,
my daughter Amelie
and my accomplice Lucy.

Chapter One

I had been summoned.

There was a voice message left on my phone in the dead of night, a taxi waiting for me by the time I got dressed the next morning and then an hour-long journey, speeding down motorways and country roads, to take me to the imposing black gates of Vomeris Hall.

"This is as far as I go, love." The driver didn't look back at me, but squinted out at the grand driveway which was obscured by morning fog. "Got my orders."

I mumbled in acknowledgement and shoved the door open. I wasn't particularly excited about the walk I'd be making in my uncomfortable work shoes.

Outside in the fresh Surrey air, the humidity nipped at my face and I immediately wanted to go back to bed. The taxi was backing out so I knew I'd have no such luck. In front of the gate, there was an unmanned brick hut with a small silver intercom on the side. Wishing I'd worn my winter coat, I pressed the button.

"I'm here to see Mr Porter." There was a crackle but no reply. "My name's Izzy Palmer."

Clumsily stuck to one of the stone lions on guard at the entrance, a video camera panned from left to right. A moment later, I heard a loud click and a door to the side of the main gate jerked open.

There was no word of welcome, which was odd yet entirely in keeping with all that I knew about Aldrich Porter. In the four years I'd worked at his company, our hermit-like owner had never set foot in the office. I figured that, even if he was about to fire me, I'd at least have bragging rights with my colleagues at this unexpected rendezvous.

Feeling like a child stepping into Narnia for the first time, I walked through the opening in the thick stone wall. The new realm I had entered felt even colder than the rest of England. The fog hung in the air, close enough to touch, and the dew on the lawn looked frozen, though we were well into August.

They said there was supposed to be a heatwave coming, I thought and a shiver ran down my back like a drop of cold water. *So much for the English summertime.*

I crunched my way up the sloping gravel drive. On either side of the path, neatly kept gardens were laid out. Topiary animals loomed over me, punctuating the long hedgerows. Eagles, stags, dragons and foxes continued the job of the security camera at the gate. They didn't welcome me to the Vomeris estate so much as warn me that there'd be trouble if I put a foot wrong.

The fog drew back like the folds of a curtain and the hall came into view. From first glance, I could tell that the main building had been constructed in the seventeenth century, whereas the wings were newer additions, no doubt commissioned by later generations of the Sherwin-Nettlehurst family who had originally owned it.

Ha, who are you kidding?

Fine. I admit it. I know nothing about architecture. I looked it up on Wikipedia in the taxi. My actual first impression was, *Gosh, that's big and ugly.*

The façade of the beige-brick house was incredibly wide. Presumably built to give as many people a view of the gardens as possible, it had ended up looking like a stretched-out workhouse, ripped straight from the pages of Oliver Twist. It was ostentatious, impressive and kind of horrible. Countless chimneys sprang up from the rooftops, stone gargoyles adorned the windowsills and each section of the building was a different height, as if a careless child had built it out of wooden blocks.

Arriving at the black front door, which was entrapped within an immense stone arch, I got the impression that nothing about this place was designed to encourage visitors.

There was another intercom, another buzz and crackle, but this time a human voice replied. "Side door," was all it said.

Once I'd followed the long path around the house, the idea that I was being sent to the tradesman's entrance was reinforced by a small metal sign which read, *Tradesman's Entrance,* nailed to an unremarkable brown door. I passed through it and the temperature dropped five degrees.

One short, dark passage led to another, with doors on either side giving on to the kitchen and utility rooms. Peering into these unpopulated spaces, I imagined that they had once been run by a pack of staff who, over the decades, had gradually been replaced by modern appliances and lower standards.

I was enjoying gawping at this strange, silent world when a sudden intrusion made me jump out of my smart trousers and blouse.

"2917!" I screamed, as a thickset, elderly man appeared from an adjoining corridor.

"Excuse me, Madam?" He spoke in a soft, deferential manner and wore a neat white shirt and black waistcoat. It seemed safe to assume he was an employee of the house.

"Oh, just a number I shout when something scares me. It's not in any way connected to my credit card and you should forget it immediately."

Smooth.

"As you wish, Madam." His kind face remained politely neutral. "If you would follow me, Mr Porter will see you in his study."

Without waiting for my reply, he turned back the way he'd come and I trailed along obediently. He was well into his twilight years and looked pretty wobbly to still be butlering. Taking us down the portrait-lined hallway, past fancy rooms that I desperately wanted to nose about in, he had to pause every ten steps to stretch his right leg.

"Old war wound." He glanced back over his shoulder to offer this explanation and I tried to do the sums and work out which war it could have been.

Battle of Hastings, maybe? The Trojan War?

Despite the grandeur of the property, there was something rather stale about the place. The carpets were old and dusty, I could see cobwebs in high corners and even the butler's uniform could have used a clean. I suppose it was all too much work for one old fella and I doubt he got any help from his bosses.

At the far end of the house from where I'd come in, my guide stopped altogether and motioned to a closed door. I felt nervous for the first time. It was not so much the idea of coming face-to-face with a man I'd always regarded as mythical, but the possibility of what lay beyond that gloomy portal. Until I opened it, I could be the new director of Porter & Porter, or headed to the unemployment centre. Let's be honest, I knew which one was more likely.

The butler limped off and I got up the courage to knock. When there was no answer, I pawed the handle gently and the door creaked open. That much was easy enough, but I was having trouble taking the next step and entering the room.

Stop being such a wimp. What's the worst that can happen?

Thanks for the pep talk, brain, but a number of terrible events could be set in motion. I could lose my job and end up on the street. Don't forget that we have zero transferable skills and are uniquely suited to our very undemanding role at Porter & Porter where no one in four years has realised how entirely unnecessary we are!

But we live with Mum-

Would you please just shut up and let me be nervous for once?

I swallowed my fears and stepped inside to discover a long room lined with bookshelves that were stuffed to bursting with green and red leather-bound volumes. Their shiny gilt lettering looked like landing lights on a runway, drawing my attention to the man sitting silently behind the oversized desk at the far end of the room.

The owner of the house was bolt upright in a high-backed, leather chair. The only photos I'd seen of him were from a decade earlier and, in the intervening years, the once stick-like Mr Porter had grown even thinner. And yet, he dominated that room despite its size. With his closely cropped grey hair and balled-up fists thoughtlessly resting in front of him, he had the look of a retired gangster surveying his kingdom.

On the wall just behind him was something equally sinister; a macabre collection of mounted skulls, with animals of every size from mouse up to moose staring back at me over Aldrich Porter's shoulders. He hadn't registered my presence and continued staring at a point somewhere up near the ceiling.

"Sorry, Mr Porter." I was still standing by the door. "I knocked but…"

I was about to deliver a no doubt sterling explanation for the intrusion when I realised that he still wasn't looking.

Oh, Gosh. Not again.

I could feel my heart pumping faster as I approached the desk. His eyes were open but his gaze was empty and lifeless. It was as if someone had pressed pause on his existence and he couldn't click back to life until the command was reversed.

There was no sign of blood, but from the stillness of his chest, as I stretched my hand out towards him, I could tell that he was most definitely-

"What are you doing in here?" His gaze twitched to lock on to me.

"Mother's maiden name: Gibbs! AHHHH!"

"Who are you, girl?" He wasn't dead after all. Just... asleep?

Urghhhh, sleeping with his eyes open. It would be less creepy if he was dead.

"Izzy Palmer, sir. You asked me to come." I felt like I'd been called to see the headmaster and straightened up to pre-empt any accusation of slouching.

"Oh, I see." He begrudgingly accepted my answer and then smiled a little as if nothing weird had just happened whatsoever.

I'm a rude person so, without any invitation, I pulled up a chair and plonked myself down – it helped me get through the heart attack I was experiencing. The room had fallen silent again and he sat looking at me like he was trying to figure out an optical illusion.

As he sized me up, the skeletal beasts on the wall behind him cried out in manifest terror. It reminded me of my bedroom back home, except, instead of posters of pop singers from my adolescence, whoever had decorated it was a big fan of death.

"I wanted to meet you in person," he eventually told me. "The woman who single-handedly tracked down Bob's killer."

"Single-handed!" I laughed at the idea that little old me could have done such a thing. "I don't do anything single-handed. My mum still has to help me get my arms in my winter coat when I'm wearing a big jumper."

He adjusted his position in his seat and continued as if I hadn't spoken. "The thing is, I don't know how I should feel about you. You solved the murder of one of my oldest friends and simultaneously denied Porter & Porter the managing director I had personally selected to take over from me."

He spoke as if the inconvenience of David's absence was a greater crime than Bob's death. I wished that my sweet, incarcerated boyfriend had been there to support me; this whole episode was far weirder than I'd imagined.

To calm myself down, I tried to take in the room around me. Porter's desk was covered with objects, yet phenomenally neat. It reminded me of a case of exhibits in a museum. Everything had its place, right down to the pens and ink cartridges that formed a neat border around a cricket ball on its stand. Nearby, there were family photos, wooden stamps shaped like lotus flowers, and a large, exotic seed pod no doubt from some large, exotic plant.

From where I was sitting, the photos were upside down but I could make out a faded image of Mr Porter on his wedding day. There was a more recent one with his five grown-up children in front of Vomeris Hall and, in the centre of the desk, one final photo of his eldest daughter, dressed in the cap and gown of her university graduation.

After years of rumour and office gossip, the combined effect of his obsessive neatness, sadistic hunting trophies and doting paternal pride was difficult to make sense of. I tried to fit it all together but it wouldn't go.

The silence had gone on too long and I was considering saying something when he spoke. "I suppose I should offer my congratulations at least. You achieved what the police couldn't."

"It was nothing." I might have blushed a bit.

You are so humble, Izzy, not to mention modest. Someone should give you a medal for how humble and modest you are.

Shut up.

"It got me wondering whether I was wrong about you." He tipped his chair at an angle and bounced gently back and forth but never stopped looking at me.

"How could you be wrong about me? We've never met before."

"True, true." His index finger flicked out in acceptance. "But I keep a close eye on the company and, somehow, you slipped beneath my radar." He looked into the middle distance and I was worried for a minute that he'd fallen asleep again.

Multi-millionaire Aldrich Porter really wasn't the person I'd expected him to be. Known as a shrewd investor, he was a legend in the financial industry. Yet, in person, he was an odd mix of hard-headed businessman and loveable grandpa. Part Steve Jobs, part Dick Van Dyke.

Snapping from his trance, he sat forward once more and opened the top desk drawer. "Anyway, it's a shame, but you'll need to sign this."

I looked at the stapled A4 document which he slid across to me. "What is it?" At least I would finally find out what I was doing there.

"I'm not someone who believes in charity." He took one of the fountain pens from its place and began to dismantle it, laying out the pieces before him, like a soldier stripping down a pistol. "Even with my own kids, I didn't want to spoil them, so I've never given them any handouts. I told them when they were young they could work for me or find another job. No one ever gave me a free ride and look what I've achieved."

I flicked to the last page where a figure stood out above Mr Porter's signature.

"£25,368? Sorry, Mr Porter, I still don't understand."

His eyebrows raised as if I'd just offended him. "Obviously it wasn't my idea. My advisor told me we should get out in front of any potential legal action so I'm offering you a year's salary plus an additional stipend. I calculated the amount based on any grievances you might have suffered."

His words clicked together in my head and I came to understand something of the man who'd been rattling off enigmas for the last five minutes. "You're talking about Bob trying to have me killed aren't you?" I had to breathe in deep to process what he was saying. "Bob, the monster you created and supported right to the end. Bob the rapist and wannabe murderer."

I thought I'd injected enough outrage in my voice but he clearly didn't catch it. "That's right." He smiled, swapping personas once again.

"And you think you can put a price on that?"

He picked up the cricket ball and tossed it from hand to hand. "What I *think* is irrelevant. I've based my calculations on hard fact. Taking into account emotional impact and inconvenience, whilst factoring in the knowledge that it was your boyfriend who turned out to be the killer. It's a more than fair settlement."

"How did you know that David was my boyfriend?"

Past tense, Izzy?

I said, shut up.

"As I told you, Miss Palmer, I keep a close eye on my business."

I couldn't bear to look at him right then, but the alternative was a lion skull or the jaws of an alligator. I turned away altogether and gazed out through the window, across the great expansive lawn. I had no doubt that Mr Porter knew the exact cost of every single item he possessed. From the topiary bushes to the antique books on their ancient shelves, there was a price tag for each of them, carefully filed away in his brain.

A surge of anger shot out of me and I addressed him once more. "In which case, you'll know that I'm not interested in money."

He laughed at me. It wasn't just a snicker, it was a full-on, stomach-shaking roar at the idea that someone could place money anywhere but the top of their list of priorities.

"Fine, don't think about the money – think what you could do with it. You could move out of your parents' house, or visit all those places you've only read about. You could go up the Nile, on the Orient Express, or over to the Caribbean."

Wow. He does know a lot about us.

I stood up from the chair to look down on him. "You think everyone has their price, don't you?"

What are you doing? You don't even like your job! Sign the paper, Izzy.

Unimpressed by my protest, he was still smiling. "I think that most people realise what a difference not being poor makes."

I opened my mouth and was just about to tell him what I thought of his offer when something stopped me and I knew that my time at Porter & Porter was over.

"I'm with you on this one, Sir. I didn't earn that money and so I won't accept it. I hereby resign my post at your company."

No, Izzy, whyyyyyy? If we're leaving anyway, you could at least take the cash!

"Very foolish." He swivelled round to look at his computer as if he was no longer interested in me. "I'd come to think you were smarter than that."

"And I think you can shove your money back where it came from."

12

Chapter Two

I couldn't wait to get out of there. I'd never in my life met someone so completely self-satisfied. It was worth being £25,000 worse off just to see the look on his face, though I could tell he would have forgotten about it five minutes later.

I don't know what had come over me. Something about that place and his manner had turned me into a rebellious teenager. I was broke now and jobless and, while I still had my pride, that wasn't going to make breaking the news to Mum any easier.

The fact is that I hated my job and should have left Porter & Porter years before. For some reason, I'd never been able to and it had taken this strange morning to force my hand. By throwing Porter's offer back in his face, I could finally move on.

Back out in the hall, I couldn't remember which direction I'd come from so it was lucky that the elderly butler emerged just then from a nearby room. I half wondered if he'd stuck around to listen.

"If you'd follow me, Madam, a taxi is on its way."

I probably didn't hide my anger very well as, instead of walking meekly behind the nice old chap, I fell in step with him, determined to understand something of the weird world I'd caught a glimpse of.

"How long have you been working here?"

He looked at me like I'd just burped out *God Save the Queen*. "Forty years in all, Madam. The Porters have only been here for thirty though." He paused to stretch his leg. "You might say that I came as part of the package when Mr Porter bought the house."

"All that time having to suffer that man's arrogance. I struggled with ten minutes."

"I couldn't possibly comment." Despite the layers of buff and polish to his voice, there was an undercurrent of roughness – the occasional note from an East London upbringing.

We crossed back through the house and, when we got to the tradesmen's entrance once more, I had something to ask him. "What's your name?"

He bowed his head to me deferentially. "Gladwell, Madam."

"No, your first name?"

"Stephen Gladwell."

I stuck out my hand for him to shake. "It was nice to meet you, Stephen. Thanks for showing me around."

He smiled and I was glad that I could lighten up the stuffy ritual of his servitude just the slightest bit. He spun on his heel, presumably off to see to his master's every whim, while I made my way down the drive.

At the gatehouse, I had to wait for my taxi to appear. It turned up fifteen minutes later with a passenger already inside.

"Hello, Izzy. I'm Mr Porter's investment manager, Audrey." She got out and fed some money back to the driver without taking her eyes off me. "I'm sorry I couldn't be here when you arrived, but I'm going on holiday this afternoon and had some things to plan."

"Good to meet you." I recognised her immediately from the graduation photo on Mr Porter's desk.

It was hard to know if it was through coincidence or design, but she fitted her name perfectly. She was dressed only in black and white, like she'd stepped out of an old film. Her obsidian hair was in stark contrast to her china-white skin and her clothes looked as if they'd been sewn for her by well-trained mice. She wore a knee-length panel dress, cut in a 1950s style, but with modern touches to it. I was pretty confident that she was the most beautiful person I'd ever met.

"Dad might not have mentioned it, but we were both very impressed with what you did. We read all about it in the paper and he even phoned the new director in your office for her account of Bob's murder."

"Oh, that's nice." I always know just the wrong thing to say.

She smiled and so I copied her.

"Really, Izzy. You did something incredible and you should be proud."

It was hard to imagine anyone more different to me. She was rich and plummy and the way she held herself was so confident it scared me. I liked her nonetheless. There was incredible warmth to her and, the more she said, the more I found myself falling for her effortless charm. She spoke as if she was about to let me into an incredible secret and I was desperate to hear what it was.

"Anyway, I mustn't keep you. It's been a pleasure though." Her smile was like the sunrise. I wanted to scream and beg her to be my friend, but she was already walking off towards the house.

Go on, do it. Ask her if she ever comes to Croydon.

Don't be ridiculous. People like her never go to Croydon and people like me shouldn't be anywhere near Vomeris Hall.

I watched as she disappeared through the side gate and had to resist calling after her. I forced myself to get in the taxi and, on the way back to south London, tried to make sense of my brief encounter with the Porters. Our esteemed patron had been so amazed by my detective work that he'd broken his long isolation to fire me in person. Perhaps he hadn't been impressed by my appearance in his home though. Maybe I should have dressed up as Sherlock Holmes and talked in riddles to entertain him.

And if that run-in wasn't enough, then there was his daughter. When I was sixteen, we'd gone on a school trip to Paris to visit the Louvre. The Mona Lisa did nothing for me. Surrounded by tourists and stern security guards, I could barely see her, despite being the tallest person there. But later that day, when our art teacher gave us half an hour to explore on our own, I found a tiny, untitled sketch by an artist I'd never heard of and stood transfixed by it. It was bare and simple, but heartbreakingly beautiful. The woman staring back at me was so real, so perfect, that she stayed with me for days. I felt the same about Audrey Porter. It was as if her image had instantly burned itself onto my retinas.

I had the taxi take me straight to P&P so that I could pick up my possessions as Mr Porter had made it clear that my resignation, was immediate.

Three months had passed since Bob's death and things had changed in the office. The new security guy was young and efficient and didn't appear to know anyone's names. He waved me through from his post at the entrance. I still felt guilty that poor old Jack – the secret drugs kingpin – had ended up in jail.

That wasn't the only difference though. There were signs all over the place about reporting workplace bullying and sexual harassment and the new manager Amara had even setup a mentoring programme to support younger members of staff. It was all change, and all the better for it.

I picked up my usual escort as I walked to my desk.

"Don't do this to me, Izzy!" Ramesh was at his dramatic best/worst. At least I'd texted him from the car so that he'd had time to process my news. "Have you thought for a second what impact your absence will have on anyone else? No, of course you haven't. You're selfish, Izzy. Entirely selfish."

I gave him a sympathetic pat on the back. "I'm taking you out to dinner on Thursday to make up for it."

That sorted him out. He was suddenly all smiles. "Ooh. Can we have Lebanese food? I have a hankering for baba ghanouj."

"We can have whatever you like. Just don't make what I'm about to do any more difficult than it has to be."

He put his arm around my shoulders as we arrived at my workstation. "I solemnly promise that I won't."

My deskmate Suzie squeaked in welcome. She made a little *chin-up* gesture so I figured that Ramesh had already told her (and the rest of the office) about my departure. I took an empty box from beside the copier and began the short, painful process of clearing my personal effects.

Ramesh lasted about four and a half seconds before breaking out in wailing tears. "Whyyyyyyyy?"

"Ra, you promised!"

"I'm sorry. I'm just a bit sensitive today." He spoke through the sobs.

I stopped what I was doing to comfort him. "You'll be all right. I know you will."

"That's easy for you to say. The future suddenly looks so uncertain." His big wet tears splashed down on me as I gave him a hug.

"I know, mate. But everything will work out in the end."

He took a deep breath and tried to get his emotions under control. "You're right. I just need to be brave."

He wasn't the only one. After I'd emptied my drawers, packed up my trademark smiley clock and stolen the stapler – which I felt rather attached to after nearly five years working together – there was no longer any sign of me in the Porter & Porter workscape. I took one last look towards David's former office and that's when the flood of contrasting emotions washed over me. I'd have managed to hold it together if Ramesh hadn't started crying again.

"It's just so sad!"

I motioned for him to come back over for a hug of my own. "For once, I agree with you. It's not that I had a nice time here; if I'd never taken the job, no one would have paid to have me killed and I wouldn't have ended up going out with a murderer, but still…" I was unable to finish the sentence because I'd buried my head in my friend's shoulder to let it all out.

As Ramesh and I continued our cry-in, Wendy came by to be rude, proving that some people never change.

"It will be so difficult to replace you, Izzy" she spoke in her happily aggressive monotone, "because I haven't got a clue what you actually did here."

Saying goodbye to the semi-human banshee of P&P certainly made me feel better about leaving. I raised myself up from Ramesh's soggy shoulder, and tried to communicate exactly how I felt about her.

"Wendy, dear Wendy, why don't you stop trying to make everyone around you feel miserable and go back to your stamp-collecting convention?" It felt oddly wonderful to finally answer back to her.

She seethed at my comment, rocking from side to side like a furious penguin before spitting out the best comeback she could come up with. "Freak!"

What's got into you, Izzy? You're a whole different person.

Too much?

No, I like it.

Some of my more pleasant colleagues formed a guard of honour for my departure. Despite everything that had gone on with Bob, Will had done his best to act human over the last few months. He was sweet and supportive as I left and made noises about meeting up sometime. Amara even made a little speech and I had to resist asking her to adopt me.

So that was my time at Porter & Porter over. I left the Croydon Number One building carrying a box filled with nothing very important under one arm and a head full of some truly mixed emotions.

It was my future I was more worried about. The last time I'd been unemployed for more than a week, Mum had packed me off to the job centre with instructions to accept anything that paid more than £5.50

an hour. I wasn't looking forward to telling her my news.

I managed to delay this confrontation for as long as possible by feigning sickness under a duvet for a few days. I spent this time trying to think up different careers that I might be suited for.

Systems Analyst?

I don't know what that is.

Astronaut.

Nope, too tall.

Life model?

Too fond of wearing clothes in front of people.

Reality TV contestant?

Too fond of wearing clothes in front of people. These are really good suggestions though. Thanks!

By the Thursday, I'd finally got up the courage to tell Mum I'd lost my job.

"That's brilliant, darling!" She is never one to go along with my expectations. "You can finally start your own detective agency."

There was no one else in the house right then. I could see my real dad tinkering with his car on our driveway for some reason, my stepdad was in his newly built studio in the back garden and Danny, my long-term crush/occasional lodger/the victim of my man-eating ways, was back in Africa healing the hungry.

"Mum, I'm not setting up a detective agency. I solved one murder, that doesn't make me a private eye." I lay back on the sofa, hoping she would run out of steam as she paced up and down in front of the fireplace.

"What are you saying, Isobel?" Her voice reached a new level of squeaky surprise. She only ever calls me Isobel when she's really worked up about something. "It's what you were born to do."

"Seriously, Mum. Don't you think you're being over the top?"

She held me in her gaze, her face a master artist's depiction of befuddlement. Instead of answering my question, she walked over to the mantelpiece where one of my stepdad's easels was standing. She flipped the pad that was resting upon it to reveal a hand-drawn logo of 'The Clever Dick Agency'. The dot on the *i* was in the shape of a bullet hole.

"This is just a rough idea that I had Greg design. Obviously the name is pending your approval, but I think it works rather brilliantly."

I would love to have given her my opinion, but I'd buried my head in a cushion so that Greg wouldn't hear me screaming from way out in the garden.

"Mum, I appreciate your input," I told her once I'd calmed down a bit. "But I've asked you not to interfere in my life so much."

"And that is exactly why I've waited until now to show you this." Everything about the way she spoke made it clear that I was being incredibly uncooperative. "Do you know how long it's been since your stepfather came up with the idea for the logo?"

The flip chart had become a regular tool in her persuasive-mummy arsenal. In the previous month alone, she'd put on a presentation on the pros and cons of sticking by David, a five-year plan to get my amateur poetry to a wider audience and a hearty testimonial on the wonders of a gluten-free diet.

I could see that some soft diplomacy would be required. "Mother – my dear, dear mother – thank you for caring so deeply that you'd go to all this trouble for me." I stood up and walked closer to her with a caring expression on my face. "Obviously, in a perfect world, I'd jump at the chance of being a detective. But have you considered that it's probably not the best paid job?"

"Ridiculous, sweetie. I popped along to see Alan at the bank months ago and he ran the figures. He predicts that, with some clever advertising and hard work, you could make more than double your previous salary."

I had to hand it to her, she'd done her homework.

I tried a different approach. "But what makes you think I'd be suitable? I imagine you've noticed that I'm rather tall. How could I blend into the background when trailing a suspect? It would make stakeouts trickier too."

"Izzy, my love, you haven't looked closely enough at what Greg's come up with. It works on so many levels!" It was as if she'd put me on mute whilst I tried to reason with her. "Clever dick? Don't you get it?" She stood in front of her display like the pretty girl on a gameshow.

"Yes, mother. I get it. I just don't know if I'm cut out for detective work."

She continued her presentation. "*Clever dick*, like someone who knows a lot, and *dick* like a private eye." She put on a New York accent for some reason. "*And you might just be both, little lady.*"

With her fingers pointed at me from her waist like two pistols, she froze in space, waiting for me to react to her inspirational plan.

"I'm lost for words."

"I knew you'd love it." She did a little dance.

"We'll have to talk about this later. I'm going out tonight and I need to get ready."

An unconvinced furrow appeared on her brow. "It's only two in the afternoon, Izzy, and I've got so many ideas to go through with you. I've come up with a jingle and an advertising campaign and we have to talk..."

I made it out of the lounge and halfway to my room before she could complain. I zoomed up the stairs, pulled my door shut then pushed the chest of drawers in front of it to make sure she couldn't follow me.

To continue the theme of that lazy week – and to push all fears of what I would do next with my life out of my brain – I spent the rest of that afternoon reading. Many people consider 'And Then There Were None' (previously known as 'Ten Little Outdated Racist Terms') to be a high point of Dame Agatha Christie's literary output. To those people I say, *yep, you're probably right.*

I have come across no other work of fiction that is so economical, so tightly plotted and so absolutely thrilling. It is the paperback equivalent of a three-minute pop song or a short-sharp plunge on a rollercoaster. It is my go-to book when I need to blow the cobwebs from my brain so I figured it was the perfect choice that day.

I got all the way to chapter ten before I was interrupted.

"Hello, Izzy?" I recognised the familiar throaty grumble. "This is Dean Shipman from Bromley."

"Hi Dean, this is Izzy from West Wickham. But I think we know each other well enough now that we don't have to say where we're from anymore."

He breathed heavily down the phone for a while in his typically stalkerish manner.

"Whatever. I'm just calling because I have something important to say."

He and I had spent a good bit of time together since our disastrous first and somewhat less horrific second date. In the meantime I'd found him to be an odd-humoured, excessively secretive and downright strange person who, for some reason, I enjoyed hanging out with.

"Don't tell me, Dean. You finally got another girl to go out with you?"

"How did you know?"

"Had to happen sometime," I explained. "Law of averages, isn't it? There's about three billion women on the planet, I couldn't be the only one stupid enough to fall for your Tinder trap."

"Well, anyway. That's the reason I'm ringing. The day has arrived for me to cash in the favours you owe me."

Chapter Three

So much for time to myself. Three hours alone at home was all I got before someone forced me back out into the world. Dean wanted me to go to his work of all places to pick up "some important equipment" of all things.

The *X-Tec Spyware* head office was on the far side of Bromley so I had to take two buses – TWO! – to get there. He'd provided no other information than the address. This didn't strike me as particularly strange coming from Dean. By his standards, it's perfectly normal to invite a lone young woman out to an otherwise abandoned factory on a wet, gloomy evening.

He'll probably lock you in a cage and make you wear his mother's clothes.

Don't be so harsh. Dean is all right really. Once you get past the various layers of creepiness, he's a pretty much decent bloke.

My brain is generally less trusting than I am.

"So who's the lucky lady?" I asked when he opened the factory door dressed in a rather nice black shirt and trousers. I'd never seen him wear normal human clothes before.

"Her name's Samantha and we've been getting to know each other online for a while. We're meeting up for the first time tonight." He wore the disgruntled look I liked to think of as *The Dean* and poked his head back out of the door to check there was no one following me.

I didn't make a snide comment in reply because I'd promised myself I'd be good. "That's nice, mate. I'm really happy for you. But, if you've already been talking to her, what do you need me for?"

He unlocked a steel door with an enormous ring of keys, once more glancing about as if someone could be in there with us. "It's different in person. I get nervous and say the wrong thing. I don't want to spend hours talking about the time I had my appendix out or complimenting her on her elbows."

I followed him up a loud metal staircase. "A guy I was dating once told me I had very attractive calf muscles. It made me worry he was planning to harvest them so I immediately broke up with him."

"Exactly." He opened one final door and we came out in a surprisingly stylish, ultra-modern office. "I genuinely like this girl. I don't want to mess it up."

I wasn't really listening because I was busy checking out the nice view overlooking a lake with woodland in the distance. "Dean, should we even be in here? Did you nick the keys or something?"

"Yes, Izzy. I stole the keys."

I immediately turned from the window and walked to the door. "I knew it. We shouldn't be-"

"…to my own office."

"What?" I probably looked a bit goofy as the reality settled in.

"I'm the boss here. This is my office."

"Oh." I probably still looked a bit goofy. "Sorry, I thought you repaired computers or something."

He fixed me with an unimpressed glare. "That's okay, Izzy. But, just so you know, I founded this company when I was still at uni and we now have offices in twenty-seven countries. So, yes. I'm allowed to be in here."

"Wait, it's your company!?" What's a stronger word than goofy? What's an adjective that describes a person with their tongue hanging out, their head a-cock and saliva dribbling from their mouth?

I don't want to be one of those women who instantly finds a man sexier because he has a lot of money but… bloody hell, Dean's loaded!

Quick, ask him out again!

Shut it.

"Okay, so… what do you need me to do?" I tried to sound normal whilst subtly wiping my chin.

"It's a cinch. I've got an app to install on your phone and an earpiece for you to listen in to our conversation. All you have to do is tell me exactly what to say throughout the date."

I had to sit down at his very attractive, evidently hand-carved desk as it was all getting too much for me. "You're Billy-Loads-of-Money, why don't you tell her that?"

He didn't seem impressed. "I don't want a girlfriend if the only reason she's with me is my Aston Martin or the villa in Tuscany."

"You have a villa in…" I'd never hyperventilated before, it was quite an interesting experience.

"My mother has always told me that I should only spend time with people who like the real me."

"The real you is a geeky Christian Grey!" I admit, I was getting overexcited.

"Izzy, get your head in the game. Are you going to help me or not?"

I was meeting Ramesh at eight at the Lebanese place in South Croydon. Dean was meeting Samantha up in town shortly after. I got halfway through my meze starter before I had to do anything.

"Start by saying how nice she looks," I said into my phone and the words appeared on the screen in neat black type. "But remember, don't single out one body part in particular. That would be weird."

"Good evening, Samantha. You look lovely this evening." I could hear everything they were saying through the earpiece.

"Tell her she's got a cool handbag," Ramesh added. "It goes perfectly with those shoes."

I grabbed the phone back from him to hide the streaming video that we were seeing through Dean's spy-glasses. "No, Dean. Don't say that unless you want her to think what everyone thinks about Ramesh."

"Fascist!" Ra replied through a mouthful of falafel.

I set the phone back down in the middle of the table and listened as Samantha and Dean made small talk about London transport. "That's good, Dean. Keep it nice and breezy like I told you. No heavy topics and try not to insult her."

Everything I said to him was turned into text by the app he'd designed and transmitted to the tiny screen on his glasses. It was a bit like Google Glass only somehow seedier. You may be wondering whether I felt guilty that we were conning this girl, but I was having far too much fun to be worried about that. How often in my life will I get to act like a spy?

"I love this place," Dean said, pulling back a chair for Samantha to sit down. "I came here once with my mum."

Though the chic Italian restaurant he'd chosen was dimly lit, I could see that Samantha was way out of his league. She had big hair and long eyelashes and I'd clearly have my work cut out.

"No, Dean. Don't talk about your mum!"

"Ahh, that's sweet," Samantha replied. "Me and Mum always go out together. She's my best friend." She launched into a five minute description of their relationship complete with photos.

Huh, shows what we know.

"Yuuuuuuum!" Ramesh spoke over her – not that she knew it. "This is the absolute best baba ghanouj I've had since the last time we came here. Waiter!" He waved his arms around like he was drowning. "Waiter? Can we get some more baba ghanouj?" Every word he'd shouted had come up on the phone to be beamed to Don Giovani's in Soho.

Dean tapped the microphone on his glasses in warning. "It's funny you should say that, Sam, because I was just thinking how much I like it when only *one* person is talking. That's the great thing about being with my mum."

Samantha looked confused for a moment and then smiled in agreement.

"Message received, Dean," I replied. "Ramesh, shut your mouth."

Dean wasn't finished. "I really like Italian food. I'd say it's better than any other Mediterranean cuisine. Especially Lebanese. I'd go so far as to say that I'm not interested in Lebanese food in the slightest."

"We understand, Dean." I shot Ramesh an evil glare. "Now stick to the talking points we worked on. You're starting to sound crazy."

"Yeah," Samantha was trying her best to understand. "I love pizza."

"I don't have anything against Lebanese people," Dean raced to clarify. "I'm just not into that kind of food."

"Oh… all right." She smiled again awkwardly. "I'm not sure I've ever eaten it."

"Dean, talking points! Ask her if she's travelled much?" I dipped a carrot baton into my hummus and grabbed my glass of wine.

"So, talking of foreign countries. Do you like travelling?"

I took a deep breath and listened to their comparatively natural conversation.

"I still haven't forgiven you for leaving P&P," Ramesh shout-whispered across to me. I knew I shouldn't have let him order wine.

I kicked him under the table. "Just because you speak in a hoarser voice, it doesn't mean the phone can't hear you. If you need to say something, cover the microphone."

"Oh, good. Because I have to tell you how angry I am." He didn't sound angry. He sounded drunk after two glasses of red.

"So, Dean." Samantha was really pretty when she smiled and she was positively grinning at her date right then. "What is it that you do exactly?"

I took my hand away and spoke into the phone. "We've prepared for this, Dean. You can do it. Just don't tell her that she wouldn't understand."

"You…" he began but then ground to a halt.

My heart was suddenly racing. I was far more invested in Dean finding a girlfriend than I had any reason to be.

"I work with computers," he finally managed to spit out, sounding not too different from a computer himself.

"Oh, interesting. What kind of thing?"

The image on my phone didn't show me Dean's reaction but I could imagine what it was like. Another ten seconds of awkward silence followed.

It finally occurred to me that I wasn't doing my job. "Say, *I have a company which designs high-tech surveillance products.*"

"I have a company which designs high-tech surveillance products."

"Impressive." Samantha certainly looked impressed. "What sort of thing do you produce?"

"Spy-glasses for one," he blurted and I thought we were done for.

"So gadgets and that kind of thing?" She hadn't cottoned on. "Very James Bond."

"I'm going to order another bottle," Ramesh announced as Sam went back to talking about her mum.

I remembered to cover the mic again. "No, you're not," I said, but he was already gesturing to the waiter. "Ramesh Khatri, you know what you're like when you have more than a couple of glasses."

"Don't be ridiculous, Izzy. I'm feeling great tonight, I very much doubt anything bad will happen."

It was too late. Our presumably psychic waiter had appeared and was uncorking a decent-looking Rioja.

As we polished off our starters, things seemed to be progressing well up in Soho. They covered all the usual first-date topics and Dean did a good job of pretending to be normal. I offered the odd pointer, but most of the hard work was his.

Sadly Ramesh wasn't doing quite so well. My erstwhile friend was in his usual three-drinks-in phase of melancholy reflection. "Everyone leaves me!" His head was laid flat on the table in front of him and the tablecloth was looking swampy from his tears. "First Smokey, then Patricia and now you." His girlfriend Patricia was finishing a Master's year in Edinburgh. As far as I could remember, Smokey the hamster was his childhood pet.

"I'm not going anywhere, Ra." I'd already reminded him of this several times but he clearly needed the reassurance. "We'll still see each other every week, just not at work."

I was only half concentrating on him as Samantha had shifted the conversation round to more serious topics.

"I found out at the end of the relationship that my ex had been lying to me for years. That's why, whenever I meet someone new, I say straight off that I will never allow myself to be treated like that again."

I swear the video feed was shaking as Dean sat listening to this. I could practically feel how nervous he was.

Luckily, I knew just what to say. "Tell her that, for you, there is nothing more important in a relationship that genuine honesty and that you're not the kind of guy to lead a girl on."

Gosh, it felt so good to be helping out my nerdy friend. As Samantha practically melted at his reply, a warm buzz passed over me.

This must be how it feels to do charity work.

The thought that we were tricking poor Samantha once more flashed through my mind and I once more ignored it and thought, *spying is fun!*

With a lot of help from me, Dean managed to navigate the rocky waters of relationship talk. He'd come a long way from our first meeting, when he'd informed me that I was too tall to work in a zoo because I'd scare the children and that my taste in movies was "wrong."

It was my other friend I was worried about. Ramesh had got up to do a karaoke version of Eric Clapton's "Tears in Heaven", only there was no karaoke at The Mezze House so he sang to the family at the neighbouring table.

I managed to pull him back to his seat and we made it through the main course without any further incident. Eleven point eight miles north from our location, Dean was growing in confidence and

Samantha was clearly having a great time. I caught a glimpse of his reflection in her wine glass and the smile on his face looked like it would burst his cheeks.

The good thing about Ramesh is that, when he doesn't stop at three glasses of wine, he perks right up again by the fifth. At nine thirty, some traditional Lebanese entertainment started up. There were two men dressed a bit like Aladdin with flaming swords that they waved about as they twirled between the tables. A dancing woman with a veil and an impressive midriff accompanied them and everyone clapped along to the music they were performing to.

Inevitably, Ramesh joined in. He did a limbo under the men's swords before twerking with the belly dancer. I'm not sure they were particularly happy about it but no one complained.

"So, Dean," I heard Samantha say rather seductively through my earpiece as they, and I, started in on desert. "Would you like to have children?"

One of the sword dancers popped up beside our table just as she asked the question and I accidentally inhaled the baklava I'd taken a bite of. It got lodged in my throat and I banged my fist down to get Ramesh's attention but he was having too much fun backing up into the poor Lebanese woman to notice.

I told you we should have gone for the pistachio ice cream.

Well, thanks for that, brain. That will be really helpful when we're looking down from heaven because we're dead.

I wasn't the only one freaking out. Dean was umming and ahhing in my ear and had taken his glasses off to clean them. One of the Lebanese swordsmen had finally realised that I was choking to death and tossed his muscly arms round me in a Heimlich manoeuvre.

I couldn't let Dean down so, when Ramesh saw what was happening, I pointed to the phone and managed to cough out, "Children! Babies!"

With one almighty compression, the baklava shot from my mouth and landed neatly on Ramesh's plate on the other side of the table. He wasn't looking though as he'd picked up the phone to advise Dean.

I couldn't hear what he was saying because the biggest cheer of the evening had just gone up for the Lebanese hero who'd saved me. Once the noise had died down and I'd thanked my rescuer, I turned to Ramesh.

"Ra, tell me exactly what you said."

He smiled like it was no big deal. "Relax, Izzy. I told Dean to tell her how he really feels." *Phew, dodged a bullet.* "But, if he wants my advice, I'd say that kids are way more trouble than they're worth."

"Ramesh, you moron!"

I grabbed the phone from him but the feed had been cut and the screen was blank.

"Dean, talk to me! Dean, are you there?"

Chapter Four

As bad as I felt when I woke up the next morning, I had the comfort of knowing that Ramesh would be much worse off than me. It wasn't that I really owed Dean anything. I mean the favours he'd done me were pretty minor by most people standards – helping me spy on Ramesh because I thought he was a murderer is no biggie, right? But I still wanted to help him and, as he hadn't answered any of my calls or messages since he'd switched off his glasses, I had to think that I'd done the opposite.

I lay in bed and looked at the sky through a slit in the curtains, as I searched for positives. Number one: I hadn't drunk too much. This is a big thing for me. I consider hangovers to be a form of fast-action karma and try to avoid them like a self-inflicted plague. Number two: All the drama of the night before meant I hadn't been thinking about what a jobless no-hoper I now was. And, number three: I didn't have to go to work so could allow myself a nice long lie in.

About seven seconds after compiling this sunny list, my phone started ringing. I picked it up and tried to make sense of the time (nine seventy-five??) and understand why I hadn't put it on Flight Mode before bed. The number flashing at me was not in my phone book and, as the only one I know off by heart is my best friend's from when I was at junior school, I didn't recognise it.

What kind of selfish person would call before noon?

I answered the phone to find out. "Hello, Izzy Palmer. This is Izzy Palmer speaking." That didn't come out quite as I was hoping.

"Evening, Izzy." The voice on the other end was distant, and not just metaphorically speaking. Judging by the greeting, they appeared to be in a different time zone from me. I glanced at my screen again and saw that it was a +66 number, which didn't tell me much.

"Hello." What else could I say?

"It's Audrey, we met the other day at Vomeris Hall."

"Oh wow, Audrey! I'm so touched that you'd call from your holiday. That was incredibly nice of you to think of me." Okay, there were plenty of other things I could have said but this is the nonsense that came out of my mouth.

"It's not a personal call, I'm afraid."

"Oh?"

"I'm about to get on a flight home and I have to ask you something before I leave. Could you come to Vomeris Hall tonight?" All the smooth assuredness was gone from her voice and she sounded tired and jumpy.

"Sorry, Audrey. I don't understand."

She stopped and I could hear her suck a deep breath into her lungs. "You're right. I'm getting ahead of myself. I do that when I'm stressed. Listen, what I'm about to tell you is in strict confidence, no matter what you decide."

"Okay." My hand had begun to shake from holding the phone up. Her nervousness was clearly infectious.

"Dad's dead. I believe someone from the house must have killed him and I need you to work out who did it."

I wondered for a moment whether this was a prank. "Are you serious?" I took her silence to mean just that. "Shouldn't you go to the police about it? They're much better equipped to deal with this than I am."

"No, Izzy. I want you there." There was a flash of confidence in her voice that reminded me of our first meeting and I knew I'd find it hard to refuse anything she asked. "If it comes out in the press that Aldrich Porter has been murdered in his own home, it will be a terrible scandal. All the hearsay and conspiracy theories that would be dragged up by the press could kill the business. The only thing that can mitigate it is if we know who the murderer is from the beginning."

I let the line crackle for a moment before replying. "I'm sorry, but I don't see what good that would do?"

"It's called getting out in front of a story, Izzy, and I won't have it any other way."

"But isn't it illegal? I mean aren't you supposed to report a death?"

"Yes, but Daddy had a friend who's high up in the local police force. My brother spoke to her and she says that, as long as we report it officially within seventy-two hours we're unlikely to have any trouble."

"Sorry, is that normal?"

"No, Izzy. Of course it isn't. But Daddy's given a lot of money to the local police society over the years and they'd like that to continue. And besides, no one's going to care about the details. By the time the police get to Vomeris Hall, you'll have the whole case sewn up for them."

That's an awful lot of trust she has in us, I thought, and I guess she read my mind somehow.

"I know you can do it, Izzy. After what happened with Bob, this should come easy." She sounded like my mum. "If you don't come now, it will be too late. The police will storm in, the damage to my family's reputation will be done and any evidence that could help you solve the crime will be bagged up and taken away."

"I'm really not sure about this." My brain ran with contrasting thoughts. The idea of incriminating myself at another murder scene didn't seem very appealing, but the image of me running about that great big house, preferably in a trench coat, fired up my imagination.

"We'd pay you of course. £50,000 today, transferred directly into your account."

"Fifty grand!?" I'm not sure I'd ever heard of that amount of money before, let alone had it.

"That's right and another fifty on Sunday afternoon when we tell the police what you've discovered." Perhaps she was trying to shock me to death.

"A hundred K!?"

"Izzy, I'm counting on you."

If she'd started the conversation by saying this, I'd have done whatever she wanted. Oh, and the money helped too. Suddenly it was no longer a case of whether I was going to investigate Mr Porter's death but how.

"I'll need to tell a few people."

Three whole seconds passed before she said, "Fine. I trust you. But please be discreet."

A checklist was forming in my brain. Things to take, people to talk to, plans to put in motion. "Of course, but I have one more question. When you say you think your dad was killed by someone at the house, do you mean your employees?"

"No. Our servants have been with us for years and they would gain very little from his death. All four of my siblings were there and I imagine that one of them is responsible."

"Do you really think they're capable of murder?" Okay, that's two questions.

She let out a sad laugh down the phone. "Oh, yes, Izzy. I'm quite sure any one of them could have done it. You'll see what I mean when you meet them." She was already resigned to having a murderer in the family and I knew right then what a weird lot the Porters were. "My plane's boarding soon. I'll have to go." I could hear her pulling away from the mouthpiece. "Be at Vomeris Hall by eleven tonight, British time."

My phone fell silent and I was about to jump from bed and get busy when I realised that, if I was starting my evening at eleven that night, I would need a lot more sleep before then.

I know it's not the most exciting beginning to an investigation – sorry about that – but if I'd spent the next two days racing around looking for clues without a wink of sleep, not only would it seem highly unrealistic, I'd have got all cranky. No, it was better for everyone involved that I got another hundred and forty winks.

I guess my brain stayed busy whilst I slept.

You're welcome.

When I woke up at twelve, not only was I feeling refreshed and ready to take on the world, I had a pretty clear idea who to talk to first.

Visiting time was two o'clock.

Chapter Five

As an unconvicted prisoner awaiting trial, David was allowed three visits a week. His parents, niece and great-aunt took up most of these slots but, whenever they couldn't make it for some reason, they'd let me know. Chloe was away with her friends at a festival that weekend and so I'd booked in to visit.

"Izzy Palmer! As I live and breathe."

"David Hughes? Fancy meeting you here!"

To avoid an excess of crying, as had occurred at one of our earlier visits, we'd worked on a number of jokey routines to lighten the mood.

"I didn't expect to see you in a place like this!" His melodic Welsh voice rose in feigned surprise.

"I heard that the food was good so I thought I'd check it out."

We were beaming away at one another. It probably seemed out of place, surrounded by largely grim-faced men in grey, discussing the harsh conditions of their confinement with their loved ones.

I've never been one to go along with the crowd and I embraced my role whole-heartedly. "Bloody marvellous to see you."

"You too, Izzy." At some point, David generally brought us back to reality. "How's everything at P&P?"

My resignation had been overshadowed somewhat by Audrey's phone call so I decided to save the news for a future visit. "Great. Will bought another silver suit. Amara is doing a really good job in your absence and Wendy is convinced that Ramesh has been eating her yoghurts, whereas I'm pretty sure that she has some form of lactic amnesia and immediately forgets that she's the one who scoffed them."

"Sounds like a case for the renowned detective, Izzy Palmer." His voice was warm and encouraging. "I'm surprised you haven't been searching through the rubbish for fingerprints."

Being the person who had brought my boyfriend to justice did make our relationship somewhat more complex than most. To be honest, my feelings towards David changed on a daily basis. When I thought back to the brief time we'd shared as a couple, I was sure that I would love him no matter what. But when I imagined him standing over our colleague with a knife, it was a tiny bit more difficult. I knew all of the terrible things that Bob had done, but murderer's moll was not a role

I'd previously dreamed of filling.

"I doubt the police would believe me." I was having trouble losing my jokey tone. "Maybe I'll win them round when I hand over Mr Porter's killer."

Smooth, Izzy. Real smooth.

David looked at me like I'd set out to offend him. "That's not very funny."

I made an inappropriate, *whoopsie!* face, which made everything a million times worse. "Sorry, David. I didn't mean for it to come out like that. It's one of the reasons I came here today. I mean, I came to see you obviously-"

"Is it true? Is Aldrich dead?" I hadn't expected him to be so shaken up.

I almost apologised again, as if I was the one who'd killed him. "Yes, I'm afraid so. His daughter Audrey phoned me this morning."

"I can't believe it. I can't believe Aldrich Porter is gone. I was pretty sure he was invincible." His gaze flicked down to the floor and he sat motionless for five ticks of the prison clock then straightened his back to speak. "When I first arrived in London, I felt so lucky to be working in the same office as this great man. I looked up to him like he was some sort of benevolent king."

I wanted to reach out my hand to comfort him but remembered just in time that physical contact was prohibited in the visiting hall. I felt terrible. As if his own situation wasn't bad enough, I'd just told him that his mentor had been killed.

What is it about Porter & Porter that attracts death and corruption?

"I'm sorry you're suffering, David. Audrey's asked me to go to their house and see whether I can identify the killer." I paused. I didn't want to rush him. "Mr Porter called me there a few days ago because he was curious about me but I couldn't get a read on him. I need you to tell me what he was really like."

David returned his focus to me. "I worked under Aldrich for seven years and can't say I truly knew him. He was incredibly supportive, had an eye for talented staff and ran his business in a way that terrified some and amazed others. I wasn't the only one who worshiped him back then but he wasn't particularly close to any of us. Even Bob didn't see him much outside the office."

I should have taken a pad to make notes. "Why did he step back from the business? Do you know what was going on with him at the time?"

"He never told anyone." David ran his hands through his hair. It was shorter than usual – a pretty standard prison cut by the look of it. "I know he'd got divorced a while before but, beyond that, I could see no real explanation."

"Did you ever go to Vomeris Hall?" I shifted in the hard, plastic seat.

"Never. Until now, the only person I'd met who'd visited was Jack's daughter Pippa. She went to the house when they paid her to keep quiet about Bob's assault. Like I said, Aldrich kept his private life completely separate. I'd met his kids at company functions and Audrey worked with us in Croydon for a couple of years but that was the end of it. He treated me like a son at work but never phoned on my birthday, if you see what I mean." David frowned despite his joke.

I let the information sink in and found my next question. "And, after he retired, how did he stay on top of developments in P&P? It was still his company; he must have wanted to know how things were going."

"That always surprised me. We sent him monthly reports by e-mail but he never responded to them. He wasn't interested in company growth or new markets opening up. The only thing he liked to influence was hiring, firing and promotions."

It surprised me too, considering what Mr Porter had told me about the close eye he kept on the company. "What about his kids? What did you make of them?"

He put his elbows on the table and let out a sigh. "Audrey's nice. We were quite good friends when we worked together. I mean, she's scarily talented – the best researcher I've ever come across and a whiz at picking her father's investments – but she's a kind-hearted person. The others were different though. Her brothers, Cameron and Edmund, were dripping with arrogance. I swear they thought everyone who worked for their father was their own personal servant. They'd turn up in Croydon and order us around like they ran the place."

"And the other girls?"

He smiled a little. "Daisy wasn't around much, but Beatrix was a

36

character. She was like a sexy vampire who haunted the office to snare her prey. I was married back then and she could never forgive me – not that it stopped her trying it on." He turned his eyes to the ceiling, as if reliving some tucked away memory. "I shouldn't be too harsh. That was a decade ago now. She's probably grown up a lot since then."

I was trying to keep my thoughts in order for when all these names had faces added to them. "The youngest of them is about my age, right?"

"Yep, Edmund's a mere whippersnapper, just like you." He looked sad again and I wished we weren't the people we were, in the place we'd found ourselves. "Listen, Izzy. I have no doubt that you can find out which one of them is responsible, but be careful. It's not a group of people I'd be desperate to spend much time with."

"Thanks, David. I appreciate you caring and I…" I'd run out of words. There were three in particular that neither of us had uttered for a very long time. In fact, we'd only said them once, just before David had been locked away from the world, but they hung over us like a storm cloud in a comic strip.

The rest of our conversation that day was cautious and controlled, as we tiptoed around important topics like his upcoming trial and the uncertainty of our relationship. We tried and failed to return to the light, jovial tone of my arrival and, when it was time for me to leave, I felt exhausted. I had one more stop to make before heading home to get ready.

I had to take three buses – THREE! – to see Ramesh. He lives in a ground-floor flat under the Croydon flyover. It's just about the ugliest house I've ever visited, and has a view of a large concrete pillar on one side and a busy road on the other, but he loves it for some reason. By the time I got there that afternoon, he was practically sober.

"Izzzyyyyyy!" He opened the door to me in a fluffy white bathrobe and shower cap. He was already crying. "Today was only the fourth day ever that I woke up knowing you're no longer my colleague."

"Why aren't you at work today?"

"I am." He spoke to me like I was trying to be obnoxious. "I told Amara I had some emotions to process and she said I could carry out my duties from home." He turned to descend the corridor.

"I can't stay long." I followed after him into the house. "I've got an important weekend lined up."

He wasn't listening, he had plonked himself down next to a large *thing* dressed in his girlfriend's coat and skirt. On the TV in front of him, a man and a dog were juggling telephone books.

"Ramesh, what is that?"

He didn't look up from the screen. "It's 'Star Bright.' My third-favourite talent show from the 1970s."

"Not the TV programme, the doll sitting next to you in Patricia's clothes."

He looked horrified, but kept watching the show. "How dare you, Izzy! She's not a doll. She's a companion pillow and she's the only thing keeping me sane."

"Does your girlfriend realise you're in training to be a serial killer?" The more I know about the other humans in my life, the less I understand. Searching for more rational companionship, I picked up Ramesh's cat, Kiki Dee. She purred wisely in reply.

Ramesh finally paused what he was watching. "As it happens, we're not talking at the moment."

"You and Patricia?" I was surprised to hear this. Though separated by four hundred miles and the Scottish border, the couple maintained a truly harmonious relationship.

"Don't be ridiculous. Not Patricia – Kiki! She's been prissy with me ever since I gave Elton the last Kitty Chow biscuit."

"I see." I tried to sound sympathetic but failed and burst out laughing. "I'm sure you'll make it up before long."

Kiki didn't agree and jumped from my arms.

"Listen, Ra. I've got something important to tell you. Someone's going to pay me to investigate a murder."

"Ahhhhhhhhhhhh!" He leaped into the air, taking his upholstered girlfriend with him. "The dream is coming true!"

"I'm on way home to pack."

He didn't listen. "So are you assisting the police with their investigation? Or is it a cold case that everyone else has given up as a lost cause but you've spotted some tiny glimmer of a clue that will enable you to unravel the truth and catch the killer?"

"No, the police haven't exactly… got to the house yet." As soon as I said this, I realised how weird it sounded. "The family want me to investigate while I still can."

All his excitement was extinguished. "Izzy, are you insane? Have you considered that they're trying to set you up?"

"Urmmm, no. To be honest that hadn't crossed my mind. But in my defence, this is an opportunity that doesn't come along every day." I looked for a way to convince him it was the right thing to do. "It feels like, if my life were a movie, the opening act is already over and nothing worth talking about happened until about five minutes ago. I think I need to do this."

"Honestly, Iz, it's not like me to tell you to be careful, but you need to look out for yourself." He was deathly serious for once but I knew how to persuade him.

"They're going to pay me a hundred grand."

His eyes had dilated. "Yep. Do it. Go for it. That's a hundred thousand reasons I can't argue with."

"I haven't got much time. I just wanted to let you know so that you don't feel left out."

His face glazed over in stony horror like he'd caught a glimpse of the medusa's glare. "You're not taking me with you?"

"I'm sorry. I would, but it's not that sort of case."

His lower lip had started to tremble. "But we're a double act. If we were on 'Star Bright', I'd be the funny one and you'd be the straight-woman. Who'd want to watch the straight-woman on her own?"

He was hugging Faux-tricia worryingly tightly, so I walked over to him. "We're not that kind of double act, are we, Ramesh?"

With a disapproving huff, he slumped down on the sofa.

"Listen, I have to go, but I promise I'll stay in touch. And, maybe, next time we can investigate together."

He pretended to be watching the TV, though it was still on pause.

I knew there was no point trying to reason with him so gave up and moved to leave. "Bye then."

I was at the front door by the time he replied. "You owe me a present!"

"Fine, what do you want?"

"Chocolate obviously."

I should really hang out with women more often – they're far less complicated than men.

"Oh, by the way, it was Mr Porter who got killed." I pulled the door behind me before the barrage of questions hit.

Outside in the street, I tried calling Dean again but it rung a few times then went to his voicemail.

"I'm sorry about last night, I really am. Pick up the phone. I've got something important to say." I waited thirty seconds and was about to call him when my mobile started to buzz.

"Where are you?" was all he said when I picked up.

"Weird question. I'm under the Croydon flyover."

"That's what I thought."

There was a screech and a silver Aston Martin pulled up at the curb.

"Are you spying on me?" I asked when the rear door opened and he stuck his head out.

"No, Izzy. I happened to be driving past and I saw you. Give you a lift?"

He scooched over and I got in next to him.

"Where to?" his driver asked.

"Urmmm, West Wickham." I was starting to enjoy being driven around, though the fact that Dean had his own chauffeur was harder to get used to. "Listen, I'm so sorry about last night. It was going really well and then Ramesh started dancing and I wolfed down my baklava too quickly just as that bloke with the sword popped up and-"

"Don't worry about it." It was hard to know whether he was teasing me. He was dressed once more in his standard utility jacket and cargo trousers – pockets as far as the eye could see – and his crumpled up mouth paused to let out a sigh. "I handled it myself."

"That's a relief. So you didn't tell Samantha that kids are more trouble than they're worth?"

"No, Izzy, I have a brain. I told her that I love the little blighters and, one day, with the right woman, just maybe…"

"You star!"

"Your job was already complete. You gave me the confidence to stand on my own. But if it hadn't been for Ramesh there, setting the perfect example of how not to act on a date, I doubt I'd have known what to say."

"So, you're not mad at me?" I brushed my hand across the fancy leather seat just to check it was as fancy and leathery as it looked.

"No, I'm not. In fact, Samantha and I are going out again tomorrow."

"That's brilliant." I was grinning like an orangutan. "Really, I'm absolutely chuffed for you."

"Let's see how it goes, eh?" For the first time since I'd known Dean, I noticed a touch of shyness in him. "Now, what were you ringing me about?"

"Oh, that…" I paused for a moment as I wasn't entirely sure I was doing the right thing. "Dean, can I trust you with a secret?"

"Izzy, I run a company that makes equipment for spies." He looked back at me like I was the one without a brain. "I'm so secretive, my parents don't even know my full name."

"All right," I took a deep breath. "My boss has been murdered and I need your help."

He looked puzzled. "Another boss?"

"Yeah."

"And you want me to act as your alibi again?"

"No, Dean. I didn't kill the last one and I didn't kill this one. You know you're far too suspicious for your own good." I pretended to be put out but there was no time for theatrics. "I've got about two days to work out who killed Aldrich Porter and I was thinking that I could just cheat."

"Wait, Aldrich Porter the millionaire?"

"I'm pretty sure he must be a billionaire actually, but yes."

Dean looked neither impressed nor surprised. "Okay, how can you cheat at a murder investigation?"

"By using your gadgets and stuff." We were driving past The Crown in Shirley, headed to the bright lights of my small town. "I thought I could set up a bunch of tiny cameras around Vomeris Hall and catch whoever done it!"

He went silent for a minute and looked down at his hands thoughtfully. "That could work. But the cameras aren't enough. You won't have time to review the footage. Tell you what, I'll get my tech squad in to monitor the feeds. They won't mind working at the weekend, they're always desperate to play with the equipment."

"Your tech squad?"

"My senior technicians at work. Imagine four people who look, sound and dress just like me and you'd be way off, because, despite all being very good with computers, they are each quite unique."

"But standard nerds all the same I'm guessing?"

He smiled. It was a rare occurrence so worth mentioning. "Standard nerds who will give up their weekend to help you."

"Sounds perfect. I don't suppose you could kit me out by this evening?"

He didn't reply directly but tapped his driver on the shoulder and said, "Giles, after we've dropped Izzy at home, we'll swing by the office then come back to West Wickham because Izzy never learnt to drive."

Giles confirmed the instruction with a nod, but no one was paying me to be quiet so I made my feelings known. "All right, matey, we can't all afford a chauffeur-driven supercar. Ease up on the sarcasm."

Dean's face ironed itself out a little. "Where would be the fun in that?"

Chapter Six

When I got to Vomeris Hall that night, it felt as if things had already changed. The front gate was open and the taxi was free to continue up the drive to the main entrance. The heatwave that the weatherpeople had been talking about for so long had finally hit.

It was a close, stuffy evening and getting out of the car was like jumping into a pot of marmalade. It was the kind of heat that's so rare in England. The kind that we wish for all year and, when it arrives, wish it would go away again.

I was already sweating by the time I pulled my Mum's oversized purple suitcase up to the front step. I don't know why I'd packed so much stuff. I was only going away for the weekend. I was about to buzz the bell when the door opened. It didn't surprise me that Audrey had anticipated my arrival. I imagine that she lived her life in constant readiness for any eventuality.

"Hi there, Izzy. I'm so glad you've come." Bit of a weird thing to say when your father's just been murdered and you're paying someone to investigate, but it's hardly an everyday scenario so I figured I'd let her off.

"Yes…" I struggled to come up with an appropriate reply. "It's lovely to be here."

Though it wasn't an occasion for smiles and laughter, there was something so comfortable about being around her again. She was rich and brilliant but never intimidating. Dressed in a beige pleated dress with a stitched pattern fringing the bottom, she looked like she'd stepped straight out of the 1940s and I wondered if she styled herself after a different decade for each day of the week.

"Welcome to Vomeris Hall." She spun on her heel, just like the butler had on my last visit, and I hurried to catch up.

As I followed along through a comparatively cosy entrance parlour, she explained the itinerary for the evening. "I've organised a chance for you to meet everyone. Gladwell and my siblings are in the petit salon, Cook will be joining us soon. I'll introduce you to everybody and then you can take a look at the crime scene."

"Lovely."

Get it together, Izzy.

I cleared my throat and tried again. "I mean to say, that all sounds highly appropriate." I think I put a posh accent on for some reason.

Her neatly bobbed hair swung from side to side as she walked. I longed for the confidence that she exuded. She was like every girl I'd looked up to at school and every successful friend I knew who'd left Croydon far behind. She strode down those familiar corridors of her childhood, whilst I bumbled along in her wake, trying not to bump into anything with my suitcase.

"Here we are."

After several hours walking, we came to a grand lounge with exquisite plush furniture upholstered in brightly coloured damask. Huge picture frames covered every wall, but in place of ancient portraits, shiny, new mirrors had been fitted. The light from the chandelier in the centre of the room shot in every direction like a star finally bursting.

Draped over the two largest sofas, the Porter children were arranged like famous actors on the cover of Vanity Fair. Audrey went to join her siblings and I could do nothing but stand and take in the beauty all around me.

"Do come in, Miss Palmer," the oldest brother told me and I did as instructed, leaving my eyesore of a case beside the door.

I sat on an armchair, a few spaces away. They were too gorgeous to look at up close and I was trying to not to think about the fact that I wanted to kiss every last one of them.

"We appreciate you coming." He spoke in a serious, considered tone. It was efficient yet appropriately funereal. "It's terrible what's happened and we'd like this cleared up in as quiet a manner as possible."

A high-pitched scoff went up from the other sofa and the first of the glamorous sisters began to hold court. "Bloody hell, Cameron. You talk as if it's a broken window or a burst pipe. Daddy's dead."

"That's right," the slick younger brother confirmed. "Dad's dead. One of us killed him and we've sent for a Miss Marple impersonator to dig us out of the hole."

I didn't mind the Christie comparison, but I objected to the cynical note in his voice.

Gladwell the butler was in one corner, serving tea from a large silver pot. I was having trouble taking much in right then though because my eyeballs were crammed with too much loveliness. Perhaps the best looking of all five siblings was the only one who stayed silent. Unlike the others who lounged and slouched across the sofas, the third sister sat very upright, her hands on her knees, her knees locked together and her back perfectly straight.

SHE DID IT! SHE DID IT! SHE DID IT!

I can't wait to get her on her own and…

Filthy!

…ask her some questions!

"Can we act like humans for just a little while?" Audrey asked, her voice lowered to reason with her wayward kin.

To help her with this task, I unexpectedly found my voice. "Perhaps someone could tell me exactly what happened last night."

"Dad was murdered." Brother number two wasn't letting up on the sarcasm.

"Please, Edmund, it was your idea Izzy should come here and we all agreed. Stop being such a brat." I could tell that Audrey was the voice of reason whenever one was required.

"As you all know, I wasn't being serious and now that she's here, I'm dead set against it." The light from on high caught his pale eyes and seemed to dwell there. Whereas his older brother was showing the first signs of mid-life spread, Edmund was sleek and well turned out. His hair perfectly coiffed into a wave-like peak and his complexion one step beyond natural, I imagine he spent more time in front of a mirror each day than I did in a week.

Audrey hadn't given up on reining him in. "Let's all try to get through this, shall we?"

He got to his feet to campaign to his older siblings. "Well, I'm dreadfully sorry to kick up a stink, but Dad's gone and you're all acting like it's no big deal."

"Calm down, E." The sister sitting closest tickled him teasingly with the toe of an elegant, black stiletto. In her purple velvet dress, she looked like she was dressed to go to a ball.

"I'm perfectly calm, thank you, Beatrix. I just don't think it's a good idea to invite a total stranger into our house to poke around."

HE DID IT! HE DID IT! HE DID IT!

Realising that there was nothing he could do to placate his brother, Cameron decided to ignore him. He turned back to me before speaking. "In answer to your question, we had dinner together last night. We were supposed to be celebrating Daisy's new job, but Dad was angry because Audrey wasn't here with us. The evening didn't go quite as planned."

The others turned to him. Daisy herself was the only one who didn't react but she'd looked petrified ever since I'd got there.

"So it was just the five of you at dinner? No partners?" It sounded like I was fishing to find out if they were single.

"No," Beatrix replied. "Daddy insisted he only wanted close family."

"And didn't Daisy get a say?" I'd definitely found my voice by this point, but my nerves suddenly reared up on me and my heart jumped in my chest as I wondered what right I had to speak to them so rudely.

They looked about at one another, clearly expecting Audrey to answer the difficult questions. "Dad could be very particular in his expectations. He preferred it when it was just us Porters here."

Edmund wasn't finished with his objections. "Why are you saying all this stuff? It's got nothing to do with her. It's not too late, we can tell this little madam where to go and send her packing."

His anguished words echoed off every wall, before silence gripped the room. Beatrix let out a groan and rose to her feet to push her younger brother back into place on the sofa. He stayed rigid and clearly wanted to resist but, with his sister's eyes locked onto his own, he gave in and flopped down.

SHE DID IT. HE DID IT. THEY ALL DID IT!

"On Sunday, the police will drag up all this stuff anyway. What difference does it make if some rando knows it?" She threaded her arm beneath Edmund's to stop him from jumping up again. "No offence, *Izzy.*"

I could tell that offence was exactly what she was going for, but I wasn't going to let it show. "None taken. Perhaps you could give me a rough idea of what time you saw your dad before bed?"

"I was the last up," Cameron replied. "I was chatting with him in his office about a business idea and left him at around eleven to retire to my bedroom." I got the impression that he got a notch more restrained when he said this. I'd have to find out exactly what they'd been discussing.

"In fact, I was the last to see him, Madam." The butler's voice came as something of a surprise. I wasn't entirely sure he was allowed to speak without being spoken to. "Mr Porter called for tea at about eleven thirty. As far as I know, the others were all in their rooms by then."

Gladwell seemed different from the last time I'd met him. He was younger and fresher somehow and his clothes looked new and neatly pressed. Perhaps the ghost who had haunted Vomeris Hall had been exorcised and it wasn't just the family who would benefit.

"So, if it wasn't Gladwell, and it wasn't any of us, clearly Cook must be the culprit." Edmund's voice was beginning to grate on me.

I turned to address the more helpful siblings. "Why are you so sure that one of you killed him? Couldn't it be somebody coming in from outside?"

Cameron peered around the group before accepting that he would be the one to reply. "There are cameras and sensors all over the outer wall of the property and the gates were closed. Dad was rather obsessive about security."

"What about on the estate? Were there any cameras around the hall?" I was trying to make a mental note of the surroundings, their reactions and anything of interest while still engaging with the conversation. It was trickier than you'd think.

"Sadly not," Beatrix replied. "He clearly never imagined the threat could come from within." She had a wicked smile on her face as she spoke and I could see why David had compared her to a vampire. With her long black hair and colourless skin, there was something vicious, otherworldly and entirely seductive about her.

"Don't start, Bea." Cameron admonished his sister and she jerked away like she'd been touched by silver.

"Which of you found the body?" I studied their faces once more.

I was surprised to see Edmund put his arm around his youngest sister and give a straight answer. "It was first thing this morning. I was supposed to fetch him for breakfast on the lawn but I talked

Daisy into going."

Her eyes flicked about uncomfortably, glancing in my direction and then rebounding around the room. She looked like a mouse in cat's claws.

At that moment, a large woman dressed in food-stained overalls appeared in the doorway. It was hard to imagine anyone looking so completely out of place – except for me perhaps, which is why I was making an effort not to catch my reflection in the mirrors.

"Ahh, hello, Cook." Audrey stood up to welcome her. "This is Izzy Palmer, the woman I told you about. I'm sure you'll give her your full cooperation."

Cook looked at me like she was sizing up a side of beef before cutting it up for the freezer. She was the spitting image of a terrifying dinner lady who had worked at my school when I was a kid. No one messed with Madge and I assumed the same could be said of the new arrival – until she opened her mouth.

"Allo, darlin'. Terrible thing that's happened. In't it awful? Poor Mr Porter going like that." She sat on the chair next to mine and put her hand on my shoulder like I was the one in mourning. Audrey looked over affectionately, while the other siblings barely seemed to register her arrival.

Gladwell brought us both some tea, served in fine bone china. This was not my first time in a posh country house with fancy crockery and I was pretty sure I was going to break it. Memories of a disastrous childhood visit to my Mum's rich cousin splintered through my mind and the cup and saucer shook as I accepted them.

Edmund had been watching me this whole time like I was about to steal the silverware. "I'm not sure I want anything to do with this, but how's it going to work anyway?" The arrogance was back in his voice.

I had an answer already planned. I'd been thinking of little else all day. "I'll have to speak to you one by one. It may take some time, but I'm confident I can get to the truth."

That would have sounded more convincing if your hands weren't still trembling.

"Whoever killed Daddy isn't exactly going to confess, are they?" Beatrix slotted her long, glossy fingernails together and looked at me hungrily. "What makes you think you can work out who did it?"

When I saw the expression on her face – a mix of superiority and apathetic curiosity – something fired inside me and the right words came to my lips. "That's not for you to worry about. I know what I'm doing."

Audrey spoke up once more in my defence. "Not only is Izzy here to help us, she's sworn that nothing that goes on in the house will go any further. She's doing us a favour even coming."

It made me feel all chirpy to have her in my corner. I looked around their beautiful faces. Daisy hadn't spoken, Cameron already appeared a little bored and Edmund's scowl still scarred his face. They were fiercely intimidating but it was my game we were playing and, as my nerves subsided, I was beginning to enjoy it.

"I'll start by visiting the crime scene." I took a pair of latex gloves from my pocket and slipped them on in a manner that I hope shouted very clearly, *Hey, don't mess with me, I have latex gloves!*

Audrey stood up and, without another word, I followed her confidently out of the room. If I hadn't forgotten Mum's case and had to go back for it, that would have been a pretty badass exit.

Chapter Seven

Walking down those endless corridors felt like a Scouts' night-hike my mum once forced me to go on. Except, instead of being poked with sticks and called names by a bunch of savage twelve-year-olds, I was off to see a murder scene. It's hard to say which would scar a person more.

Nah, no competition. Jenny Jackson and her band of psycho-Barbie clones were far more disturbing.

The hanging lamps in the hall had motion sensors. It was eerie how we would walk into a patch of electric light just as the previous one clicked off. Looking back down the corridor, it was as if the path behind us had been plunged into oblivion. I felt like Gretel in the fairy tale, coming to realise that breadcrumbs weren't the best choice after all.

"Here we are then," Audrey said outside the library, as if she was about to invite me in for coffee. She looked rather nervous.

"I'll be fine. It's not my first corpse, as you know." I shut up for a second and realised that I wasn't the one she was worried about. "You don't have to come in if you don't want to."

She emptied her lungs in relief. "Oh, thank you. I really don't think I could take it."

I put my hand on her shoulder to comfort her and felt like a fool for trying. "Just wait out here for me, would you? I'll probably get lost if you leave."

She clamped her lips together and nodded.

I put my hand against the door and pushed it open, expecting to come across a similar scene to the one that had greeted me there four days earlier. But not only were the lights all off, when I managed to find the switch and bathe the room in the warm glow of the velvet-shaded uprights, Mr Porter wasn't at his desk.

I caught sight of him and staggered forward unconsciously. It wasn't the violence of his death that shook me but the sheer effort that must have gone into it. Three-time British businessman of the year winner Aldrich Porter was suspended a few feet off the floor. His outstretched arms were secured in place through the antlers of two great stags' heads and his feet were resting upon the skull of a grizzly bear. The rest of his torso was trapped in by the mounts of various smaller animals, and, on the wall behind him, a great channel of blood had redecorated the wall.

Somewhat belatedly, Ramesh's warning came back to me and my brain started freaking out.

What if they called you here in the first place to shift the blame? A fired employee who returned to get revenge; you're an easy target.

Me? What happened to *We*?

Without thinking about it, I had placed one gloved hand on Mr Porter's glass-topped desk and now jumped back for fear that I was dropping DNA or microscopic fibres about the place.

Too late for that, matey.

There was no sign of a weapon so I assumed it was still buried in his back. Pulling my torch from my pocket I searched the carpet at his feet for any tiny clue and couldn't see so much as a crumb. Though the bookshelves were clearly dust magnets, the desk and the area around it were perfectly clean.

There were splotches of blood at the base of the wall and a few more between there and the desk, but the front of Porter's clothes were spotless. I stood back up to look at him more closely. His head was dangling awkwardly so that his half-open eyes were on me. He looked more drunk than dead; a barfly at closing time, propped up by his sober mates. In actual fact, he'd been there for the best part of a day and his skin had taken on an unnaturally waxy hue. He reminded me of a really bad Michael Caine figure I'd seen on a trip to Madame Tussaud's years before.

I tried to put some facts together in my brain. He must have been stabbed from behind and-

Pfff another stabbing. I was hoping for a shooting this time.

Quiet, I'm trying to think!

Stabbed from behind, then dragged over to his precarious final resting place. There was no blood on his chair so it was unlikely he'd been killed sitting down and the only bloodstains on the carpet were a few feet from the body. It surprised me there weren't more. He wouldn't have died instantly either. It didn't quite add up.

Unless he'd been drugged before the knife went in, the only thing I could think was that someone had held him there to make sure he bled out. Either that or the shock of knowing his murderer was too much for him and he'd fainted. Aldrich Porter was slain by someone he was close to. If it was one of his kids who'd done the deed, he could have died looking into their eyes. The same blue-grey eyes that he'd passed on to them and that – even as these thoughts ran through my head were – looking down upon me.

In the ten minutes I'd spent with him at the beginning of the week, Porter didn't come across as a particularly good person. That didn't stop me feeling sorry for him though. I thought about my first time in that library and couldn't help wishing that he was dreaming with his eyes open.

Two minutes had passed in silence, but there was more work to do. I walked the long way round the desk to avoid having to step over the bloodstains. It was bad enough that I hadn't thought to cover my shoes with plastic bags. There was more to discover, I just knew it, so I stood back and tried to play a party game. I closed my eyes to remember the room as it had been the last time I'd been there. Opening them again, I could see the differences as if they'd been marked up in fluorescent pen.

In the left corner of the room, by one of the lamps, an occasional table had been setup to hold a tea tray. On the desk in front of me, the photograph of the five Porter kids was missing. In its place was a faded outline between the two remaining photos. The cricket ball was off its stand too, knocked from the table to land some metres away across the carpet. The obvious conclusion would be that it had been dislodged in a struggle, and yet Porter's fountain pens and ink cartridges were still neatly arranged in the middle of the desk.

I got down low to see if anything else had fallen. The floor under the desk was once again free of the tiniest speck of dust and the same was true around the chair I'd sat in on my visit.

I took a look at the tea tray in case it had a tale to tell but there was only one cup and it hadn't even been drunk from. I thought that I'd have to give up altogether and retreat with barely a clue to go on, when I returned to the centre of the room and something caught my eye. If I hadn't had my torch, I wouldn't have seen it. I'd already walked past the spot twice but, beside the right-hand wall of bookcases, a small, shiny object now sparkled in the beam of light.

There turned out to be quite a haul in fact. A trail led from the dislodged cricket ball to the nearby wall. Going by the orderly way in which Mr Porter lived his life, it seemed fair to assume that these items had ended up there on the night of the murder.

The first stop on my treasure hunt was an ivory domino, obscured by the deep, shaggy fibres of the carpet. It was inlaid with six black dots on each half and was well worn by years of play. Most interesting of all though was the dab of dried blood clearly visible on top of it. I left it where it was but made a careful note of its appearance in my mind.

Next, buried between the edge of the carpet and the base of the shelf, was a small glass bottle. It looked incredibly old, the kind of thing you'd have found filled with gin if hotels in the seventeenth century had minibars. I brought it to my nose and caught a strong, bitter smell that reminded me of my great aunt's practically inedible almond cakes. But then cyanide and bitter almonds have an incredibly similar scent.

The last object to find was an ornate brass key with a filigree handle and a tiny crown on the bow. The less I disturbed the crime scene the better, but that key was too good a clue to resist so I carefully pocketed it and headed back to my guide.

"Did you…" she hesitated over her words, "…find anything?"

I thought it was better not to give too much away. "I don't know who the killer is yet, if that's what you mean."

"It's almost a relief." She looked distressed and struggled to get the words out. "It's not as if I want you to cart my family off to prison."

For the second time that evening, I realised she needed my reassurance. "I'm only here to work out what happened, not judge anybody."

This seemed to put her at ease and a troubled smile cut across her face. "I appreciate that and I know you'll remain impartial. That's one of the reasons I wanted you here instead of the police."

"I was meaning to ask you about them." I looked for the right way to phrase it without offending her. "Are you sure what we're doing is legal? I mean, your dad's corpse is literally rotting in there, forensic evidence is deteriorating. Couldn't we get into trouble for not reporting the crime early enough?"

She looked at me like I was being naïve. "Izzy, there are two things you may not have considered. First, if there was any chance that the killer had left a bloody handprint behind that could prove their guilt, they'd be on a plane to the Caymans by now. And second, this country was built for families like mine. Rich people have been getting away with murder for centuries. But that's not what we're trying to do. We just need a little time to put our house in order."

There wasn't much I could say to that. It was too late to change my mind now anyway.

Typical Izzy, trying to have your cake and eat it.

What would be the point of having cake if you couldn't eat it?

Audrey's tone softened. "I'll show you to your room. Then, if you don't mind, I think I need a drink."

She needn't have promised me alcohol to get me to follow her, her company was too good to turn down. Yanking mum's case behind me, with its broken wheel scraping loudly along, we climbed the stairs up to the west wing.

"I hope you find the accommodation suitable. Dad wasn't one for entertaining and Gladwell didn't have time to get it spick and span." She pushed the first door on the landing open.

My, oh my! My brain sounds like a southern belle when I get excited for some reason. *Lordy! Why, I could live here forever!*

I followed Audrey into a room the size of my house. It was split into a lounge and sleeping area with a brown leather Chesterfield dividing the two. On the far side of the room, the biggest four-poster bed I'd ever dreamed of was sitting prettily. If Audrey hadn't been there, I'd have run straight over and jumped on it.

I turned to her and, casual as possible, said, "It's quite nice."

She walked to one of the matching armchairs. "I haven't been in here for years. Sorry it's so musty."

Having checked that her seat wasn't dirty, she settled down and I watched as her eyes scanned the wall in front of her. All around the door, a thousand framed photographs filled the space. The Porter progeny's entire childhood was accounted for. I could see various birthday parties, a young Daisy on the beach, Edmund looking cool on his first bike, Beatrix on stage in a school play with a dagger in her hand and Cameron holding up a prize catch. But it was Audrey who dominated the display. There were countless photos of her clutching certificates and, right in the centre of everything, a large print of her dancing with her father at a wedding. The only person missing was the children's mother. There wasn't a trace of the former Mrs Porter in any of the photos.

Perhaps she never existed, perhaps they were born by miraculous conception. No doubt the rich can afford such things.

"I've no idea why Dad put up all those photos in a guest room." There was a touch of disapproval in the way she spoke. "I used to come up here when I was a teenager to get away from everyone; rather ironic when you think about it. I'd sit right on the floor and relive the highlights of my golden youth. It makes me nostalgic being up here again."

Her voice had gone all dreamy but, as if remembering her responsibilities as a host, she snapped out of it and, in her usual sympathetic tone asked, "What was your childhood like?"

I was perched on my suitcase halfway into the room, like I was scared the furniture wasn't really for me and that Audrey was playing a trick. "Nothing like yours. I didn't have any brothers or sisters and my parents barely spoke until I was fifteen, at which point they suddenly started arguing and decided to get a divorce."

She smiled understandingly and I got a glimpse of a more down-to-earth Audrey Porter underneath all the elegance. "Well, we have that much in common at least." She hesitated as if she was worried she'd offend me. "Izzy, would you please come and sit down? You're my guest here, not the cleaner."

I reluctantly trailed over with a goofy blush to my cheeks and took the armchair across from her. She put her hand under the marble-topped coffee table between us and pressed a hidden bell.

A moment later Gladwell's voice crept politely out of a small speaker in the corner of the room. "Yes, Madam. How may I help you?"

"A bottle of whisky and two glasses to Miss Palmer's bedroom, please Gladwell."

I thought about asking for some orange juice to mix with it because

I'm a wimp.

"What age, Madam?" There was a slight pop on the microphone as he spoke.

"I'll trust your judgement, Stephen. But Macallan obviously."

With the order made, I decided to trust her with some of the details of what I'd discovered at the scene of the crime.

"I found a few items that I don't understand in your dad's study." I watched her calm, curious reaction before continuing. "There was an ivory domino on the floor not too far from his desk. It had a spot of blood on it. Do you have any idea what it could mean?"

"A domino? Like the game you mean?"

"Yes, it's old and a little worn."

She paused before replying. "There'll be a set down in the games room. My brothers used to play when we were kids. I've no idea how it could have ended up with Dad though."

"And what about a tiny glass bottle, antique, I think. Is there anywhere in the house with a collection like that?"

She seemed amused by this. "There are collections of just about everything in Vomeris Hall, though I can't say that any bottles spring to mind."

I debated whether to mention the key and finally decided against it. I wasn't going to play all my cards until I could be sure who to trust. An awkward silence descended between us. It was the kind that often occurs when two people know each other just the wrong amount to stimulate conversation.

Before I knew it, some words had popped out of my mouth that I didn't think I had the guts to say. "Where's your mum in all the photos?"

"Ha, good question." She did not sound amused despite the laughter. "You can just about make her hand out in a few of them but Daddy chose the ones without her in. Even before they split up, he considered my mother a terrible disappointment. I have no doubt he loved the twenty-three-year-old he married, but the plump middle-aged woman who had sired his children didn't fit the picture."

"What happened after they divorced? Do you still see her?"

She looked away from the photos at the heavily curtained windows. "I didn't for a long time. The comforts of Vomeris Hall were too great a pull and my father made sure that Mum left the marriage with very little. But that wasn't all. He told us straight out that he didn't want us to see her and I was a good little daughter and did as Daddy said. I was under his spell completely."

I knew that it was my job to shake things up and see what would fall out, but the reality of meddling in someone else's family affairs was far more difficult.

She turned to face me, her watercolour eyes catching hold of mine. "I should probably have started off by explaining that my father was not a good man. I've loved him deeply my whole life but that doesn't make him an angel."

She paused as if to acknowledge to herself that she'd just said these words out loud. "He brought us up to treat our mother inhumanly. We made jokes at her expense, acted like she was ignorant and beneath us – the only one without the precious Porter blood." She pulled a breath back in before continuing. "We made her life miserable and it took me years to realise how cruel we'd been. When I finally did, I reached out to her. I wrote so many apologies but it was too late."

"She wouldn't talk to you?"

"No, it wasn't that. She was living in a tiny flat in Mitcham with barely a window. I went to see her as often as I could, but she told me there was nothing to forgive. She wasn't a strong woman and believed every word we'd ever said to her. She died of cancer before I could prove to her she was wrong."

A silence descended and held there between us like a ghost waiting to scream. I let my mind wander to that tragic apartment of Mrs Porter's final days. When Gladwell knocked on the door, a moment later, my nerves were as tight as piano wire and I jumped in my seat.

"Your drinks, Madam." He sailed into the room with a silver tray bearing the whisky and two glasses. I had no idea how far he'd had to come but he'd got there pretty fast. "I must apologise, Miss Palmer, for not being able to welcome you earlier, I was attending to the family."

As he served us both unhealthy measures of whisky, Audrey smiled up at him. "We'd be lost without our dear Stephen."

The butler didn't react to the compliment but stood back from his service and, with a respectful nod, retreated from the room. I noticed that he paused for a half moment to stretch his bad leg before closing the door.

Alone once more, I was determined to return to the topic we'd been discussing. "What you said about your mother, do you think it could have had something to do with Mr Porter's death?"

"You mean someone killed him because of the way he treated her?" She paused over the question like she was holding her breath. "I very much doubt it. My siblings aren't the sentimental types, and, besides, we were just as much to blame as Dad."

Picking up my glass, I took a slug of whisky and immediately regretted it. I was about to follow up with another question when she spoke again.

"If you do your job properly, Izzy, you're going to uncover all sorts of dark secrets in this place. My brothers and sisters aren't exactly innocents but one of them is hiding something truly despicable." She sounded faintly sickened by this fact. "I'm sure you'll get it out of them."

When she looked at me like that, I actually believed her. "Are you so certain that your staff weren't involved?"

She sipped her drink and showed no sign that her throat was in the poker-hot agony mine was still suffering through. "One hundred per cent. I see no reason why either one of them would have had a hand in it. And besides, Cook would surely have put poison in his dinner and, as for Gladwell… *The butler did it* is a bit too obvious, no?"

I let the information swirl about my brain for a moment
Only four suspects! This should be an absolute cakewalk.

Yeah, except that we do sometimes have trouble walking and eating cake at the same time.

I changed tack. "When I was trying to work out who killed Bob, it took me far too long to question who he really was. I focussed too much on the suspects and not enough on the man who was killed. So will you tell me as much as you can about your father before I go any further?"

"Of course I will." She finished her drink and put the empty glass down beside her – still showing no sign of permanent bodily damage. "But not until the morning. I'm exhausted after my brief sojourn in the sun."

"I'm sorry you had to cut your holiday short."

"So am I. I managed two days in paradise before my family forced me back here." She stood up and straightened the folds on her dress. "You know, perhaps that was the real reason he was killed. My siblings couldn't stand the idea of me having a holiday and did whatever was necessary to get me back." There was no lightness in her voice, I think she was genuinely examining the possibility this was true.

I took one last sip, to confirm how horrid the drink was, but this time it must have shown on my face.

"You don't like whisky, do you Izzy?"

I thought about knocking back the rest to prove her wrong, but couldn't handle any more. "No, sorry. I'm more of a cloudy lemonade sort of person."

"Dad always says…" She came to a sudden stop and sadness invaded her face once more. "Or rather, Dad always *said,* that people don't get anywhere in this world if they don't ask for what they want."

"He probably knew what he was talking about." I risked a cheerful grimace. "Then again, I got here so I don't think I'm doing too badly."

She perked up a little and clicked her heels efficiently. "I'll be in the east wing if you need anything. My brothers and sisters are there too and Gladwell is always on hand."

I could tell that she was physically and emotionally exhausted but something about her made me want to stay up late to share all our secrets. I wanted us to have a midnight snack and braid each other's hair. I wanted to do all the things that teenage girls do that I never got to because my only friend at high school was a nerdy boy called Martin, who got really nervous the one time I organised a sleepover and his parents had to come and collect him.

Audrey paused at the door as if she had something more to say but then shook her head and disappeared with a slight smile shaping her pretty face. I finally got to jump onto the bed but I couldn't be happy about it because I was feeling guilty for not staying in touch with poor old Martin.

Chapter Eight

"Dean, can you hear me?"

It was one in the morning but my techy friend only gets about three hours sleep as he runs a successful company in the daytime and spends his nights playing very dull, strategic computer games on the internet.

"Dean, are you there?" I was pressing the button on the side of my spy watch just as he'd told me, but nothing was happening. I decided to do what I always do when a gadget fails me and shout at it. "DEAN? IS ANYONE HOME?"

"Calm down, would you? I'm here." His grumpy voice came out of the small speaker and I didn't feel quite so alone anymore. "Shouting down the line at me isn't going to make me want to help you more."

"Sorry. I didn't think the mic was working. Are your friends there yet?"

He sighed like I was being extraordinarily unreasonable when, actually, I was only being averagely unreasonable. "They'll be here in the morning. Do you know what you have to do?"

I'd unpacked my case and extracted the silver box he had given me with the equipment in. "I think so. I have to decide where to put the cameras and hope for the best. Did you manage to find the plans of the house?"

He gave a yawn, but I'm pretty sure he was putting it on. "More or less. Vomeris Hall was requisitioned during the war for use as an army training centre and some local interest group put a plan online with all the main rooms on. If I was Aldrich Porter, I'd be furious. Talk about a security risk, anyone could-"

"Thanks, Dean. I'm sure he'll be very upset. Can we get on with this?"

I put the tiny Bluetooth earpiece in my ear and began the search for the best possible locations to spy on my clients. Dean had tried to convince me to wear the glasses as well but that was a step too far, and besides, I'd need a prescription pair.

"Okay, I've worked out some obvious places to hide the cameras and they're small enough that you won't have to worry about them being spotted. Go out of your bedroom and head downstairs."

I did as instructed, despite the fact that it was really dark out in the corridor and I'm pretty sure that old place was haunted. It's not that I saw, heard or even really sensed any ghosts, but sometimes it takes more than facts and evidence to prove something; it takes vague suspicions.

"Keep going straight along the corridor, and when you get to the end, take the second door on the right."

Even more dangerous than the possibility of post-life apparitions was the amount of sticky-out furniture everywhere. By the time I got to where I was going, my lower body probably looked like I'd been attacked with a hammer. I was bruised and deterred before we'd even begun.

I wound my way around the building, accompanied by the smell of polish and potpourri. Dean directed me to a large dining room and, using the light from my watch screen, I hid the first camera within the glass casing of a clock on the mantelpiece.

"Good, now on to the library."

Two minutes later, I was back at the scene of the crime. "I'm not going in there."

Dean huffed down the line to me. "Why not?" He sounded like a grumpy puppet from a kids' TV show.

"Because this place is terrifying enough already without poking around a dead body in the dark."

"I'm not suggesting you carry out a post-mortem. Just go into the room, hide the camera and then leave."

I resisted for about five seconds, then folded, as is my wont. "Fine, but I'm going to be making this sound the whole time, ooh ooh ooh ooh ooh ooh!"

I dashed inside, found a space in the first bookshelf I came to and tucked the black mini-camera into the spine of an old book.

"Ooh ooh ooh ooh and… I'm out." I carefully pulled the door shut with relief that… well I'm not really sure what I was relieved about, but I'd made it out in one piece.

"You'll have to go back in," a particularly annoying voice in my ear declared. "There's something blocking the shot."

"Ooh ooh ooh ooh ooh!" I was there and back in fifteen seconds but

I still felt the need to make a sound like I was walking on hot coals.

We moved on to other areas of the house. I left cameras in the front parlour, the games room, the grand salon and a bunch of rooms and passageways that probably had names too but I don't have a clue what they were.

I was on my way to the kitchen with only one camera left to place. "It's a shame we can't see what's going on in the bedrooms."

"Don't even think about it, Izzy." Dean had hardly been chirpy company throughout my task. "If anyone got a whiff of what you were up to, they'd track down the other cameras no trouble."

"Sometimes, talking to you is like talking to my mother – if my actual mother wasn't the opposite of you in every respect."

"Madam?" a voice just behind me enquired and I froze where I stood. "Is everything okay?"

I turned around and came face-to-face with the butler.

"Urmmm. You probably heard me telling myself off for being both like and unlike my mother. You see…" I searched for an explanation that might in some conceivable universe make sense. "She's a wonderful woman and I wish I could live up to her example yet I'd hate to be so conformist as to succeed."

Ignoring nonsense must be an important skill they teach in butler school. He nodded his head demurely and asked another question. "Is there anything I can get for you?"

I thought fast. "Actually, I was just on my way to get a drink of water from the kitchen."

Bravo!

"Very good, Madam. Though there is a sink in your room…"

"Yeah, of course, but I prefer bottled water."

"…and a well-stocked fridge. You could have found water in there as well."

I did my best impression of someone who was deeply surprised by something. "Oh, that's a fridge!" I'm not a good liar but I am a committed one. "I thought it was a washing machine!"

He smiled and pointed down the corridor to the kitchen. "Why don't you come with me?"

I'd been distracted throughout the conversation by Dean's smug laughter in my ear. "Impressive stuff, Izzy. You are a master of subterfuge." I couldn't even tell him to shut up. It was torture.

Rather than dwell on the fact I'd come across as an idiot, when we arrived at our destination, I decided to make the most of it.

Good thinking. No one would ever imagine that an idiot could solve a murder.

"Would you like to join me for a nightcap, Stephen?"

He eyed me uncertainly, then looked down at the bottle of Evian he had just fetched. "Do you mind if I have something a little stronger?"

We sat at the kitchen table, a huge slab of wood like a butcher's block, complete with a century of scores and scratches on its beautifully patinated surface. Gladwell had opted for a cognac while I sipped at my water.

Single use plastic, Izzy! Wasting the world's resources just to avoid messing up your murder investigation. You should be ashamed of yourself.

My brain has become a real green-shamer ever since we watched the opening ceremony of the Rio Olympics.

"Mr Porter's murder is a terrible thing," my drinking buddy began. "Makes me think about those kids differently, you know?" There was something relaxed about his manner that made me feel at home.

"I can imagine." I studied him as I spoke. "You saw them all grow up, can't be nice to think that one of them could be a murderer." I looked about the kitchen at the racks of shiny copper pans and old-fashioned skillets which hung from the walls. "But does it surprise you? I mean, they're not exactly a normal family."

"I'm not sure I know what a normal family is." He let his drink mellow in his mouth before swallowing. "All I know is that those children were little angels when they were small. Each one of them was the friendliest, most affectionate child you could hope to meet and I'll never think bad of them."

His London accent was peeping out again. I was seeing the real Stephen Gladwell, not the polished mannequin who served the family.

"So was it you who killed him then?" I threw the question across to him, hoping to catch him off guard.

His friendly face stretched out in a smile. "You mean, did the butler do it? Isn't that a bit of a cliché?"

"Yeah, but that would make a good double bluff. It's so obvious that no one would take it seriously." I was playing with the bottle top but still kept my eyes on him for any sign of guilt.

"What would I get out of killing him though?"

"Who's to say?" I allowed myself a moment to think, my brain running with conspiracy theories. "Maybe you were working with one of the Porter children. Maybe they'll let you in on the inheritance."

"Ooh, that's a clever idea." He laughed and it made everything I'd been thinking seem ridiculous. "There's only one problem with that. Mr Porter was good to me. I know he wasn't everyone's cup of tea, but I spent a lot of time with him and, for all his faults, he had good intentions."

I was pretty sure he wasn't about to confess so I changed the topic. "What were his faults? What dark deeds did the famous Aldrich Porter get up to?"

His eyes cast off to the ceiling in remembrance and he swirled his drink round in his glass. The liquid caught the light of the low hanging lamps above our heads and shifted between shades of gold, peach, amber and brown.

"He was a businessman and a damn good one. But the very word has negative connotations these days. We think of the world of business as heartless and self-serving. Well, Aldrich could be all that and worse. He might not have set out to hurt anybody but he believed that the world was a giant set of scales and, for one person to do well, another would have to lose out. I heard him say this a number of times and it was often at entirely the wrong moment."

The room fell quiet so I prodded him along. "How do you mean?"

"I mean, I was here twenty-five years ago when he let the rest of the domestic staff go. He didn't do himself any favours. He tried to comfort them by explaining how much better off he'd be if he didn't have to pay their salaries. Some of the kitchen staff had been here for forty years and never found work again. They were in tears. I reckon he only kept me and Cook around so he could boast that he had his own servants."

The chair I was on was very slidey beneath my skirt and I had to keep pulling myself back up. "Is there any chance that one of the people he upset came back here for revenge?"

He didn't need to think over his answer. "No way. Even without the insanely expensive security system that guards every inch of the perimeter, all that was decades ago. Most of them have moved away and the others all died."

"So you really think one of his kids did him in?" I was still having trouble with the idea.

"Well I don't reckon Cook was behind it and I certainly wasn't." He tipped his head back to get the last warming drops from his glass.

"I'll let you go to bed, promise I will, but I have one last question." I paused to take in his reaction. "Of the four who were here, who do you think had it in them to kill their father?"

He was silent for a moment before answering. "At a push, I'd say…" He came to a halt, gave his empty glass a shake and stood up. "I'd say that it's your job to work that out."

He took up the stiff, upright posture of his profession – like he'd donned his uniform afresh – and put the glass in the sink.

I couldn't let him off so easily. "Fine, I have one more question before bed or I won't be able to sleep." He returned to the table and nodded his consent. "You served Mr Porter before bed, did you happen to notice a domino in the library?"

"There was nothing out of the ordinary on his desk, if that's what you mean."

I started over. "It wasn't on the desk, but down low, by the right-hand bookcase. Do you know if it was there when you left him?"

"I don't think so." He shook his head. "But then, there's no guarantee I'd have noticed it. My eyes aren't what they once were."

"And do you have any idea why a gaming piece would have been in the library in the first place?"

"I can't say I do."

Realising there was no further to go with the topic, I pulled my chair back to accompany him out. "I'll have to talk to you more formally tomorrow."

"I'm here whenever you require, Madam."

An idea came to me that was too good to resist. "And I think I'm going to need your help if I've got any hope of catching the killer. What do you say, Watson?"

Breaking character once more, a smile blossomed on his face. "As you wish, Mr Holmes."

Chapter Nine

I dreamt of nothing that night but, when I woke up in that luxurious bed, surrounded by plump pillows and high-thread-count bedding, a story was playing out in my mind. Related images had been floating around my head ever since I'd laid eyes on Vomeris Hall but now the full movie was screening.

As I listened to the beams of the house creaking with the rising morning temperature and the sounds of the world waking up, I saw myself on a childhood summer trip with my mum. My holidays back then tended to be with one parent or the other, in theory because of their work, though, by age eleven, I was coming to realise that my parents couldn't stand being together for any extended period of time.

Mum's cousin Elizabeth had come from serious money and lived on a vast estate near Derby that had once belonged to the royal family. Castleton Square Manor fitted its name perfectly in that the house looked both castle-like and very square.

Despite, or perhaps because of, my mother's own humble beginnings, she had lived her life in thrall to this incredibly wealthy wing of her father's family. It was a poorly kept secret that the Castletons had made their money in the slave trade and, when abolition arrived, cashed in their pot to make a tidy sum.

The sins of her forefathers lay heavy on Elizabeth Castleton's shoulders and she over-compensated for this by acting superior to everyone she came into contact with.

"The place is a miracle," I remember my mother declaring as servants transported our meagre luggage up the great stone staircase in front of the house.

"You're family, darling," Elizabeth reminded her, not so much in welcome, but explanation for why she was putting up with the intrusion. "And you're only with us for a few days."

Elizabeth was a large, cheerless woman who looked like she'd been left out in a storm. Her skin was chapped and red, her hair dishevelled, and her clothes were perennially autumnal.

Standing proudly beside her, in front of the gigantic front door, my second cousins, Tedwin and Noémi flanked their mother. They looked like Victorian ghosts from a horror film.

"You remember little Isobel, don't you children?" Elizabeth's words were a warning, cautioning her children not to get too close to their poor relative. "Run along now."

My mother looked briefly worried about me, then got to work on her thankless task for the weekend; doing whatever it took to impress her cousin. I trailed after the children into the Olympic-size front parlour where a pair of grand staircases scrolled towards us. Though a century more modern, Castleton Square Manor made Vomeris Hall look like a garden shed.

The walls were painted with intricate friezes, featuring angels, cherubs and a cornucopia of culinary delights all depicted in soft pastel shades. Velvet curtains adorned every window. Crystal chandeliers dripped from the stuccoed ceilings and, as I crossed the gigantic space to go upstairs, a line of maids and servants stood in rigid silence.

As soon as we were out of sight of the grownups, Tedwin and Noémi sprinted away from me, giggling cruelly as I struggled to keep up. The first floor was a rabbit warren of curving corridors and neatly arranged antechambers, from which a hundred doors led off. I quickly lost the little brats but followed the sound of their mirthless laughter through studies and bedrooms. Silence eventually fell and, for the first time I can remember in my life, I felt entirely alone.

My hopes for that holiday had been stoked by my mother's vivid description of the palace we'd be staying in. She'd made me dream of the fast friendships I would make with these relatives, who I'd previously only seen at large family gatherings. But it wasn't all Mum's doing. I was excited about the holiday because I'd spent the last few months burrowing through Agatha Christie's books and was looking forward to meeting the wealthy socialites and charismatic aristocrats who frequented large houses such as Castleton.

The contrasting reality came crashing down around me as I ground to a stop in a small, comparatively humble library. Tears shot from my eyes and I was about to wail out – and fulfil my part in the cousins' spiteful game – when I noticed a book on one of the shelves.

I scanned the spines and found large collections organised by author. Dorothy L. Sayers, G.K. Chesterton, Mary Roberts Rinehart and a hundred more. It wasn't so much the names that stood out to me as the dramatic fonts and racy sounding titles. "Murder Must Advertise", "Enter a Murderer", "Murder at Mid-Day" and "The Box Office Murders" gave me a sneaking suspicion that I had just stumbled across a lifetime supply of murder mysteries.

Still emotional from my ordeal, my hands trembled as I reached for a small green volume. "Malcolm Sage, Detective" by Herbert Jenkins was a short story anthology that I'd never heard of before. Sitting cross legged in the middle of the room, I flicked to the first chapter and began to read "The Strange Case of Mr. Challoner". I've got to be honest, it wasn't great, but it transported me to a familiar world of crime and swiftly apportioned punishment which, at that moment, I longed for more than anything.

By the time I got to the brilliant Detective Sage's revelation of the murderer, Tedwin and Noémi had given up hiding.

"You were supposed to come looking for us," Noémi told me, standing in the doorway in her black pinafore dress, with her ankles together and her hands at her sides like a porcelain doll.

"You were supposed to be sad," her brother added. He was round and squidgy like a toasted marshmallow.

I stood up and put the book back in place without saying anything, then turned to show them just how little their trick had got to me. "And you were supposed to welcome me as a guest. It seems that none of us have lived up to expectations today."

I pushed past them and traced my steps back through the house, determined to revisit the detective library many times before my stay was up.

As I relived this painful episode in my room at Vomeris Hall, I realised that, though the visit was mentioned often in my family, I had not recalled the events in any detail for many years. That was just the beginning of course. Tedwin and Noémi weren't done with me yet, but the morning was creeping by and I had a murder to solve. I cast off the sheets and got dressed.

I'd had a nightmare deciding what clothes to pack. I simply didn't know what to wear to a country house murder investigation and fashion was one area where Poirot and Miss Marple were less than suitable role models. I'd ended up bringing a mix of my smartest going-out clothes and my most casual Sunday loungewear, none of which went together.

I jumped into a baggy t-shirt with a smiley face on it and a rather slinky, grey pencil skirt then went off in search of breakfast.

They should have given us a map when we got here.

Totally, it's like navigating a theme park.

"Anything to report, Dean?" I whispered into my iTechno-cyber-e-watch-McGadget (not very good with technology, sorry) as I hunted for the dining room.

There was a short delay before Dean replied. "My staff have only just arrived. They're going to go through last night's footage quickly but we'll be with you live from then on."

"I'm here too Izzy," a faint voice in the background declared. "And I'm still not talking to you!"

"Is that Ramesh?" I knew he wouldn't be able to leave me alone for two whole days. "What are you doing there?"

"I've asked him to prepare me for my date tonight." Dean's voice was even shiftier than normal and I could tell that he hadn't revealed to Ramesh the exact details of the help he'd be providing.

"That's right, Izzy. Some people appreciate my input."

I considered telling him that the only reason Dean wanted him there was to learn exactly what not to do, but I'm not that mean.

"Ahh, that's nice. Two of my boys playing sweetly together. I probably won't be able to talk much today, but I'll check in when I can."

They didn't reply. Ramesh had begun to break down his seven rules for successful romance before I clicked my watch off.

It took me long enough to find a dining room and, when I did, it was empty. Headed towards the kitchen, I spotted someone through a window and made my way out onto the lawn.

"Take your time, sleepy head." Edmund was already in a combative mood. "You're not going to solve much from your bedroom."

"Leave her alone, E." Beatrix didn't look up from her P.D. James novel as she reprimanded her brother. "It's becoming boring."

The five siblings were arranged around an ornate cast iron table in the sunshine. Dressed in tennis whites, they looked like they'd been cut and pasted from the nineteen-twenties. The back of the property was less austere than the main façade, with rose bushes growing up the walls at regular intervals and pretty wooden shutters pinned back beside each window.

"Are you hungry, Izzy?" Cameron pulled up a chair for me, but it felt wrong somehow so I stayed on my feet.

The selection of food laid out before them was better than any hotel breakfast I'd come across. There were all types of dainty French pastries, cold meats and sliced cheeses. On a well-stocked fruit plate, kiwis and a pineapple had been carved up into animal shapes. I got the distinct impression that most of it would go to waste.

"I'm not that hungry actually." I grabbed a croissant and shook it like a tiny bell. "I'll take this to go."

Daisy at least made eye contact this morning and I considered speaking to her first, but Audrey got in before her.

She cast her napkin off and rose to standing. "How about we go for a walk?"

I nodded, as my mouth was already full of light, buttery dough. I should have taken a few more cakes for the road.

"Did you sleep all right?" she asked, once we were out of earshot of the others, our feet crunching down the gravel path.

I grunted a distracted, "Yes," as I was already thinking up the first question I wanted to ask her. "I need you to tell me what came into your head when you found out your Dad had been murdered."

She didn't answer immediately but looked down at her neatly pleated skirt and the spotless white pumps beneath. "I thought, he'd finally gone too far. I mean, he often loses his temper but obviously things turned serious."

"You mean, your father got angry and someone snapped back?"

There was a sad frown on her pale, pretty face. "Not Dad, it was almost impossible to get a reaction out of him. I'm talking about Edmund. No doubt you've noticed he can be a little provocative. Definite youngest child syndrome, I'm afraid. He's always been impetuous, but recently he's taken things too far. Shouting at the servants, moaning to Beatrix whenever he doesn't get his own way. That's not to say I ever imagined he'd be a murderer but, now that it's happened…" She paused to assess what she was saying. "I can't say it's a shock."

70

"So what was the issue between your dad and Edmund?"

She looked more troubled the longer our conversation went on. "Perhaps I'm reading too much into it, but Dad disapproved of my little brother's lifestyle. He's never had a career and tends to coast through life on his connections, which was something our father deeply disagreed with."

We'd reached a walled garden and cut inside to discover a trail of carefully directed rose bushes which wound around metal fences to create a sort of open maze. I was trying to concentrate on what Audrey was saying but my brain is often a bit fuzzy in the morning and didn't help things by singing an irritating song from my childhood.

What would you do if you couldn't find the loo?
In an English country… garden.
Pull down your pants and you'll suffocate the ants,
In an English country… garden.

It was the only verse I could remember and it was repeating over and over.

I finally managed to focus. "That doesn't explain why Edmund would kill him."

She looked uncertain of herself and I thought she was going to take it all back. "No, you're right. But I can't help feeling that's what caused it." She sat down on a metal love seat in the middle of the garden and I squished in next to her. "Listen, I adore Edmund, I honestly do. You haven't seen the good part of him yet. He can be kind and generous, warm and funny, but his temper always lets him down." Her voice suddenly rose higher. "Even if he did kill our father, I wouldn't be able to condemn him for it because I know how difficult it was to be around Dad."

I could see she was struggling and decided to put her at ease once more. "Audrey, you don't have to feel guilty all the time about sharing your suspicions. You've called me here to find evidence, not canvas opinion. No one will be going to prison without absolute proof that they're guilty." She smiled back at me and I felt a little proud to have had that effect on her. "Listen, why don't you tell me about your dad? Tell me the things that only you would know about him."

It was still before ten, but the sun was in full attack mode. I'd have to make this a short conversation if I wanted to avoid my skin turning carnation red.

"I'm sure that the others will tell you all sorts of terrible stories, but he wasn't all bad. I know that he loved us, even if he struggled to communicate it. The problem with Dad was that he knew the answer to every question imaginable. It didn't matter if it was right or wrong, his answer was the only one that counted." Audrey's creamy skin glittered like pearlised snow in the daylight. "This house and the money in his bank account were all the proof he needed."

"But the two of you were close, weren't you? He had a photo of you on his desk."

She cast her gaze away to the blood-red roses that had entwined themselves around the intricate metal bench. "Well, Daddy was very proud of me; it's no secret. He trusted me and put me in charge of his investments after I graduated, but that doesn't mean he was any closer to me than he was to Gladwell or Cook even. In fact, sometimes it was better not to spend time with him, it only served to show how little love he had for anyone but himself. Which is why I was supposed to be on a Thai beach right now, all on my own."

"Did your brothers and sisters feel the same way?"

She laughed for the first time that day and it still sounded sad. "Actually, I'm pretty sure Beatrix never noticed. All she worries about is where her next Hermes handbag is coming from. Daddy liked to say he never spoiled us, but that doesn't mean he brought us up to value anything more than the mighty pound."

As I let the information sink in, I realised that nothing she'd just said really surprised me. "Can I be honest, Audrey? There's so much history to wade through in any family. So many rivalries and alliances that it's hard to know where to start. I got a picture of what Mr Porter was like from David and you've backed it up, but tell me what you think I should know and what I need to ask the rest of the family. At the moment, I'm scared I haven't got what it takes to find his killer."

A change came over her and it was as if she'd put all her doubts and concerns away to focus on mine. "Ask them straight up if they loved our father and I've no doubt they'll fall apart like a house of cards. Daisy and Edmund especially – Daddy used to say they were weak like their mother, but the truth is they just care more deeply than he ever could. Cameron and B will be the tougher nuts to crack but, if you can set them off guard, they'll tell you what you need to know."

I didn't feel I could take my pad out and make notes there in front of her, so I tried to organise my thoughts into neat columns in my brain. I assigned the headings, Suspects, Clues and Hypotheses, and felt certain they'd be filling up before long.

"You said on the phone that any one of your siblings could have murdered your father. What makes you so sure?"

A robin landed on a bush a few feet from us to listen in, but Audrey paid him no heed. "That was one thing Dad passed on to all of us. He might never have slashed someone open or pulled a trigger, but my father was a killer through and through." Like in some elaborate painting of the Virgin Mary, she was perfectly framed by roses. "When he was starting his business in the seventies, he had no friends – only acquaintances and sworn enemies. He bankrupted rivals, chewed through staff and never cared who he hurt along the way. He didn't know loyalty and he *never* knew fear."

She bit her lip nervously before delivering her final salvo. "Whoever murdered him did so with the same efficient brutality that he had practised his whole life. He was in their way and now he's not. Problem solved."

"Are you suggesting that he wasn't murdered for the inheritance so much as the power he still wielded over you all?"

"I think…" She hesitated, drawing her hand across her face to clear a single stray hair from one eye. "I think I could spend a millennium trying to work out what was going through my brothers' and sisters' heads and not come close. I was rather hoping you might do that for me." She got to her feet to show that the preliminary discussion was over.

I remained where I was. "You go ahead. I need to think for a while before I start the interviews."

"Very good, but don't take too long." There was a brief flash of confidence in her eyes. It was just enough to remind me that she was the boss and I was there to do a job. "The clock's ticking."

I watched as she walked out of the rose garden, her tiny skirt swishing prettily with each step. When she had gone, I opened the app to call Dean.

"Listen, with all the spy equipment you have, is there any way to check whether Audrey really was in Thailand when her dad was murdered?"

He didn't have time to answer. "Izzy? This is your mother. I'm deeply disappointed in you."

Nothing new there.

"Mum, why are you in Dean's office?"

"Ramesh told me he was here so I came over. Now don't change the subject. Why didn't you tell me that you were investigating another murder? How is *The Clever Dick Detective Agency* ever going to get off the ground if you don't keep me informed of developments?"

There were so many things wrong with what she'd just said, but there was no time to correct her. "I told Greg where I was." Yep, I trusted my stepdad far more than Mum to keep a secret. "I didn't want to make you worry. Now, can I please talk to Dean?"

"Not a chance." The line was quiet for a moment. "At least, not before I tell you something important. I've had a thorough debriefing from his tech squad and I think, at this point, I'm well qualified to tell you that the butler did it."

I sighed down the line at her. "Mum, that's just a cliché. It's not even that common in crime fiction. And besides, Gladwell would gain very little from Mr Porter's death so why bother murdering him?"

"I haven't got to the motive yet, darling," she cleared her throat officiously, "but I'm confident of the culprit."

"Thank you, Mum, now put Dean on."

"I'm here, Izzy." His voice sounded distant and I could tell that the mic had been wrestled off him.

"I'm sorry about this. If Mum and Ramesh get in your way, you can chuck them out."

"How dare you," Ramesh's voice came back. "If it weren't for the fact I'm not talking to you, I'd give you a serious piece of my mind."

I ignored him. "Dean, did you hear my question before about Audrey?"

"I heard it, but there's not much I can do. Short of hacking into Thai border control, I can't say for sure if Audrey was where she says she was. Is it important? Do you think she's involved?"

"Not particularly. I figured we should check it out though." I wasn't quite sure how to phrase the next question. "So... that hacking you mentioned, is it something that one of your friends might fancy trying?"

"What you're suggesting is highly illegal, but…" There was a murmur of voices and one excited, "Ooh!" before Dean came back on the line. "I'll have to get back to you on it. Listen, Izzy. There's an audio file you should hear. We went through last night's feeds and came back with nothing. But, about ten minutes ago, we caught two of your suspects talking."

The sound of his office died away and I could hear the two Porter brothers whispering back and forth to one another.

"Stop being such a baby. You're worrying about nothing."

"Why did you and Audrey ever think this would be a good idea?" I'm pretty sure this was Cameron's voice.

"For the last time, I was joking. And as soon as Audrey bought into it, I made my objections very clear." Edmund was even whinier than the night before. "If you'd backed me up, that interfering nobody would never have ended up here."

"And make everyone think I was the one who killed Dad? No thank you."

Edmund let out a resigned sigh. "It's fine. She won't get anywhere, she's a total amateur."

"For goodness sake. What if she does?" Cameron sounded desperate. "We all have secrets that we'd rather not air. What if she works out what I…" There was a sudden thud and the recording cut out.

"What did he say next?" I asked into my watch. I'm pretty sure I didn't have to hold it to my mouth, but I liked doing it. It felt very Star-Trekky and cool – if that's not a contradiction in terms.

"Someone must have come in. We think it was probably the butler judging by his movement on the other cameras." This side of Dean's personality was impressively business-like.

"Good work. Keep me updated if you catch them again."

"Izzy?" Mum was back, speaking far too loudly into the mic. "I have every faith in you and I know you can crack the case wide-"

I pressed the button on my watch and ended the call.

Chapter Ten

There were various factors working against me if I wanted to crack… if I wanted to find the killer. Time was the obvious one. As Audrey had reminded me, the clock was ticking. I had a little over a day left to work out which of these beautiful, conniving creatures had murdered Mr Porter and why. But, for one simple reason, I wasn't as nervous as I probably should have been.

Back when I was looking into Bob's death, I'd had to do everything on the sly. I couldn't ask direct questions for fear that someone would work out what I was up to and stop my covert investigation. This time, everything was different. Even if Edmund wasn't happy about it, I could talk to whoever I liked and go wherever I wanted. The fact that everyone there knew they were a suspect was liberating and it made me think that, if I could have spent a few hours grilling my ex-officemates. I'd have come to the right conclusion much sooner.

A bigger problem now was that this was all new to me. I was confident I could work out any puzzle and see through my suspects' lies, as long as I had a clear plan for what needed to be done. The crime scene was there at my disposal, but I had the feeling that the clues I'd found – the bottle, the domino and the old key – would mean nothing if I couldn't hack open my suspects heads. Metaphorically speaking, of course.

My mind kept coming back to Stephen Gladwell. Unlike me, a butler can glide around the house practically unseen. He had witnessed these people grow up, been present for every scandal and argument and surely knew them better than they knew themselves. If I was to get anywhere, I'd need him on my side.

On my walk back to the house, I decided on my strategy. Though it was tempting to jump straight in with Edmund, or see what was keeping Daisy so quiet, that would need preparation. Gladwell was the key; I was more certain of it by the second. I'd talk to him first, then see what Cook might know, before moving on to my main suspects.

Another advantage to my surveillance network was the fact that I could easily find out where someone was last seen. A quick message to

Dean informed me that Gladwell had recently left the house through a side door.

"Hot day for it." I tried to sound casual, as I strolled across the yard to the shade of a large outbuilding where he was sitting polishing the first in a line of leather shoes.

"Good morning, Miss Palmer." He bowed his head politely. "Lunch won't be served for a couple of hours so I'm trying to get a jump on some work."

I stood watching his careful administrations. "Can you run me through the events of Thursday night while you do?"

He paused his brushing and looked at me, as if the light of day could have told him something far more revealing than his sightings of me in the ancient house.

"Certainly, Madam. I started preparing-"

"You don't have to call me Madam, or milady or anything like that. My name is Izzy. I know it's your job to stand on ceremony, but it's not necessary with me."

That made him smile. His beautifully wrinkled face creased up even more. "I started preparing the dining room for dinner straight after lunch and the children arrived between four and five."

"Do none of them live here anymore then?"

"Only Audrey lives at Vomeris Hall. The others have flats up in town, except Master Cameron who has a house not far from here. As it happens, Master Edmund arrived the day before the party so we'd had the pleasure of his company for a little longer."

"Do you know why he came down early?" The sun had sneakily popped up above the roof of the building and I had to shimmy round into the shade to avoid being roasted.

"I'm not sure that it's my duty to report on family matters." He was slathering thick, black polish onto a man's boot and didn't look up at me.

"Is that the butler's code or something? Like doctor-patient confidentiality?"

"I wouldn't know about that. But I reckon it's only right I should repay the trust that the Porters have placed in me with a bit of discretion."

"It's the Porters who are paying me to find the killer and it's the

Porters who will suffer if I don't resolve this situation quickly." I paused to let my words sink in. "Think what a field day the papers will have speculating over which of the five children could have been responsible. They'll drag each one of them through the mud. Beatrix and Daisy will be painted as feckless party girls, Edmund a chancer, Cameron the snob. Even Audrey won't escape, despite being half the world away."

There was still no reaction, so I pressed my case. "It'll be much better for everyone if we find the murderer before the police get here. So are you going to help me or not?"

He eyed me wearily before answering my original question. "From what I overheard, Edmund got here early because he needed to talk to his father about a financial matter."

"Did they argue?"

He let out a deep breath and began to brush the boot more forcefully. "Yes. For about the thousandth time in his life, on Thursday night Edmund attempted to convince his father that there was no sense in having all these riches if he didn't share them with his family."

"I bet Mr Porter enjoyed that."

"Well." I could tell how hard it was for him to cough up dirt on the family he'd served so faithfully for so long. "In a way, he did actually. My old master liked nothing more than a good *discussion* – his word. He restated his usual argument that his children would be able to fritter his fortune away, as soon as he was good and buried."

"And what did Edmund say to that?"

Stephen stopped his work and looked for his words. I was worried for a moment that he might never find them. "It was the heat of the moment. He didn't mean anything by it."

"What did he say?"

He swallowed hard. "He said that it might happen sooner than Mr Porter expected. They'd been playing billiards together in the games room and Edmund threw his cue down and stormed out." Unlike the night before, his speech never veered back to his east London accent but held with the smartly clipped phrasing he'd learnt for his trade.

"Do you know why he wanted money so desperately?"

"No, I don't. I was not privy to that information." There was a determination in his voice, but it never broke over into anger. At the end of each sentence, his warm grin would reappear to show there were no hard feelings.

"I appreciate you telling me all this. Could you continue with the details of Thursday night? What happened once everyone had arrived?"

"An aperitif was served in the grand salon to celebrate Miss Daisy's new job. They were all in good spirits and-"

"Wait." I crouched down low so that I could once more escape the encroaching sun and look him in the eyes. "That's not true. Last night, Cameron told me that Mr Porter was angry because Audrey couldn't be there. Stop trying to cover for everyone. For your own benefit and theirs, tell me the truth."

He held my gaze for a moment and I could see that this was not the same person I'd shared a drink with the night before. It would be difficult to get the messy details out of him when he was on duty.

"Fine. In the ballroom after dinner, some more words were said. Edmund was still furious about the money. Daisy was upset because her moment was overshadowed and Cameron was cagey and morose. It was only Miss Beatrix who seemed to enjoy herself."

"Did it continue like that all night?"

He picked up a second boot. "More or less, though Beatrix did her best to entertain everyone. She got them all up for a dance and they finally seemed to have some fun."

"What sort of music did they listen to?"

"It was something from the sixties. Motown, that sort of thing. Why are you interested?"

"Nothing for you to worry about." All right, I admit, I only asked this to sound a bit quirky and weird. I didn't actually care what they were dancing to.

"What happened next?"

"I served drinks. The kids all went up to bed and Mr Porter retired to the library to do a bit of work. He called me to bring him tea at eleven thirty and that was the last time I saw him."

"And what about the rest of the household. Did you see anyone else that night or hear anything strange?"

"Not a soul. I stayed up till around one as usual – I'm not much of a sleeper."

"And where were you before bed?"

He shifted the boot round in his hand and looked up at me with a hint of appreciation. "I was in a room not far from the kitchen, shining up the silverware."

"Would you have known if anyone had gone into see Mr Porter?"

"If they'd been coming from that side of the house. I dare say I would."

"Thank you." I allowed my thoughts to consume me for a minute and he patiently polished another boot. "I've got one last question, but I need you to keep this to yourself."

He put his cloth and polish down and looked up at me tellingly. "I think you can trust me."

I took the brass key out and held it in the handkerchief I'd wrapped it in. "Do you know where this could be from?"

He laughed then. It was a sudden burst like a clap of thunder breaking into a cloudless day. "There are a million keys in this house. All I can tell you is that it's not one of my regular bunch." He fished in his pocket and showed me a mess of silver on a large ring. "I imagine it's from a cabinet, but even that doesn't narrow it down."

"Would you know if one was missing?"

He studied the key. "I'm afraid not, but it looks a little familiar. I'll have a think where it could have come from."

"Thanks, Stephen. I appreciate your help." I breathed out and the tension broke. "Seriously, I think I'm going to be needing it a lot."

We shared a nice, smiley moment then I headed back to the house to cross off the other servant from my list.

There was no sign of anyone in the main kitchen and I was about to head off for a little explore around the house when Cook appeared with a butcher's knife in one hand and a leg of lamb in the other. She really was one of the scariest-looking people I'd ever met.

She did it. She did it. She did it!

"Good morning, m' lovely. Beautiful day for it." She again seemed to be unaware that the *it* in question involved working out which of her masters was a murderer. "If you're peckish there's some sausage rolls just made."

Oh, joy. Oh heavens. I take it all back. She's the most saintly woman I've ever met.

My brain gets a little emotional when I'm hungry.

"Thank you so much, I'm starving." I helped myself to (several) sausage rolls from the tray on the kitchen table. They were still piping hot but too good to resist.

"Master Cameron loves my puff pastry. I like to make him little treats whenever he comes to visit."

I made some inappropriate noises of appreciation as I devoured the homemade delights. It wasn't the most professional start to an interview but, as I'd long since discovered, my love of baked goods generally trumps my work ethic.

I licked my fingers and tried to put on a stern face. "Cook, what's your real name?"

With the bloody limb in place on a chopping board, she raised the cleaver above her head. "Cook *is* my real name." The knife came down with an impressive *thwack!* "Brenda Cook."

I was tempted to ask her whether her surname had been the inspiration for her profession but doubted it would shed much light on the murder.

"Would you mind taking me through the events of Thursday night?"

She pulled a chunk of flesh from the bone before answering. "I made a beef casserole. We always have casserole on Thursday when the family are here. I made some savoury scones to go with it – I've always found it a funny combination but that's what Mr Porter enjoyed best. He said there was nothing like scones dipped in beef stock."

Though I was hoping for juicy details, this wasn't what I had in mind. I decided to help her to get to where we needed to go. "And what was for dessert?"

"Sweet scones, of course. With clotted cream and my raspberry jam. I always make the two kinds together and no one complains."

Ask her if she makes a good lemon meringue pie. I love lemon meringue pie.

Shhhhh!

I made a mental note of the menu. I very much doubted it would factor into my investigation but it might come in handy one day if I ever throw a dinner party. "Okay, so after you'd finished cooking, what do you remember of the evening?"

"Well, I had my supper here of course, as I tend to. Back when my hubby was about, I'd go back to our place. Now he's gone, I spend more time here in the evenings."

I put on my most sensitive voice. "Oh, I'm truly sorry for your loss."

She gave the bone another whack. "He's not dead. I slung him out. He's a miserable old fella, my husband, and I'd had enough of him." She went from grandmotherly sweet to terrifying in the space of a sentence. I decided not to rule her out so swiftly after all. What if Mr Porter had fallen foul of his faithful chef?

Would she have had the strength to lift him up onto the wall though?

Yes, she would. She definitely would.

"Oh." I picked over my words. "I'm glad you're rid of him then."

"I had my dinner here in the kitchen and finished up with a glass of sherry. I'm not much of a drinker, but it helps me sleep."

"Did you see anyone after dinner?"

She stopped her chopping then and looked over at me rather sadly. "No, not down here. The family don't tend to come round this way. I'm not sure that anyone but Miss Audrey even knows my name to be honest."

I hadn't taken the time to consider her a real human being until that moment. She was a cartoon character of a cook. Big, ruddy cheeked and with a rolling pin never far away. But, as she looked at me then, I realised something about her that I doubt anyone else knew. She was a groupie, a hanger-on. Though they lived at the same address and she could talk in great detail about each member of the Porter family's favourite dishes, it was second-hand information, passed along to her through her sole remaining colleague.

Beatrix, Cameron, Daisy and Edmund didn't know her any more than they knew the postwoman or the gardeners. And though she was locked away in the kitchen and only caught glimpses of them down distant hallways and through windows, she loved them like a mother.

It made me want to give her a hug and have a good cry so I pressed on. "You said you have a house of your own?"

"That's right. I've rooms above the stables. It's cosy up there. My fella used to call it my granny flat, not that he gave me any kids."

I didn't know how to respond to that and stuck to my questions. "So, did you notice anything out of the ordinary when you walked home on the night of the murder?"

She hesitated and I could see the same reluctance in her that I'd noticed in Gladwell. "Urmmm… yes actually. I heard a scream."

"What time was it?"

"It was about twelve o'clock and…" Her words dried up for a moment but I nudged her on with the tilt of my head. "I thought it was someone messing around, but the sound was from the front of the house. Now that I know what happened, I realise it must have come from the library. I… I just wish I'd gone to see. I could have saved him. I know I could."

She put the knife down and supported her weight on one arm on the table. At least I had an idea of the time of death now. I wasn't sure if it would help me work out who killed him but it was good to bear in mind.

"Don't think like that." I was trying to be sensitive again. "Who knows what would have happened if you'd gone to the library. You could have joined Mr Porter up on the wall."

She froze, a tear descending one cheek. "Did they string him up like an animal? Those savages!"

"Urmmm… well, yeah. Sort of." *More sterling work, Izzy.* "I'm sorry to upset you, but what exactly did you hear?"

Her eyes fell down to the butchered lamb. "There were no words, just a long drawn-out shriek of horror. I'll never forget it. That sound will never leave me."

The sudden fear that had overtaken her as she recounted the moment, had infected me too. I shivered as a feeling like someone's fingers teasing the top of my spine passed over me.

Casting off the eerie silence, I fired up my next question. "What time did the family finish dinner?"

Cook perked back up. "Oh, I'd say at about nine. They eat quite early round here."

"Uhuh. So what were you doing between then and twelve o'clock?"

She looked guilty again. "I… well, the truth is… I feel a bit silly about it actually but…"

"There's no need to be nervous. It's a simple question."

She tried again. "The truth is, the sherry went to my head and I fell asleep here at the table."

Had I just caught her out in a lie? "So you were asleep that whole time? Didn't Gladwell come in to make tea at some point?"

"Oh, no. We have a drinks room between the breakfast room and the smoking room. Stephen serves all the drinks from there."

A drinks room? Of course they have a drinks room! Ooh, I wonder if they have a dessert room too. We should probably investigate in there.

"So that was it? You woke up just before twelve and went to your apartment?"

"That was it. I climbed into bed when I got home and didn't think about the scream again until yesterday morning, when I heard the news of Mr Porter's death."

I didn't reply. I sat turning over her answers in my head in the hope I might find some chink in her evidence. Perhaps her only crime was helping herself to too much sherry and dozing off, but there was a nervousness to her that was hard to square with the rest of her character.

"Sorry to love you and leave you, but I'd best be getting on." She wiped her hands on her apron and flicked the tear off her chin. "Plenty of mouths to feed. It's been a while since the kids have all been here together for so long. It makes a nice change."

"Thanks for your help, Cook." I stood up from the table and headed to the door. A sudden thought occurred to me and, Columbo-like, I turned around at the last moment. "Just one more thing…"

She paused her preparations and looked up at me innocently. "What's that?"

"I don't suppose you could make a lemon meringue pie, could you?"

Chapter Eleven

I was debating which of my four suspects to begin with when I walked past the games room and decided to have a poke about in there first. It was a large, wood-panelled space with a full-size snooker table that occupied the centre of the room.

On one wall, a glass cabinet was stocked full of boxes. Games of every kind from Backgammon to Yahtzee were neatly piled, with barely an inch of space around them. There was a key in the lock but it was an entirely different shape from the one I'd found in the library.

That would have been too easy.

On the central shelf, a beautifully carved wooden box caught my attention. It stood out for being by far the oldest piece in the collection. I put my gloves back on and carefully extracted it. The top of the box was decorated with flowers and abstract patterns, but, when opened, the lid displayed a gruesome tableau with slaves being pulled on chains and whipped by their masters. It was not the obvious design for a child's toy.

The dominos within were stacked on their sides in two neat rows. I took one out to ensure it was the same style as the ivory piece at the crime scene and noticed there was just enough space for the missing piece to have been housed there. The tile looked almost identical to the double six I'd found. I was about to flick through the other pieces to confirm the absence when a sudden noise made me jump out of my nice comfy t-shirt.

A large china vase came flying into the room to smash against the far wall. By the time I'd made sense of what had happened, whoever was responsible had bolted off down the corridor. I could hear their heavy footfall as I ran over to the door but, when I stuck my head out, they'd already disappeared.

This is getting dangerous.

I don't think the vase was aimed at me. I think it was a warning.

I walked to the other side of the snooker table to inspect the remains. Like most things in the house, it looked old and expensive. It had a bold design of large purple flowers on a blue background and I didn't need to hunt long to find a William Moorcroft signature. The maker of the vase that someone had chucked at me – who happened to be my deceased grandmother's favourite – was another piece of evidence that I very much doubted would lead me to the murderer.

"Dean, please tell me you can work out who just ran past the games room."

He came straight back to me. "We only caught a flash of them as they passed the camera in the hall. They must have come in from the garden and I don't understand where they disappeared to after."

"What about who it wasn't? Can you work out where everyone is right now and eliminate anybody?"

He hummed and hesitated a little before replying. "I can try. We might have to go back through the footage a bit to be sure. I can tell you that Cook and Gladwell have been in the kitchen for the last five minutes."

"That's what he wants you to think, Izzy," my Mum shouted, to the amusement of Dean and his team. "The butler did it. You have to believe me!"

"Okay, thanks, Mum. Dean, buzz my watch if you find anything out."

"Yep." He huffed into the earpiece for a moment and I knew he had more to say. "Izzy, don't you think you're a bit underdressed?"

I motioned to the top of a cabinet where I'd stashed the tiny camera. "Push off! This is my comfiest t-shirt. What would you say is more appropriate for detective work?"

"Urmmm... pretty much anything?"

The microphone crackled and I heard Ramesh barge his way in. "He's got you there, Iz. You look like someone stole your school uniform and you had to get dressed from the lost property bin."

There was more laughter from the nerds in the office. My mother didn't hold back either. I pressed the button on my watch again and hung up on them with great satisfaction.

Figuring that, if someone had gone to such lengths to disturb my snooping, I was on the right track, I went back to look at the dominos. There was no double-six tile to be found, so it seemed safe to assume the one in the library had come from there. The Clues column in my head was getting longer but had little relation to the far spottier

Hypotheses and Suspects list.

I went to look at the snooker cues on the off-chance that one of them had been used as a weapon. I knew that Edmund had argued with his father, right there, on the night before the murder. What more fitting way to drive his point home than by stabbing a snapped-off cue right into Daddy's back? Sadly, my theory didn't play out. Every space on the rack was full and none of the cues looked damaged or bloodstained.

I thought I should check out the dartboard for a similar reason when a figure darkened the doorway.

"Come on, Izzy. No time for games." Edmund sounded as smug as ever. "Follow me, please."

I noticed that he'd arrived from the same direction that the vase-chucker had disappeared off to. "Wait, where have you just come from?"

He turned to go then paused again, his hand resting on the door frame. "My room. Why?"

I felt my watch vibrate and subtly accepted the call.

"He's telling the truth, Izzy," Dean told me. "We traced him all the way from the east-wing staircase. I don't think he was the one."

"Never mind that." I made sure to hit back at Edmund in my toughest voice. "Why should I go anywhere with you?"

He smiled. It was the kind of look that would either make you fall in love or launch yourself across the room to slap into oblivion. "Because I think it's high time I incriminated myself." He closed his flapping mouth again and slipped from the room.

The plebs in the gallery seemed to enjoy his parting line. "Woooh!" One of the lady-nerds hollered. "Pretty smooth." It was followed up with some clapping and lusty noises.

"He is hot stuff!" Ramesh inevitably added.

"Izzy darling?" Mum had her mind on other matters. "Perhaps you could stop off at your room on the way. You must have a nice blouse or something to go with that skirt."

And… click. Bye for now, my faithful support crew. I have enough voices in my head to be going on with.

Edmund was so confident in his powers of persuasion that we'd gone halfway across the house before he looked back to see if I was following. I was of course, but at a safe distance. That way, I could pretend I was tailing him like a real detective, instead of going along at his command.

We travelled to the wing where the Porter family had their rooms, and ascended the Restoration-era staircase – which Wikipedia had assured me was one of the finest architectural features of Vomeris Hall. He glanced down at me from the landing and I had a brief, nasty flashback to my pursuit of Tedwin and Noémi aged eleven.

He feigned nonchalance, but I could tell that he had lingered there to guide me onwards. By the time I caught up with him, he was safely ensconced in his own territory. His door was wide open so I entered without knocking.

"There you are." He was sitting at a broad, wooden desk that seemed too big for the space it occupied.

"Here I am."

We were in an entrance area to the main bedroom, which was still bigger than my lounge back home. On the wall behind where he sat, there was a vast collection of weapons on display. Axes and daggers and knives fought for space among guns, clubs, maces and hammers.

"I'm impressed," I said, as I sat down in a ridiculously uncomfortable, hardwood chair that I had to assume he'd chosen especially for me.

He peered over his shoulder to look at his arsenal. "You soon forget they're there."

"The fact you managed to find an even more macabre decoration scheme than the one in your father's study is almost more impressive than the collection itself."

He cleared his throat and straightened his posture self-consciously. "It was Dad who put them there. I think he was trying to toughen me up or something."

"Did it work?"

He didn't reply, but his smile returned. I couldn't tell if he was trying to charm me or patronise me.

I pressed on. "So, Master Edmund, why did you want to see me?"

"There's no need for formality, Izzy. Mr Porter will suffice." He laughed and I failed to hide quite how skin-crawlingly self-satisfied (yet head-explodingly handsome) I found him.

"Very droll."

He crossed his arms. "Oh come on, I was only joking. I thought that was what we were doing. A bit of back and forth. A bit of banter. How about we start again?"

"Fine. Why did you bring me here, Edmund?"

He paused once more before speaking and I knew that he was incapable of giving a straight answer to the simplest of questions. Everything he said would have a gloss and spin on and I'd have to be on my guard to see through it.

"I want to tell you my side of things. I'm sure that my brother and sisters will all have something very worthwhile to say about me, but you can't believe everything that falls from their lips. After all, one of them is a murderer."

"So you didn't kill your father?"

He drummed his hands on the empty table top in front of him. "No. I. Did. Not."

"And why should I believe you? I'm sure it will come as no surprise that, up until now, you're my prime suspect."

He ran his hands delicately through his hair, as if scared of disturbing it. "I'm flattered, I really am. But think of it like this. I'm the black sheep of the family, I've known it all my life. It was practically written on my hospital band when I was born. What hope would I have of getting away with murder?"

I full-on scoffed at that argument. "A higher probability of your guilt can't be used as evidence that you're innocent."

"Think about your beloved Agatha Christie." He jutted his head out like he'd made a killer point. "That's right, Izzy, Dad showed me your little write-up in the Croydon Herald."

Croydon Advertiser, but whatever.

"'The crime-fiction fan who brought a murderer to justice,' isn't that how they put it? You know that, in detective stories, it's never the obvious suspect who ends up being the killer. It's the quiet one no one notices or the benevolent member of the community with a guilty secret."

Get him, Izzy. Prove him wrong.

"Actually, that's not true." I might have let a smirk creep across my face. "It's quite often the first person you consider. Good writers trick you into thinking that the black sheep, the ex-con or the adulterer couldn't have done it, only to reveal at the last moment that it was them all along. Perhaps that's what you're doing right now – coming up with reasons why it couldn't possibly be you."

He fell quiet for a moment and looked me up and down, like he'd only just noticed I was there. "You're beautiful when you're angry."

"And you're disgusting." I swallowed the bile that was rising in my throat. "I mean, not aesthetically. I'm not going to lie; you are basically the most attractive man I've ever shared the same air as." Thoughts of David and Danny attacked me and I fought them off. "But looks aren't everything and the idea that your tacky comments could ever convince a woman to sleep with you makes me physically sick."

"So you *do* find me sexy?" Trust a man like Edmund to reduce an argument to who finds who sexy.

"Well, if that's the best you can offer as proof of your innocence, I'll be off."

I stood up to leave and he raised his right hand.

"I'm sorry, Izzy. I'm not trying to seduce you, I just…" He searched for some way to explain his odiousness and eventually gave up. "Please, sit back down and give me a chance to tell you what happened on Thursday night."

I hesitated for a moment but eventually gave in. Audrey wasn't paying me to make friends. I was there to find a killer and, truth or lies, whatever Edmund had to say could help me reach that goal.

"If they haven't already, I've no doubt someone will tell you that I'd been arguing with Dad over money." His tone had changed once more. He was serious, concerned even. "It's true, of course. Dad hasn't given me a penny since I was sixteen years old. He introduced me to rich friends and found me internships in the city but that was his world, not mine."

I tilted my head to look at him. "You're doing an excellent job of showing why everyone thinks you did it."

"Thank you. That's exactly what I expected, but give me a while longer and we'll see what you think." He opened a drawer in the desk and took out a financial brochure to fan himself with. Most of the house retained that distinctive, stately home chill, but up here, with the door to his room open and the windows piping in summer air, it was stifling. "I'm telling you this stuff to show I have nothing to hide. I think that should work in my favour at least a touch."

The fingers on his free hand drummed faster. "Yes, I argued with Dad the night before he was killed and again at dinner but I had a good reason to. I'm broke. Completely wiped out. I've tried earning money, as he always told me I should, but it's not so simple. I've come to the conclusion that there are people like Dad who have magnetic fingers, which money zooms towards, and people like me who don't."

"Thanks, Edmund. You've proven that you had the motive and the anger to kill your dad, if you could just sign a confession, I think we'll be done."

"Will you please listen?" He was getting more desperate and sounded like he genuinely needed my understanding. "I can't prove to you that I didn't kill him, but I can tell you why it could never have been me."

I let his words fade away before replying. "Okay, I'll hear you out."

"I came home to try, one last time, to convince him why he should share his wealth with us. It's not just me. Cameron's in a bad way and I was worried he'd do something stupid."

I might have snorted a little in disbelief.

"I'm not suggesting it was for entirely selfless reasons. I'm about to lose my flat in Richmond, my girlfriend split up with me because I couldn't keep her in the style she was accustomed to and none of my old contacts will answer my calls. Yet none of that matters because I knew I could move home whenever I wanted. I had zero desire to live with Dad, but it wouldn't have been so bad."

"So you're saying you didn't kill him for the money, because money's not that important to you?"

He sat up and looked comparatively cheerful. "Well... yeah. Unlike my brother, that's exactly it. And there's more."

He spun in the black leather executive chair he was sitting in, to look up at the potted history of man's most violent achievements. He reached for a short-handled dagger, which looked like it had been passed around a prison yard more than a few times, and plucked it from the bracket on the wall.

I gasped involuntarily. For some reason, I hadn't imagined them being so easy to remove.

"This isn't me, Izzy." He turned back round and pressed the tapered point of the blade against the end of one finger. "Dad never cultivated the killer instinct in me that he was hoping for. He constantly told me that I wasn't ambitious enough and he was right. I could never be the savage businessman that he was, just like I could never have stuck a knife in him."

I was quick to jump on that. "How do you know he was killed with a knife?"

"It's an expression damn it." He cast the dagger down and it skidded across the polished desk towards me. "And besides, all my weapons are accounted for." He motioned to the wall once more where, I have to admit, every other bracket was occupied. "Can't you see that I liked the old guy? We fought and argued and I could never get my head around his stinginess, but that was all part of the fun with us."

Silence fell and I could tell that he'd come to the end of his defence.

"Fine, if you didn't kill your father, who did?"

He put his teeth against his upper lip and took his time to answer. "That all comes down to who Dad was most successful in shaping in his image. Which of my siblings achieved the ruthlessness that I lack?"

"And the answer is?" I flicked the end of the discarded dagger so that it spun like a bottle.

"Well, Cameron's desperate enough, Beatrix's cruel enough and Audrey's certainly clever enough to have got one of the others to do it for her."

"But not Daisy?"

"No, not little D. She's too sweet. If it wasn't for Beatrix leading her astray, she'd be off working as a missionary somewhere or helping poor people learn to recycle."

"Forgive me if I don't take your word for it."

"Do what you like, but, given that Audrey was in Thailand, if I were you I'd focus on Beatrix and Cameron."

Reaching the end of its spin, the dagger came to a rest. It was pointing straight at Edmund.

I thought back to the conversation between the two brothers that Dean had played me. "You said that Cameron is desperate. Why's that?"

He smiled and I got another flash of his arrogance. It helped remind me not to invest too much in anything he said. "I'm not going to dump him in it. You'll have to ask him yourself."

"You're such a loyal brother." I wasn't serious.

His smile went full grin. "You really think you know me, don't you, Izzy? Since the moment you walked into this house, you thought you'd got us all sussed out."

"I know a slimy bloke when I see one."

"I'd hold fire on that if I were you. You might discover this weekend that you can't judge a book by a cover after all."

"In my experience, book covers give you a pretty good idea of what's inside." I stood to leave. "But let's have this conversation again once I know for sure who hacked up your father."

"Great." His eyes stuck to me as I backed out of the room. "There's nothing I'd like more."

Chapter Twelve

I'd completely failed to ask him any of the questions I had planned, but can't honestly say I'd expected any useful answers from him. He'd got right under my skin just like his father. It was a less than endearing family characteristic and made me feel like screaming again.

I couldn't let him get to me. I had a job to do and, seeing as I was already in the east wing, I figured I'd have a poke about there. I needed to calm down after my clash of heads so I was happy that there was no one around to set me off on another intense interview quite so soon.

Through the door next to Edmund's, I found an almost identical room to the one I'd just been in; an entrance parlour leading to a larger bedroom. This one appeared to be used as a makeshift dressing room. There was a broad wooden desk on one side, but it was piled high with clothes and the rest of the space was taken up by ancient, wooden wardrobes, which again reminded me of Narnia.

Go on, climb inside. You never know!

Behind the desk was another elaborate display, this time with a hundred glass cases, each with a selection of brightly coloured butterflies pinned in place. It was beautiful and tragic and I was instantly confident that this was Daisy's room. The heaps of clothes weren't gothic-looking enough to be Beatrix's either and, when I peeked inside the main bedroom, I could see pictures of Daisy with friends and lovers, displayed on a low bureau near the door.

There was an enormous four-poster bed against the opposite wall but the rest of the room was oddly sparse for such a grand space. I thought about looking through her clothes or the chest of drawers but I knew nothing about the youngest daughter at this point and it felt intrusive and premature.

I went back outside and darted up another staircase to the second floor where I correctly guessed that Mr Porter's own bedroom would be. It occupied most of the upper level and had clearly once been divided into smaller spaces. I was surprised to see how sparse his quarters were though. I'd imagined him having an en suite bathroom at the very least – perhaps matched with a home gym and Jacuzzi.

Instead, he'd opted for a plain white room with the original small windows of the house and a single bed in the far corner.

The one concession to luxury was a huge walk-in wardrobe which I made sure to walk into. As I opened the door, a light flicked on to reveal a long rail of expensively tailored suits in fifty shades of blue. Saville Row, I cleverly deduced, based on the labels which said Saville Row on them. His shirt and tie collection was equally vast and a good bit more colourful. I very much doubted there was a single polyester fibre in there and I let my fingers dance across the exquisite fabrics.

Beneath the hanging rail, there were shelves of shoes interspersed with grey filing cabinets. Even here, business had its place. My latex gloves back on – in fact, from now on, let's just assume I put them on whenever necessary, all right? – I opened the top drawer of the first cabinet I came to. The files inside were arranged by year, dating way back to the early eighties. I wondered what grubby secrets an accountant could have extracted from them. Sadly I was the one reading and had no idea what any of it meant. Seriously, how could anyone need the information *65589425PL* in the column *Transaction Data*?

The next three cabinets spanned the decades but offered no new revelations so I gave up and searched on high for what I was looking for. A shelf above the suits held a number of boxes and I brought a small, red leather case down, expecting to find cufflinks or tiepins but it was nothing so prosaic.

I'd never touched a gun before and wasn't tempted to, but the neat silver revolver in its black velvet housing that I found inside was oddly pretty. The case even had spaces for six small bullets which pointed up at me, begging to be taken out and loaded.

Why would Porter have a gun?

Why would he have half the stuff there is in this house? Perhaps it was a gift. It clearly hasn't been fired and no one's been shot so let's file it under *presumably useless evidence,* shall we?

I moved on to a plain brown cardboard box that was conspicuous in its inconspicuousness. Opening the flaps, I discovered a jumble of family photos.

"That's more like it," I said out loud as I hadn't uttered a word for literally minutes.

It was the one trace of a personal life I found in Mr Porter's entire personal space. I wondered if they were the leftovers from when he'd planned out the photo wall in my bedroom as I saw several repeated photos and it was difficult once again to find a trace of his ex-wife.

There were more shots of Beatrix on stage in various amateur productions plus a few of her posed in a studio. Edmund paraded through most of them in camouflage with a rifle over his shoulder and Cameron looked constantly bored. Whenever there were babies to be held, Audrey would be the one doing the mothering. In the group shots, it made me sad to see how well they'd got on as children, I couldn't imagine such loyalty still held true with a murderer in their midst.

After five minutes searching, I finally found a picture of Daisy with her mother. It must have been the day she was born as the poor woman was dressed in a pale green hospital gown and looked drained. She had the waifish appearance of her daughter – a far cry from the strong, recognisable features of Porter himself. Her face was tentative and serious, like she wasn't quite sure what to make of the whole experience. On the back of the photo, in faint, elegant handwriting, someone had written the date, the name of the hospital and "Daisy Elizabeth Porter, 6.3lb."

Once I was sure that I hadn't missed anything important, I put the box away and moved onto another one. There were photos in that one too, but they couldn't be described as personal. There were snaps going back to the foundation of Porter's company, staged like the annual class photographs we had to take in primary school. In each one, Mr Porter stood in the centre of the group, which grew bigger with each passing year. Few of them had anything written on the back and what I could find was smudged or faded.

The only thing that surprised me was that the waifish woman from Daisy's baby photos made an appearance in several pictures. I hadn't realised that Mrs Porter had worked at P&P. Seeing how business was Aldrich Porter's whole life before he retired, I guess it only made sense that he'd have met his wife at work. She looked happy in some of them, but never healthy. A frail, almost ghostly woman who did not match up to the picture I'd had in my head when Audrey had talked of her mother.

Bob featured heavily too of course. As time went by, his position in the photos moved steadily closer to his boss. It was no great shock that he was just as repulsive in his youth as when I knew him.

No doubt there were interesting conclusions to draw from all this, but I wasn't there yet. Figuring I could always come back for another look if necessary I put the box back on the shelf, had a quick look for a safe that didn't appear to exist and headed back downstairs.

I was eager to see the other bedrooms and find out what each sibling had on the wall of their dressing room, but then a bell rung out from another small speaker. I might have jumped a bit as, even though Audrey had given me the freedom of the house, I still felt like I was trespassing.

I assumed the bell I'd heard was the signal for lunch and descended the staircase to find out. In planning my investigation, I'd failed to take into account how much of rich people's time is taken up by eating.

There was no one around, so I took the opportunity to check in with my team. "Dean, have you found anything out from your surveillance?"

"Nothing much," Ramesh replied for him. "This spying lark is a lot less fun than I'd imagined."

"Feel free to go home whenever you like, Ra."

He didn't listen. "Most of the time it's just a bunch of videos of empty rooms. And even when people do appear they tend to sit and read a magazine or something. It's like a live feed of Love Island but everyone's got far too many clothes on."

I decided to ignore him and repeat my original question. "Dean, have you found anything out from your surveillance?"

"Well, I can say with great certainty that Edmund seems nervous about your presence there," the grumpy genius finally replied. "He's been on edge all morning. We saw him first thing, pacing about in the salon like he was trying to reach his daily step count. He took a call from someone too and was shouting and waving his arms about the whole time. We couldn't hear what he was saying as he went out in the garden, but I caught his reactions through the window."

"Anything else?"

"Yeah… Audrey is the only one who does anything to help with the running of the house. I've yet to see her brothers and sisters even acknowledge the presence of their staff. Daisy seems permanently morose."

"You said it," Ra confirmed. "I've never seen such a mopey woman. What's she got to be so sad about?"

"I feel for her, I really do," a new voice added. "She's like a lonely princess trapped in a tower."

"Dad, is that you?"

"That's right!" He sounded happy to be there.

"I asked him to come," Mum explained. "I found his perspective to be truly invaluable last time round and I'm sure he'll help me build a case on that old devil Gladwell."

I let out a tired sigh. "I'm surprised you haven't dragged Greg along too."

"I'm here as well, Izzy," my stepdad confirmed. "Your Mum's car has a problem with the starter motor so I had to drive her over."

"Feel free to throw your opinion in any time you fancy, Greg. Everyone else has." I stopped walking and tried to get a sense of where I was. "Hang on a second, I've gone the wrong way again. I'll ring you later."

Though I was almost coming to understand the layout of the house, there were so many areas set aside for serving food, it was difficult to know in which direction to head. There was no one in the dining room or the ballroom. The breakfast room was empty – as I suppose was only logical – and the terrace by the back lawn was equally deserted. I figured the only solution was to go to the one person in the house who had told me anything with any certainty. Only, I couldn't find Gladwell either so I headed to the kitchen in search of Cook.

"Cook, do you have any idea where lunch-"

"On the veranda, Miss." She was pulling out a big dish of something delicious from the oven.

Oh, man. I wish posh people were killed more often so we could go to their houses and eat all their food.

SHHH!

"Sorry, where is the-"

"Beside the vineyard, Miss." She spoke through a cloud of steam, but presumably caught a glimpse of how absolutely clueless I was, as she immediately followed up her reply. "Which is a way beyond the stables."

98

"Thanks! I appreciate it."

I walked through the kitchen and was about to leave through the side door when she called after me.

"Izzy?" She had a great big grin on her face. "There might be a treat for you after the main course."

Yayyyyyyyyy! Piiiiiiiiiiiie!

I gave her a really cheesy thumbs-up and ducked out.

The stables were the set of outbuildings where I'd found Gladwell working that morning. As I made my way past them, Daisy caught up with me.

"Do you know where the veranda is?" I admit it was a stupid question, but I was still unsure if she was capable of speech. "I'm a bit lost."

"I've lived here most of my life." Her voice was just as delicate as I'd imagined it would be. "I know where everything is."

"Great, you couldn't draw me a map could you?" I let out a long, irritating laugh, like what I'd said was impossibly hilarious.

I do this thing with people who don't say much where I become excessively chirpy and talkative. It's just not natural for me to be quiet for so long. I've tried countless times to put an end to this quirk of my personality but I soon fall back into it. She was lucky I hadn't put my arm around and told her we were going to be friends forever.

"They call them the stables but I don't see any horses!" At least I didn't do funny hand gestures like an over-insistent clown (this time).

"They're on the other side of the building." She smiled like she had a stomach ache that she didn't want anyone to know about and I concentrated hard to avoid spewing out any more inanities.

I'm pretty sure that the awkward silence that followed was worse than what came before. The noise of the loose stony path beneath our feet was almost unbearable. This encounter did not make me look forward to interviewing Daisy. I'd probably end up leading her in a show-tune medley or doing a dance to cheer her up. When the veranda came into view, I let out a happy sigh and accelerated towards it.

"Izzy, I'm glad you found us." Audrey seemed pleased to see me, which helped me forget the excruciating twenty seconds I'd just lived through.

The veranda was probably the prettiest part of the estate. The wooden trellis held a mix of honeysuckle and climbing grape vines, under which a long table was laid out ready for lunch. A perfectly white table cloth matched everyone's neat outfits and I wondered if I could sneak off behind one of the rows of vines to at least turn my acid-house t-shirt inside out.

The vineyard itself stretched into the distance across a gently rolling hill and, with the un-Britishly hot weather we were having, it was easy to imagine we were nestled in the Provençal countryside instead of southern England.

"What's she doing here?" Edmund had arrived a few seconds after us and wasn't nearly as happy to see me as his sister. "We don't normally let *the help* eat with us."

Gladwell was serving wine already and I spotted a slight reaction from him. He put his feet together and straightened his back which caused Daisy's drink to splash down a little more noisily in her glass. By butlers' standards, I imagine this was tantamount to a rebellion.

"Izzy is our guest, as you know full well." Audrey put her rebellious little brother in his place. "If I were you, I'd try to be a bit nicer."

Sitting down opposite me, Edmund audibly scoffed. "Or what? She'll have me locked up?"

There was silence then as the reality of what he said sunk in. It was weirdly dramatic as everyone peered around at one another. It made me a little excited to think that I was responsible for the fear they were all experiencing. Four of the siblings knew they hadn't murdered their father but they'd still be wondering who had. Perhaps they were afraid that the killer would strike again or that they would get framed for the crime.

Just like in a bad soap opera, the silence lingered. It was Gladwell who finally broke it.

"If you're all quite ready, I will serve the first course." The level of poshness his voice could attain when he was addressing the family was impressive. He marched back to the house and I was worried we'd have to spend the whole meal with only the scraping of cutlery on porcelain and the sound of ice in our glasses for accompaniment.

"So, have you solved the mystery yet?" Beatrix looked over at me with a wolf-like glint in her eyes. Perhaps silence was preferable after all.

"I believe I'm making progress."

"Why don't you tell us what you're thinking and maybe we can help you out?" Cameron suggested.

That was the last thing I wanted, but all eyes were on me and Audrey hadn't come to my aid as I'd been hoping. "I don't think your father was killed for his money. I think it was more personal than that."

"She's a genius." Edmund was back to his old self.

"Quiet, E." Even Beatrix was tired of his sarcasm. "Let her talk."

"Obviously the inheritance is important but it isn't enough in itself. I believe that one of you wanted to punish Mr Porter for something in your past." I hadn't actually realised that this was my working hypothesis until that moment but, as I said it, I knew it must be true.

"Yes," Cameron agreed. "That's very interesting. I can see that now, I really can." His eagerness to encourage this theory made me wonder what was in it for him.

"Dare I ask if you've found any clues?" Edmund adopted an innocent smile.

Though she remained silent, Daisy's sorrowful gaze floated over in my direction.

"I've gathered a lot of information." I took a sip of water and the time to collect my thoughts. "I haven't been dusting for fingerprints or searching for tyre marks if that's what you mean. The police can do that when you call them tomorrow. Audrey has already pointed out that, if there was forensic evidence linking the killer to the crime, one of you wouldn't have stuck around for the investigation. I'm here to work out why your Dad was killed and when I know that, I'll be able to tell you who was responsible."

"So have you actually got anywhere?" Beatrix kept changing between serious and snide and I couldn't get a handle on her. Even in her all white outfit, she had managed to maintain her gothic look. Her eyes were ringed with mascara and her lips were a shade of scarlet that I could never get away with.

"One of you threw a vase at me, so I think that shows I'm on the right trail."

Sitting on either side of me, Audrey and Daisy took a short, sharp breath. Edmund and Cameron looked less surprised and Beatrix went so far as to smile at this new development.

"That's too much." Daisy directed her comment straight at Edmund.

"And it had better stop," Cameron said, looking at his brother too – Edmund was clearly the bookies' favourite. "Whoever is responsible should remember that Miss Palmer is here at our request."

"Oh my, it's just terrible," Edmund spat the words back across the table. At least he was angry at someone other than me. "We all think that Izzy should be allowed to conduct her investigation without fear of assault just as we all think it was terrible what happened to Dad. Maybe the butler killed him after all."

I thought that things were about to blow over into a full-on argument but Gladwell arrived at just the right moment with a large silver tray in one hand.

"Actually, it's an urban myth," I said, as a starter of cold tomato soup was served.

"What is?" Cameron asked. "Gazpacho?"

"No. The idea that the butler is usually the killer in country house mysteries. It doesn't actually happen very often and never once in Agatha Christie's books. It's a self-fulfilling cliché really. The idea has been spoofed so much that people think it's true."

"That must be a relief, eh Gladwell?" Audrey looked up fondly at the family's long-serving attendant, who continued with his task with just a nod of acknowledgement.

"I'm more of a military-history man myself." Cameron raised one eyebrow apologetically.

Edmund threw another filthy look at his brother. "You do surprise me, C."

"Personally, I enjoy a bit of *murder*." Beatrix stressed the final word and took pleasure in her family's response. "The bloodier the better."

Unlike her siblings, Daisy showed no horror, but turned to me with a question. "What made you fall in love with murder mysteries in the first place?"

It was something people had asked me many times but I still enjoyed explaining. "I had a pretty innocent childhood. Mum and Dad didn't let me watch any TV until I was sixteen and the only films I saw at the cinema were cartoons."

"Wow." Audrey let out an elegant laugh. "If Dad had tried that with us, he'd have been killed off years ago."

"They thought I'd get corrupted by soap operas and daytime TV for some reason. Mum loved Agatha Christie though, so I was allowed to read detective novels. I thought they were super racy when she first gave them to me. And, later, when I discovered they were about as risqué as an old cardigan, I never turned my back on them."

"So this must be a dream for you?" Cameron correctly predicted.

Edmund put on a voice like he was recording an advert. "The Porter family; making dreams come true."

It felt good to be having a civil conversation with them all for the first time. It was a break from all the death and suspicion, but then I remembered that time was short and decided not to waste my opportunity to get information from them. "I was meaning to ask you, why was the business called Porter & Porter? Did your dad set it up with another member of the family?"

They all laughed before Beatrix replied. "Nope. Dad was so important to the company he felt he should get two mentions. He was both Porter and Porter."

"Don't be unfair," Audrey scolded her sister, but kept a cheerful look on her face. "He chose the name because he thought it sounded more professional."

"I'm not sure it's possible to be unfair to Dad's legacy." Beatrix's pastel-coloured eyes shone brightly. They were full of mystery and mischief in the sunshine. "We'll never find the words to describe half the nasty stuff he got up to."

"I can tell you this now." Cameron raised one hand resolutely. "I'm not going to be the one who reads the eulogy. No matter what you say."

Edmund sat up in his seat and straightened an imaginary dog collar. "We are gathered here to remember Aldrich Zachary Porter. He was not a good man… In fact he was a total skunk but we are here today to confirm, beyond any doubt, that he is a dead man."

The mood had been bordering on friendly until this moment and I'd enjoyed seeing them act like a normal family. Edmund's sketch had rent the peaceful atmosphere in two though and Audrey was the first to react.

"You're being too harsh on him. Dad wasn't perfect but he was good to us; you know he was."

Having kicked things off, I was surprised to see Edmund back away from the argument. He turned his attention to the food and politely sipped a spoonful of soup.

"He was good to *you*," Beatrix told her sister, her voice steely and sharp. "He loved you because you did what he told you to. He couldn't stand the thought of one of his children growing up to be anything less than his clone."

"You're exaggerating." Audrey turned away and I saw once more how conflicted she was over the memory of her brilliant but brutal father.

"No, she's not." I wasn't expecting Cameron to get involved. He seemed too hesitant, too flaky somehow to stand up to his fierce older sisters. "Dad never let us be ourselves. It was his way or no way and that's why he was so proud of you, Audrey. Because you conformed."

"Oh, please." Audrey rolled her eyes, unimpressed by an argument she must have heard many times. "As if you didn't try, Cam. You wanted to be Daddy's good little boy just as much as he wanted to have one."

He was really worked up now. "I was foolish to even try with the great Audrey to live up to. If I'd never bothered, then I wouldn't be…" he cut himself short and his eyes dropped to the traces of blood-red soup left in his bowl.

Beatrix opened her mouth to join in the argument but caught sight of me and the words never came. The discussion flared out just as quickly as it had started and an awkward hush descended. Daisy was the only one who hadn't contributed. Having emerged a little from her shell a few minutes earlier, she now carried out a full retreat and sat looking across the vineyard in silence.

"Wonderful soup," Edmund said with a smirk. "I'll have to get the butler to tell the chef."

Chapter Thirteen

In all of the private conversations I'd had with my suspects up until this point, each one had professed an underlying affection or respect for Aldrich Porter. I suppose this was a natural strategy in a murder enquiry. I mean it hardly looks good if you come straight out and say, *I bloody hated the victim. I had every reason to kill him.* And yet, that's what Beatrix had expressed over lunch. No one had tried to make out Porter to be a saint but she was the first I'd heard really lay into him.

It wasn't just the soup that was cold, the rest of the meal was consumed in a frosty hush. It reminded me of dinners when I was a kid and Mum and Dad weren't speaking. Nasty memories flooded through my mind and I suddenly understood where my instinct comes from to clown around whenever I'm with quiet people.

Huh, you learn something new every day.

I wonder what traumatic childhood memory could explain the nonsense you spout minute after minute.

My brain didn't respond because dessert had just been served and it was too busy screaming, *piiiiiiiiiiiiiiiiiiiiiiiiiiiiiiiiiiiiiiie!*

To be fair, Cook's lemon meringue was so good that it was worth reliving any number of infant nightmares – as long as I got a second helping.

I suppose it was inevitable that spending time with another family would force me to reflect on my own. I hadn't had the most normal of upbringings but I did have four parents who loved me. I'd always thought I wanted a little brother or sister to add to the picture; I could see now that siblings brought their own unique set of challenges.

Having presented a single, united front when I'd arrived at Vomeris Hall, cracks had begun to appear in the Porter family. One of them was a murderer and I knew they all had secrets to uncover. How difficult would it be to split them apart altogether?

It was obvious who I'd have to talk to next, but my plan for the afternoon was interrupted when coffee was served.

"Madam," Gladwell whispered into my ear in a professionally discreet manner. "There's something I think you should see."

I dabbed my lips theatrically with my white cotton napkin and quietly got up from the table to follow the butler back towards the house. As soon as we were out of earshot of the others, he started freaking out.

"I didn't know what else to do. This is insane, this is." His accent had slipped entirely and, glancing back over his shoulder, he was all nerves.

"Calm down, Stephen. What's the matter?"

"I've seen a lot of things in my life. I've seen men killed and I knew why it was done. When Mr Porter was murdered, I accepted it was a family matter and didn't even think of quitting. But this is a step too far, I have to tell you."

Instead of taking the path to the Hall, we forked off towards the stables. We soon came to a u-shaped building with high doors on one side where the horses were kept and pens for chickens, pigs and sheep on the other. The straw in the central enclosure was stained red and I could that see channels of blood had poured out of it, to mix with mud and manure in the yard.

I was suddenly gripped by fear. "Oh, no! It's not Cook, is it?"

Gladwell looked similarly terrified. "Cook?"

"She hasn't been murdered?"

"No, it's a pig." He sounded put out by my poor guesswork. "I don't know who could have done it, but they're savages in my book."

It was my first non-human criminal investigation – well, the second if you count the steak someone nicked off me at university. I found the culprit back then and I was determined to do it again.

Gladwell pointed at the pen. "I came to give Geoffrey some scraps of food that were left over after lunch, when I found him… like that."

A huge pink corpse occupied most of the space. On first glance, I could have imagined he was sleeping but there was one problem with that image.

"Where's his head?"

"That's the thing!" Gladwell was really worked up. "Some monster has murdered the poor fella and made off with his head. He wasn't bred for butchering. He was a pet."

Weirdly, I felt woozier looking at big, dead Geoffrey than I had finding big, dead Bob, or big, dead Aldrich for that matter. It occurred to me that poor Geoff wouldn't have had much hope of fighting back.

"When was the last time you saw him alive?" I had never imagined asking that question about a pig before.

"I heard him squabbling with the chickens a couple of hours ago." Gladwell had sat down on a farrier's stool to get his head straight. "They must have done it since then."

I glanced around the stables. It was a bit sad that all the other creatures were getting on with their lives as if nothing had happened. I doubt they'd be much use as witnesses. "Does no one come in to look after the animals? And what about the vineyard and the gardens? Do you and Cook run the whole estate?"

"No, of course not." He wasn't impressed by my line of questioning. "There's all sorts of people who tend to the grounds but I rang to stop them coming while Mr Porter's still here."

"Hmmm…" I tried to sound like I knew what I was talking about. "Sensible thing to do."

This case was getting weirder by the minute. I had plenty of theories for why someone might want Mr Porter out of the picture but no solid evidence to tie it to one of the suspects. Nothing that had happened so far made any sense and, to top it all off, someone had just murdered the family pig.

"I'd better get back to work." Gladwell wiped his brow with a bright white handkerchief from his top pocket. "But I've had enough of this. If you come and find me a bit later, I'll tell you whatever you want to know and more."

"Thank you, Stephen." I smiled at him despite the sad circumstances.

"Poor Geoffrey…" He glanced one last time at the pigpen before leaving. "I don't know what the world's coming to."

I don't know who would go to the trouble of decapitating a pig.

I clicked my watch on. "Dean, please tell me you've got video of someone carrying around a pig's head."

"Dean's having lunch with his friends," Greg replied. "He left me in charge."

"He didn't leave you in charge." Mum didn't sound happy. "He said that you seemed like the least likely person to break something."

"What's a pig's head?" Dad asked.

"It's not a euphemism. I'm talking about the literal head of an actual pig."

"Why would someone be carrying around a pig's head?" Ramesh already sounded grossed out. "They're not Satanists are they? I read an article in Heat magazine once about how the English upper classes dabble in the occult. It's how they maintain their wealth."

"Okay, thanks for your input." I already had my finger on the *End Call* button. "You've been a great help."

"How do we hang up? Stupid computers are all the same. They never work how they're supposed to," I heard Mum say, just before the line went dead.

If there was no footage of the pig killer, traipsing blood about the place, I'd just hit another dead end. While I waited for the family to return from their endless lunch, it occurred to me that there was one clue I'd yet to investigate.

"Hello again, Cook!" I was truly joyful to see her and dashed into the kitchen to give her a hug.

"Oh. Hello, dearie."

"I'm so glad you're alive."

"Oh…" For a moment, she was lost for words. "Someone clearly enjoyed my lemon meringue pie."

"Absolutely. In fact it was better than my dad's, but don't tell him that." Enough chatter, it was time to get down to work. "On a more serious note, do you happen to keep almond extract here in the kitchen?"

I probably changed the topic too swiftly as she still seemed overwhelmed by my greeting. "Well… I… Yes, I do. I've got a bottle of it in the pantry. Miss Daisy has always loved my cherry and almond tarts."

She dawdled off through a doorway in the corner of the room and returned a minute later with a confused expression on her face. "I know I had a brand-new bottle in there a few days ago. I don't understand where it's got to."

I was not so surprised. "And does anyone else go in your pantry usually? Gladwell for example?"

"Oh no, he doesn't help me with food prep. Occasionally a delivery might be brought in by a driver but there haven't been any since the beginning of the week." She shook her head resignedly. "I don't understand where it's got to."

"And so you haven't seen anyone in the kitchen recently? Not even one of the family?"

"Well…" She thought for a moment. "Mr Cameron came to ask for a snack one afternoon last weekend. But I was with him the whole time. What's the world coming to when even a bottle of almond extract isn't safe in the pantry?"

The domino, the old bottle and the key. None of them had given me much idea of who was responsible for Mr Porter's murder, but I was beginning to understand the killer's thinking.

I went back to my original plan and waited in the garden for Beatrix to return from lunch. Sitting on the grand lawn, in the shade of a willow tree, with the perfectly warm breeze rippling my hair and stroking my bare arms, I had time to put my thoughts in order.

The five Porter children weren't as complex as they wanted to believe. It was their father I was having the greatest trouble figuring out. Just like when I'd met him, there was little of substance to get a grip on. He loomed like a tower in the minds of his children and yet none of them had given me a clear idea of who he really was. It made me wonder if his skills at self-marketing were an even greater achievement than the wealth he had accumulated.

Porter was feared as much as admired by his business associates and I could see now that his family felt the same. It was hard to know which of his children were putting on an act for my benefit. As far as I could tell, Edmund was the only one who had stood up to the lofty patriarch. Audrey was the high achiever, Cameron the try-hard and, as for the two younger sisters, they had opted out of the race entirely.

Yet one, more than all the others, must have suffered. One of the five must have lived their lives with the scars of their father's treatment. One was telling nothing but lies, the other four had presumably uttered the truth from time to time. All I had to do was work which was which.

Chapter Fourteen

I didn't have to wait long before Beatrix reappeared. She was the first to come back from lunch and I flagged her down before she disappeared into the cool of the house.

"Wait up!" I yelled across the garden, sweating already after a twenty second run. The heat was too much and I slowed to a jog as soon as she spotted me.

"How may I help you, Miss Marple?" Her voice was far from sincere.

"Time for a chat, Miss Porter. Where would you like to discuss your innermost secrets?"

Beatrix led me back to the east wing in silence and only started talking once the door to her dressing room was shut and the rest of the family were far away. I was beginning to see how essential each child's space was to them. I can imagine that, in a place like Vomeris, territory is everything.

The wall of Beatrix's dressing room was covered in rosettes.

"You know, the first thing I'm going to do once we have control of the estate is sell the horses and burn down the stables." She paused to look up at the display.

Mixed in with the multi-coloured ribbons with phrases like "1st Place – West Sussex Gymkhana" and "Silver Dressage Event – Commendation" were photos and certificates. A girl, aged variously between five and eighteen, beamed out of every frame. I knew it was Beatrix but something in her had changed since then. The girl in the photos looked so optimistic and full of hope.

"You'd better warn Cook first," I replied and continued studying the tribute to her equestrian accomplishments.

"Why's that?"

"She lives above the stables. I imagine she'd like a heads up."

Beatrix looked disinterested and turned to head into her bedroom so I did the same.

The room was laid out similarly to Daisy's, with another gigantic bed beside the right-hand wall, but was still unlike anywhere else in the house. Faded posters of gothic-looking bands from years earlier covered every inch of space. Names like *Sisters of Mercy, She Wants Revenge* and *Switchblade Romance*, contrasted with the innocent scene in the dressing room. But then, I think that was the point.

Beatrix sprawled across the bed, her head supported by a clutch of plump pillows. "So, dear Izzy. What would you like to know?"

I took a chair from beside the dressing table and sat beside her with my first question clear in my mind. "Did you love your father?"

Her fingers curled up into fists and I knew the gamble had paid off.

"That's not a question I've ever asked myself." She was watching her curtains as they played in the wind. "If you'd asked me whether my father was a good man, the answer is obvious. If you asked me whether I admired him, I'd give a resounding yes, but love is so much more complicated."

"All I've heard from your brothers and sisters is how ruthless he was, but I still don't understand what that meant for you all."

Her eyes flicked back in my direction and I caught some of Audrey's magnetic strength in the way they locked on to me. "Aldrich Porter wasn't so much a father as a curator. He tried to control every detail of my life from the moment I was born until two days ago when someone could finally take no more."

"Is that so unusual? I mean, my mum's pretty interfering and I'm unlikely to murder her anytime soon."

"Did your mum decorate your dressing room in a style of her choosing or give each of your siblings a mahogany desk so that you'd grow up to know the importance of business? Did she choose a fiancé for you?"

I shifted in my chair guiltily. "I don't have a dressing room or any siblings for that matter. But, no, she's not that bad." Mum's logo for The Clever Dick Agency flashed in my head but I knew that it came from a place of love.

"Everything he did for us had a clear purpose. He didn't buy us birthday presents that we wanted or because he loved us, he bought them to further his goals. He was determined to create a little army of businessmen, just like some fathers dream of breeding a whole football team."

"I can see that was hard for you as kids, but it's not as if he was actually cruel."

A low, troubled sound came out of her which might otherwise have turned into a laugh. "But it *was* cruel. He raised us to compete and thrilled in the idea that he was better than his own children. If he'd at least shown us a bit of love, I might be able to forgive him. But we were just data to him; an experiment that didn't work out as planned."

"What about your mum? Did she try to compensate for the way he treated you?"

"She loved us." Beatrix felt the edge of her longest nail on the palm of her hand. "She was kind and gentle but Dad made sure we didn't see it. Mum was an innocent, like Daisy, but he thought she made us soft so he sent her away."

"That must have been horrible for you." I should have been able to come up with more than empty words.

"No, what's horrible is the way he did it. He made us his accomplices. I was only fourteen when he got the whole family together in the dining room and told Mum that she didn't fit in any longer and would have to leave. He didn't divorce our mother, so much as fire her from the company."

Tears peeked out of her eyes and it made me wonder if she'd expressed these thoughts out loud before.

"I'll never forget the way she looked at me that day. What we did to Mum was far worse than the knife in Dad's back."

OMG! How did she know he was stabbed from behind?

It's a turn of phrase, dummy. And, actually, maybe Daisy told her.

"Is that why you killed him?" I timed my question to catch her out and she drew her head back like I'd thrown a punch.

"I wish it was me." She laughed and the first tear crested her cheek. "I might sleep better at night if I'd done it."

"So, if it wasn't you, who's the killer?"

"The others all say it was Edmund but I can't see it. He's just too selfish." She wiped off both sides of her face with the back of her hand. "Planning a murder, covering it up. It's too much hassle for little E."

Though laid out on her bed like Potiphar's wife, her expression was deadly serious. "If you really want to know, I think Cameron did it.

He has the most to gain and the most to lose. He needs Dad's contacts for his work and without them he'd never be able to pay the mortgage on his house or his wife's enormous credit card bills. Of all of us, it's Cam who tried hardest to be like Dad and Cam who disappointed him the most."

"In what way?"

"Okay, look at it like this." She pushed herself up to sitting and I sensed she was about to give me her perspective on the whole family. "Daisy, Edmund and I never came close to the others – for us, failure was our rebellion. It was Audrey and Cam who went into the family business. Audrey looked after Dad's investments and Cam set up his own financial company. The problem is that, even with all the backing that Dad's old-fogey contacts could give him, Cam is no great financial wizard and his company has always struggled. Add that to the fact that he was up against Audrey and the poor kid didn't stand a chance."

From my comfy chair several feet away, I studied her for a moment, and she seemed happy to let me. "Is he in debt?"

"Oh definitely. He's up to his Windsor knot in it. His whole existence is one great long list of numbers and they're all in red."

I took my time to put my words together in just the right way. I didn't want to lead her into an answer. "Do you think he has the temperament to murder someone?"

She smiled the same reluctant smile that Audrey had shown me when I'd asked a similar question. "Absolutely. He may be all genteel on the surface but, underneath, Cameron is as savage as they come. I did a bit of work for his company one summer and he ran that place like a prison. He's nastier than Dad ever was to his employees, I can tell you that."

"What about you? If business isn't your thing, what is?"

She played with the tassels on the corner of a cushion as she spoke. "For dad, work was a holiday. For me, holiday is a holiday. I prefer working as little as possible and have made all my important life decisions with that goal in mind. From the men I've dated to the places I've lived, even without handouts from dear Papa, I've managed to avoid too much hard graft over the years. I'd recently come to the conclusion that I'd have to let Daddy pick some rich, useful idiot for me to marry. But now that he's dead, I think I'll be fine on my own."

"So you had a good reason to kill him then?"

She didn't hesitate in her answer. "Money is a good reason for anything. I may not be interested in counting it or studying it, but I do like having it. Now that Dad's gone, I've got more than ever."

Her smile was so warm right then, so contented, that she could have been talking about a puppy or a beautiful sunset. It was almost refreshing how honest she was, but that didn't mean I trusted her.

"What about Daisy? You and Edmund make out like she's some kind of angel. Are you really so sure she wasn't involved in the murder?"

She hugged the cushion to her and smiled as she thought of her little sister. "Not a chance in hell, my friend. Even if Daddy had pushed her, hit her, abused and insulted her, Daisy would never have snapped like that."

She paused again to watch the light behind me pouring in through the French windows. "I imagine you've already dismissed that scenario anyway. You see, we Porter women would do our homework before carrying out a murder. We're the slow methodical types. We'd only go through with it if we knew we wouldn't get caught. I can imagine Cameron messing it up or Edmund half-arseing it, but I can tell you right now that Daisy wasn't involved. And besides, would she even have the strength to lift his body up so high?"

"Would you?" I watched for a response but she barely flinched. "There are surely ways to hoist a body up onto a wall." I wasn't sure how I felt about this possibility but moved on to the next question. "Do you know why your dad stepped back from P&P?"

Without warning, she jumped off the bed and walked to the balcony to throw the doors open. She took a silver case from her pocket and held it out to me. I found myself drifting towards her without thinking and, for some stupid reason, I broke the habit of a lifetime by accepting a cigarette.

"Daddy never retired, not really. He just spent less time travelling to and from work."

"How is that possible?" I took a puff of smoke deep into my lungs. "I worked in the Croydon branch for four years and he never once called in to see us."

"As long as the annual profits were okay, he left the hands-on details to David. But he still pulled the strings when required. He used to spend all day in his office keeping track of everything."

"The library, you mean?"

"No, a room in the west wing. It's like a monument to business in there, you really should see it."

"So, stepping down as the head of the company had nothing to do with your parents' divorce." I coughed back out the smoke as she let out a perfect, slinking line into the balmy afternoon sky.

"Nope, they'd been separated for years by then. The divorce was just an extra bit of paperwork for Dad." She turned to look through the window at the front lawn below. I watched as her eyes traced a path around the maze of ornate hedgerows.

"Will you take me to his office?"

She looked at me like this would be too much hassle, then dropped her half-smoked cigarette to the stone balcony and stamped the life out of it. I was relieved to be able to do the same.

Why on Earth are you smoking?

I have absolutely no idea.

There was no single corridor running through the upper levels of Vomeris Hall so we had to return to the ground floor and work our way back through the house to reach the west wing. I followed her like a child chasing an ice cream van as she threaded us through corridors and up staircases. It once again annoyed me just how charmed I was by each and every Porter child.

"I don't suppose you know why your dad would have had a domino in his office?" I asked as we climbed the final flight of stairs.

"Not a clue." She didn't turn round as she replied.

"No. I didn't think so."

"This is it," she told me, finally looking over her shoulder as she barged the heavy wooden door open on the second floor of the building.

The immediate hum of technology floated over and it reminded me of lunches with Ramesh in the P&P server room. For about three seconds, I longed to be back there, eating carrot batons and joking around with him, before murder and suspicion had consumed my life.

We emerged in a room with several server stacks blinking in the sunshine beside two rows of computers. It looked as if it had been setup ready for a class of IT students. On the other side of the room, a row of filing cabinets held more Porter empire secrets and there were shelves on every wall with a library's worth of folders and books.

"You see what I mean. He never gave up his work." Beatrix peered around the room like she was trying to make sense of it herself. "Hiring David probably started out as a fun little experiment on Dad's part but the Welsh wonder was good at his job and Dad never went back. Even if he was happy to let the business bump along without too much interference, he still spent Monday to Friday in here."

I walked over to the first monitors which displayed a series of constantly updating charts and figures that I am confident I will never understand. Further along the row, there were screens with currency information and, at the end, several monitors showing surveillance footage.

"That's my office," I told my guide as I watched Will and Amara working together in David's old room. The rest of the space was displayed in smaller, black and white boxes underneath. I unmuted the footage and their voices burst through speakers around the room.

Beatrix came to stand beside me. "I told you. Nothing changed for Dad. P&P was still his baby and he was just as obsessed with it as ever."

"But these aren't the regular cameras." I took the mouse to scroll through different live feeds. There were angles and locations I'd never seen before. I found Will's office, the conference room, Jack's now abandoned cubby hole and a bunch of different shots of the main floor.

Mr Porter had told me he was surprised I'd managed to solve Bob's murder and now it made sense. He'd been watching my work that whole time and never thought much of me. Worse than that, he'd probably been listening in to every ridiculous conversation Ramesh and I had shared. "He must have had them fitted in secret. Even the police didn't find them after Bob was killed."

Bloody hell, Izzy. You know what this means?

"He had footage of Bob's murder. He could have gone to the police with it but he didn't."

Urmmm… I was going to say that he leaves these monitors on every night wasting energy but that's important too.

Beatrix had a smug look on her face. "Do you see what I mean now? He was no normal neglectful father. Dad was a full-blown psychopath disguised by his business suit and Bentley."

116

Chapter Fifteen

Everything comes back to Bob.

Robert H. Thomas with his racist, misogynistic – not even vaguely funny – sense of humour. Bob Thomas with that scent of stale tobacco trailing after him around the office. Bob: murdered by my boyfriend and captured on hidden camera by Aldrich Porter.

Once Beatrix had gone, I navigated through folders in search of the right date – that Wednesday night which already felt like a lifetime ago. It wasn't hard to find. The surveillance system automatically stored the files on Mr Porter's servers, cut up into neat hourly chunks and arranged by room, date and then time. It was easy enough to fast forward through the video until I saw David enter.

Do we really want to see this?

No. But we have to.

He already looked distraught when he sat down in Bob's huge leather chair. The camera was well located to capture the whole room. It must have been hidden in a ceiling tile or behind a picture or something as I'd never noticed anything in the position it was recording from.

I should probably have skipped the video on but it made me feel oddly calm to have David there with me. I could hear his breathing through the speakers and his feet tapping an impatient rhythm on the carpet.

When Bob finally swaggered in, champagne bottle and glass in hand, it was as if I'd sunk through the floor. The sound of his voice as he berated David and accused him of spying, perving and interfering made my nails feel like they were coming loose. The very sight of him after so long set my whole body shaking. He was the corpse that wouldn't stay dead.

David stayed firm. He made Bob sit down and listen, but the odious man prattled on about his rights and necessities.

"You can't do this." I could hear the total disbelief in my boyfriend's voice and I remembered why I loved him. "You can't put your own selfish desires before everyone and everything else."

'What you gonna do, Davey-boy? Tell my wife? Tell the police?"

He let out a snorting laugh. "I'd wait a while longer if I were you. The worst is yet to come.'

It all happened exactly as David told me. Reaching across the table as if to serve himself a drink, he grabbed the bottle and sent it crashing into the side of Bob's head. I watched that look of unexpected amusement on Bob's hideous face as he slumped into his seat. Then David grabbed the knife to finish the job.

It was a curiously inoffensive video. Far less gruesome than a thousand movies I've watched and yet it hit me harder than the gory horror films Ramesh makes me sit through. When it was over, I sat staring at the blank screen. I couldn't bear to watch any of the other clips – of Will's humiliation or David's departure. I sat at that computer – just as Mr Porter must have after he'd discovered Bob had been murdered and wanted to find out who was responsible. I sat there, with my hand on the mouse, unsure whether to delete the file or not.

When the police come tomorrow, they'll find it. It's absolute proof of David's guilt. You have to get rid of it.

No. It's absolute proof of what a terrible man Bob was. If anything it shows what David was up against.

It hit me that the servers wouldn't just have videos of the killing. There'd be every nasty word Bob had spoken in the office in the last months of his life. Every insult and cruelty and, better than that, footage of him paying to have me murdered. Assuming they were admissible in court, the files could help David's case more than hinder it.

I had no idea how far back the videos would go. I imagine they would be deleted after a certain length of time to reduce storage space, but perhaps Mr Porter had saved key moments. He would surely have reviewed the footage of Bob with Pippa, the intern who'd been assaulted. My stomach lurched again as I realised that Porter knew exactly what had happened and chose to cover it up. I was coming to understand why someone would have killed the man.

I turned all the monitors off to save energy…

Thank you very much.

…and left the computer room behind.

The experience had unsettled me. The very idea that Porter had been watching us for so long was bad enough. But why wouldn't he have done something to stop Bob if he'd known how abhorrent the man was? And why hadn't he gone to the police after the murder?

I thought back to our meeting in the library. There was something very hollow about him. His emotions didn't seem to line up with the world around him. Beatrix had called him a psychopath and perhaps she wasn't far off. A man who doesn't feel things the way most people do – even with the glaze of respectability – cannot be considered normal.

The more pressing issue was how this knowledge would help me find his killer. Was he murdered for his unfeeling attitude? Had he done something even worse to one of his own children? New hypotheses wrote themselves out on the list in my head but it was still all conjecture. I needed proof.

I'd made it back out to the garden when my watch started buzzing.

"Good news, Izzy." If this was the case, Dean's voice betrayed no hint of happiness. "My head-programmer Emilia managed to get the information you wanted from the airport in Bangkok."

"So Audrey was definitely there then?"

"No doubt about it. I'll send you the footage of her passing through security. She flew back yesterday, just as she told you."

"Thank Emilia for breaking the law for me. I appreciate it." I took a deep breath as I now felt even further from working out why Mr Porter had been killed. "Have you got anything else for me?"

He cleared his throat. "Nothing concrete. The family haven't been back from lunch long and Cook and Gladwell have been busy with their jobs. I still reckon Cameron's acting weird. He never sits still for one thing and, whenever we catch him on a mic, he's short-tempered and nervous. I reckon he's worried you're on to him."

"Don't listen to Dean, Izzy," Mum shouted in the background. "It's the butler! The butler did it."

"I'm not so sure." My dear biological father spoke at his usual slow, steady pace. "That Beatrix seems like a wild one to me. And the way she speaks about her father... I know he might not have been a kind man but she clearly isn't mourning the loss."

I waited for Ramesh to throw a theory in. "No, Ra? Have you got nothing to add?"

"Oh, so now you want my opinion, do you?" He still sounded put out. "If you ask me, they're all guilty. But Cook's the scariest of the lot so let's say she did it."

"Hi, Izzy! This is Fernando, your Mum's hairdresser. I bet you didn't think I'd be making an appearance!"

I was beginning to feel sorry for Dean.

"I invited him, Izzy." Mum was back on the line. "Not only does Fernando have some very interesting opinions on the murder, he's agreed to style Dean's hair for his big date."

"That's right." Fernando was from Penge but he spoke with an Italian accent for some reason. "My money's on Daisy. That butter-wouldn't-melt routine doesn't work on me. Why is she so quiet? Perhaps it's because she hacked her father to death and is living with the guilt."

"Thanks, Fernando. I'm sure that will come in handy. Can I speak to Dean privately for a second?"

There was a click and the background noise died away as Dean transferred the call to his handset. "This is Dean speaking. What can I do for you?"

"I just wanted to remind you, if that lot are getting too much, you can throw them out. Has Mum brought her flip charts with her?"

Dean didn't get the chance to reply because my mother grabbed the phone from him. "How ungrateful, Isobel. I heard that!"

I hung up before she could tell me off and went looking for Gladwell. He wasn't in the kitchen and, back at the veranda, all signs of lunch had been removed. I finally found him over by the stables, smoking a mournful cigarette as he cast his eyes in the direction of Geoffrey the pig's lifeless body.

When he saw me, he let out a long drag before speaking. "I haven't smoked one single ciggy in twenty years, but this week has got me so cut up that I had to beg one off Cook."

There was no time to sympathise with him. "You said you had something to tell me?"

He looked about suspiciously, it reminded me of Dean. "Where to start? This family has done some terrible things, I can tell you. I serve 'em cos that's my job but I can't imagine they'll keep me around long after this anyway. Mr Porter was the worst of 'em of course but I'm coming to think that some of the kids ain't much better."

A switch had been flicked inside him and all his loyalty has disappeared. He was steaming like a kettle.

"Do you have any specific details?"

"Well, he did a right number on his poor wife. I can tell you that for nothing. She was nice, Mary her name was. Always treated us staff with respect and remembered our birthdays, that kind of thing. Well, when he got rid of her, he made sure she got nothing in the divorce."

I knew all this. "Yes, Audrey told me."

"And did she tell you that her dear daddy made up all sort of lies to cut their mother out? She'd signed some sort of agreement before the marriage and all he had to do was say she'd had an affair and she was left penniless. Just imagine! To say such a thing after what he put her through."

His anger was loosening his lips better than the cognac had the night before and I jumped on his comment. "What did he put her through?"

He let the air whistle out between his lips and it seemed to calm him down. "Well…" He hesitated and I knew that I shouldn't have interrupted. "Let's just say that loyalty wasn't his strong suit. I don't like to speak ill of the dead but he really had it coming."

Reading between the lines, it didn't take much to add three and three together and come up with sex.

Ha, classic! Some jokes are worth repeating.

"So he was having an affair? Who with?"

He paused again. "To be honest, I don't know all the details and I don't see that such ancient history would be relevant now anyway."

I moved things on. "What about his kids? What do you know about them?"

From where we stood, we would have seen anyone coming ten seconds before they arrived, but he scanned the yard just in case. "In my job, I overhear things I'm not supposed to. If I were you, I'd look into Cameron's finances." Another flick of the eyes, another quick check. "Up to his silk bowtie in debt he is. He'll lose his house if he's not careful, he's re-mortgaged it enough times. Money is always a good reason to kill and I don't reckon he has much."

"What about the other siblings?"

He didn't reply at first because he was smoking again. He held the cigarette in all five fingers like he didn't want it to blow away. The contrast to Beatrix's elegant technique was striking.

"Audrey always treats us right, much better than the other kids, but she's a shrewd businesswoman. More like her father than she'd like to admit, if you ask me."

"Yes, but Audrey wasn't here at the time of the murder. Do you have any reason to believe she's behind it?"

He thought for a moment, looking up at the cloudless sky. "Not really. I was just saying, that no one in this place is an angel. If I had to pick one of them though, Edmund's the most savage. Typical spoilt youngest son. Never done anything with his life, despite all the opportunities he was born with. And talk about a temper on him. The way he speaks to me sometimes-"

He was beginning to ramble so I cut him off. "What makes you say he's savage? That's a strong word to use."

A cloud of smoke floated up between us. "Edmund is a thug in a Ralph Lauren shirt. He always gets his way in the family because he threatens anyone who tries to stop him. I caught him in the games room once, about to give Audrey his hand across her face. I don't know what she'd said to upset him like that but there was the devil in him, I can tell you."

He paused, perhaps trying to put his suspicions in order. "What I'm saying is, he's the last person I'd want to cross. You know all them weapons on the wall of his room? Mr Porter didn't put them there for decoration. Edmund had shooting and fencing classes, he was in the army cadets too. His dad trained him up to be a good little killer and I reckon that's just what he became."

"You were in the army, weren't you?" I remembered his comment about an old war wound and the way he carried himself in general reminded me of my mum's uncle, Captain John. "Does that make you a murderer?"

Something in his reaction told me that Gladwell didn't like it when the focus was turned on him. "Not the same. Back in my day, we knew how to control ourselves. Edmund is a nasty piece of work, through and through."

"What about the other sisters? Is there anything to say that they're involved?"

His cigarette had burnt down to its stub but he took one last puff, savouring every ounce of nicotine. "I can't say I'm particularly fond of them. Cook talks about them like they're sweet little fairies but there's no heart in Daisy and no warmth to Beatrix."

"Why do you say that?"

"I shouldn't be so harsh, but after her father called off her wedding, Daisy became a shell of a person. No – worse than that – she's a ghost; wandering around after all the life has gone out of her."

"So she was already like that before the murder?" Perhaps I would finally learn something about the innocent girl who no one could imagine being the killer.

"Well… She'd got a bit better recently, I suppose. She got a new job in a gallery up in town and seemed pretty excited about it. Then all this happened and she's right back to where she was six months ago. You know that her father threatened to disinherit her if she married that boy she'd fallen for? Porter really did a number on those kids. I never speak ill of the dead, but he had it coming."

I was surprised how worked up the butler had become. Having previously hidden his feelings so well, all the dirt and family secrets were suddenly spurting out of him. I wondered if it was the death of his friend Geoffrey that had done it or there was something more.

"Anyway, that's all by the by." His face brightened and he looked at me like we were old friends. "I have an idea where your key might fit. It takes me a while to remember these things, but I normally get there in the end."

With the precious chemicals sucked from his burnt-down paper tube, a slightly smoky Gladwell was free to lead me back to the main building. There were doors all along the rear of the house to enter by, though some were clearly more acceptable for staff like us to make use of. We slipped in through a quiet corridor between the ballroom and the smoking parlour.

"The place is an absolute maze." He paused to stretch his leg. "It'll take you a while to get to know it the way I do."

We crossed the main corridor and came to a seemingly unremarkable alcove with a small table at the end of it and a framed hunting scene displayed above. Without warning, Gladwell pushed against the right-hand wall to reveal a door, perfectly disguised by the textured plaster which covered it.

"I didn't realise it existed until years after I started working here."

He held the door open for me and I walked through.

From a tiny window high above us, a sharp beam of light penetrated the dusty space we'd entered. The room gave onto a bare, wooden staircase which I began to mount.

"What is this place?" I asked, starting to feel creeped out.

"These were the servants' stairs. We don't use them much these days but they're useful if you want to go up to the attics or some of the spaces that aren't easy to get to without a ladder. You'll see now."

This could explain where our mystery vase-thrower disappeared off to.

Yep. And there's fresh prints in the dust. Could be Gladwell's but they look too large for his dainty feet.

On the first landing, there were another set of doors, sunk into the plasterwork. It was quite a large area to be hidden away like that and I could see signs of the Porter children having played there decades before. On the wall near where we entered, all five of their names were written in smudged pencil and, in the corner of the room, piles of once-loved toys lay abandoned. A musty porcelain doll stood waiting for someone to play with her.

Waiting to come to life and curse us more like!

Gladwell put his arm against the wall to catch his breath. Poor old thing, I wondered how long he'd be able to stick at his job, even if he wasn't turfed out by the heirs to the manor.

"One more to go," he said and continued up the stairs.

The second floor was an exact copy of the one below, except, in place of old toys, it was filled with stacks of magazines and newspapers from fifty years earlier.

"The old man who Mr Porter bought Vomeris Hall from was a bit of a hoarder. The attics are full of this sort of thing."

"Can you get to them through there?" I pointed to the final staircase.

"That's right. You can walk from one side of the house to the other up there, not that you'd want to with all the junk it's stuffed with," Gladwell explained and, when I didn't reply, he moved towards the corner of the room. "Here we are."

He pushed one final hidden door and we stepped through to be bathed in darkness. Pulling on a cord above his head, he turned on a dangling lightbulb which swung gently on its cable, sending shifting light across the room.

"We call it the armoury," my guide explained as I took in a museum's worth of helmets, breast plates, chainmail and gauntlets in the cool, windowless space. "It was never meant for such a purpose of course but, after the Porters moved in, this stuff was considered surplus to requirements and packed away."

I inspected the artefacts as he searched about for something. Beside the left wall, a line of hollow soldiers stood to command. Covered in a cotton-like layer of dust and cobwebs, eight full suits of armour, in a neat regimental row, had been awaiting their orders for the last three decades.

"There it is."

I turned to see Gladwell in the opposite corner, lugging a small canon out of the way. I gave him a hand, noting further scrapes in the carpet of dust beneath our feet. With the heavy weaponry removed, we were free to access a tall cabinet which held about a hundred drawers. It looked like it had come from an ancient department store and I could have spent an hour rifling through it.

Only the large drawers at the bottom appeared to have keyholes so I fished in my pocket and tried the first one. The key that I'd found so close to Mr Porter's body stuck a little as it turned, but soon enough, the lock clicked open and the drawer came sliding out. I'd been imagining something unique and magical inside. Obviously what I found was a bunch of weapons.

"When I first worked here – and Lord Sherwin-Nettlehurst was still the owner – all of these were on display around the house. I remember them lining the corridors and even in some of the grander salons downstairs. He was a military man, of course."

I looked at the twenty or so flintlock pistols, pinned carefully in place on a bed of green baize. "It's all a bit macabre, isn't it? Perhaps redecorating this place was the one thing that Porter got right."

"Hmmm… I dunno. I rather like the old way of things. People had better manners when I started out." There was a nostalgic tone to the butler's voice. "Anyway, I finally remembered the key from back when I had to shift everything up here. Must be twenty years at least since I've been in."

I moved on to the next drawer which was filled with rusty spurs and bayonets. A third and fourth revealed similar forgotten treasures but it was the bottom one where I found what I was looking for.

"There's one missing," Gladwell pointed out, as we took in the collection of daggers and the one slightly cleaner spot with four unoccupied pins surrounding it.

"I guess we know where the murder weapon came from now."

My assistant smiled proudly. "Glad I could be of help."

"But why go to the trouble of taking a knife from here when there are a million all over the house the killer could have used?"

Gladwell straightened up and stretched his back out with a click. "Perhaps whoever killed Mr Porter wanted to make it more dramatic. The way he was killed was very theatrical, don't you reckon?"

I turned to look up at him. "That's exactly what I was thinking."

After I gave him an appreciative tap on the arm, his pride shone even brighter.

It's useful having another person with me during my investigations, it means I don't have to talk to myself so much.

I noticed and I'm starting to feel left out.

Chapter Sixteen

The shadow of a murder weapon seemed to be just about all I could expect in the way of a clue for this investigation. The intangibility of everything I had discovered so far was rattling me and it was hard to make any plans or comprehensive theories. I still had plenty of questions to ask his children, but even knowing how and when Mr Porter had been killed didn't bring me any closer to understanding why it had occurred.

What I really needed was someone unrelated to the case to bounce ideas off. I needed... – I really hadn't expected to have to say this – I needed my friends and family.

Gladwell went off to do to his real job and, as soon as I was alone, I rang Dean.

"Have you got anything for me?"

"Not really. They all seem perfectly calm except Cameron. Edmund is having a doze in one of the lounges. Beatrix is sunbathing on the lawn and Audrey has gone to her office on the ground floor."

"No sign of the pig's head?"

"Nope. Nor Daisy, we haven't seen her on our feeds since lunch."

I left the armoury and sat on the floor of the landing, among the piles of papers. "Dean, I don't know how to ask this... are Ramesh and my folks still about?"

"We're here, darling." Mum sounded ecstatic to be needed. "How may we be of assistance?"

I believe there was a hint of contrition in my voice. "I was wondering if I could run some ideas past you."

I closed my eyes and imagined myself over to Dean's office, to the site of the latest Hawes Lane Crime Squad reunion. Mum was standing in front of her flip charts, a marker in hand as her devoted male followers – one ex, one current husband, her hairdresser and her daughter's exuberant former-colleague – waited on her every word.

I pictured Dean and his gang of techies squashed over in the corner in front of a row of computer screens showing all of the data and video feeds they could access.

"Oh. So now you want my input, do you?" Ramesh asked down the party line.

"I want everyone's input. I'm sorry if you thought otherwise."

"At last, Izzy," Mum replied, and I knew I would regret my decision. "Gladwell must be the killer because he has the softest feet and could sneak up on a sleeping bear. Plus he always wears gloves so he'd leave not a trace behind him."

"I disagree," my father began. "The way I see it, one of the kids must have done it. They stand to gain the most and I reckon that Edmund has the savage nature for patricide."

Ramesh wouldn't be outdone. "Well I'm starting to think it was all just some horrible accident."

This was exactly the kind of nonsense I needed to hear to help me put my slightly saner thoughts in order. "An accident? He was stabbed from behind and then suspended off the ground on the skulls of a bunch of dead animals."

"Stranger things have happened, Izzy." He sounded like a child who was sad because his marbles had been stolen or… you know… lost.

"Hi Izzy, Fernando here. I think I might have cracked it actually. What if Mr Porter-"

It pained me to interrupt. "Sorry everyone, I was thinking that I could give you an update on what's been happening here and you could tell me your ideas after."

There was some murmuring and Greg stepped forward to be the voice of the group. "Go ahead, Izzy. We're listening."

"I'll work through the main suspects one by one. When I spoke to Beatrix, she was incredibly honest about her relationship with her father. I'd say she had the most evident dislike of the man but then, why would she show me that if she's the killer? At lunch, I could tell that it wasn't just her dad she's angry with. There are schisms forming in the family and I'll be interested to see where Beatrix's loyalty lies when everything falls apart."

"Surely it's Edmund who has reacted most violently to your presence there," my dad put in. "I was rather worried about you when you were alone with him."

"You're right, Dad. And it's his name that his sisters keep

mentioning when I've asked them about motive. He'd argued with his father on the night of the killing, he wasn't afraid to show his anger and we know he's capable of really losing it. Gladwell even said that he saw him being physically violent to Audrey on one occasion."

"Gladwell can't be trusted, Izzy. You mark my words."

"Yes, thank you, Mum." I ignored her and retraced my train of thought. "But I think that we have to bear Edmund's argument in mind. He's the black sheep of the family, they were bound to blame him. Perhaps whoever killed their father knew that. Losing your temper isn't the same as stabbing someone to death."

"That doesn't mean he didn't do it though," Fernando of Penge helpfully pointed out. "Which brings me onto my point about-"

"Hang on a second, Fernando." I was fighting to get my thoughts in order. "There's something else I wanted to ask you all. Can anyone think of an explanation for why someone wanted to kill Geoffrey the pig?"

"Perhaps he saw something that the killer didn't want anyone to know." My mother often finds her own jokes hilarious and she really let rip with the laughter this time.

"Perhaps he stuck his snout in where it wasn't wanted," Dad suggested.

"Or someone fancied some bacon?" Ramesh couldn't be left out.

"Well, thank you. That's marvellously helpful." Their bad jokes weren't getting me anywhere so I changed the subject. "Dean are you there? Gladwell mentioned that Cameron is in financial trouble. Can you look into his situation somehow? Maybe his company website has private access you can login to or he keeps his bank statements online somewhere."

Dean's nasal voice buzzed in my ear. "Izzy, are you asking me to break the law by hacking into Cameron Porter's private files?"

"Urmmm, yes?"

"Great, just checking."

A thought occurred to me. "Oh, and Dean? How's the preparation for your date going?"

"Ramesh has been incredible, Izzy." There was a spring in his voice I wasn't used to hearing. "He has an uncanny way of showing me all the mistakes I've made on past dates. I really think tonight's going to go well."

"Ahhh, buddy. It's all you." I could hear my ridiculous best friend blushing down the line. "You listen to everything I say and learn from it. That's the key to success."

"Izzy?" It was Fernando again. "I just wanted to mention that I don't think you can dismiss Audrey entirely. Just because she was out of the country at the time and she's paying you to investigate her father's murder, that doesn't mean you can-"

"Hmmm, good point, Fernando. I'll bear it in mind." While it probably hadn't brought me any closer to identifying the culprit, the distraction had no doubt helped me arrange my thoughts. I felt more confident about what I had to do next. "I'm off to speak to Cameron. Do you know where he is?"

Dean already seemed disinterested and no doubt wanted to get back to his spying. "No, sorry. He went downstairs about half an hour ago."

"Okay, thanks. Keep me updated."

I picked myself up, brushed the dust off and walked downstairs to start all over again. Emerging through the hidden doorway, I wondered if my vase-smashing assailant really had used such a passageway to escape. I should probably ask Gladwell about any other secret spaces in the house. Perhaps I'd find Geoffrey's face stashed away in one of them.

The house was far too big and I didn't have a clue where Cameron could be so I went to ask the one person who seemed to know what was going on at all times.

"You might find him in the bowling alley," Cook informed me. She was already getting dinner ready.

There's no way that she could be the killer. She spends her whole life in this kitchen.

You've changed your tune.

And that's the power of lemon meringue pie.

"There's a bowling alley here?" I struggled to hide the excitement in my voice. Ten-year-old Izzy's greatest dream was to have a bowling alley at home.

"That's right. It's at the far end of the house, next to the grand salon. Mr Porter had it installed when the children were young. Cameron often spends the afternoon down there when he comes to stay."

"Thanks, Brenda!" I gave her a smile.

"Oh, and Izzy? One more thing." She paused for tension. "I'm making chocolate mousse for dessert!"

I jumped up and punched the air. I really hoped that Cook wasn't the killer. Despite the fact she looked like she should be working in the kitchen of an ultra-secure prison in some convict-breakout movie, I kind of loved her.

That house was biiiiiiiiiiig – well, loooooong anyway. I was a bit disappointed that I'd had to leave my own watch at home because, for the first time in months, I might actually have met my step-count target for the day. It took me ages to walk from the kitchen but, by the time I was halfway there, I could hear the unmistakable sound of falling pins.

I peeked into the grand salon and everything was golden. Every wall was covered in gilt-inlaid, carved panels, depicting famous scenes from the bible. Three great chandeliers sparkled above me and a long table was laid out for a banquet like I'd popped by to see Miss Havisham.

It was odd to walk around that exquisite, antique dining parlour, slip through a doorway between two enormous renaissance vases and find myself in a single-lane bowling alley. Even odder was the fact that it smelt of beer and feet, just like every other one I'd been to. In fact, the only thing that marked it out as different was the fancy, fleur-de-lis wallpaper running down both sides of the lane.

"Here for a game, Izzy?" Cameron sent a ball skidding away from him to topple all ten pins. A familiar mechanical whir and clatter echoed back to us as I reached the players' bench.

"I'm not particularly good I'm afraid," I told him with a humble smile.

"Do you mind if we play all the same?" He maintained the upright, polite manner I associated him with. "I mean, if you're here to interrogate me, you could at least let me show off my skills."

I went to the eighties-style monitor and slowly entered my name. Well, it came up as Iszxy but it was far too much trouble to change.

He was up first and managed a half strike, arrogantly strutting back in my direction without waiting to see the outcome of his second throw. I decided not to get into the interview just yet, I wanted to see how good a bowler he was first.

"The key to bowling," he told me as I chose a ball, "is calm and concentration. Though the pins may explode in a chaotic symphony, inside you must always be Zen."

Oh no, one of those pretentious bowlers. They're the worst.

I sent my first throw down the gully and, on a screen hanging from the ceiling, a mocking cartoon declared, "Gutter Ball!"

"You almost had it. Try again."

"Oh, wow. Do I get another go?" I waited for the only medium-sized ball to return to me. I wasn't being fobbed off with some insanely heavy thing that would break my nails and sprain my wrist.

I managed a six on the next shot, and celebrated like I'd won the world championship. He didn't reply, he just smashed another ball down the lane, leaving two awkward pins still standing that he didn't quite pick off with his follow-up.

"Tell you what." He had a self-satisfied look on his face. "If you can get a strike with your next ball, I'll answer any question you've got for me."

"A strike?" I've never been one for jargon. "Is that where you get all the skittles down in one go?"

"They're pins not skittles." He didn't like that and the civility in his voice suddenly vanished. "But yes. If you get all ten down, you can fire away with your questions."

I watched him for a few seconds to check that he was serious, then retrieved my ball. I got my eye in, started the run up and released the shot at the optimum moment, with the weight on my fore-leg balanced just right. Happily, all ten pins toppled and I was free to walk back to Cameron with a grin.

"The key to bowling isn't just concentration," I told him. "It's angle of entry, pin carry and hook potential. But then I'm guessing you didn't spend every Thursday afternoon from the time you were six being taught all about it by your dad."

Okay, so I never mentioned that I'm a pretty good bowler. It's not that I was keeping secrets, I just hadn't found the moment to slip it in. I promise that all my gifts are now accounted for. I bowl, I'm good at solving murders – when there are a very limited number of suspects at least – oh, and I got up to grade eight on the accordion. That's it.

132

Nothing else. Well, nothing that I can think of right now.

"You hustled me!" Cameron was furious.

I hit straight back with my first question. "Did you kill your father because you're drowning in debt?"

"I can't believe you tricked me like that." He was definitely more upset about the bowling than the accusation of murder.

I sat back down on the bench. "Did you?"

"No, of course not. I loved my father – idolised him. Even if he thought I was a failure."

"Take your shot."

He kept his eyes on mine for a moment before relenting. The pressure was on him and he only managed a seven off the next two throws. I followed up my strike with a split.

"You were the last to see your dad on the night he died. What did you talk about?"

Already looking dejected, he stepped up for another turn. "Nothing important. I showed him a few pictures of his grandchildren, not that he gave a damn about them."

"You stayed up late to show him photos of your kids that he has no interest in?" I didn't believe him for a second. "Try again. What did you really talk about?"

His score was even lower this time, a five in total and things weren't looking good. "Fine, we talked about money. He knew the situation I was in and would do nothing to help."

"What about the debt?" I asked. "Why are you broke?"

"None of your business." His softness had vanished and I was seeing the side of his personality that Beatrix had told me about.

"You made a bowling bet." I may have struggled to contain the shock in my voice. "You *never* go back on a bowling bet. And besides, it very much is my business. You're paying me to investigate."

He huffed out a breath and sat down on his side of the alley with his back to the wall. "I'm in debt because I don't make enough money and have a very high cost of living. I'm in debt because I haven't told my wife that we have issues and she continues to buy royal jelly and caviar like they're jam and margarine." He spat the last word out like a mouthful of bad milk. I can't imagine the Porters have ever eaten anything so common as margarine.

"That doesn't explain why you didn't want me here. I know you told Edmund that you regretted employing me. What are you so scared of?"

"That little grass." Edmund hadn't actually told me anything, Dean's microphones had captured their conversation earlier that day. "I'm scared that you'll find out about the money I owe on my house and my car and essentially my children and assume that I killed Dad. But then I guess you already have."

I took another throw and sat down in a seat opposite his. "Your brother tells me he's pretty much penniless and Beatrix and Daisy are hardly high-flyers. I wouldn't have thought too much of it if you hadn't been acting so strangely today."

Until now, he'd managed to keep up the pretence of being a willing, helpful host whenever I was around. It was only Dean who had caught him freaking out before, but the mask had slipped and there was no longer any point trying to hide who he really was.

"It's a widely held truth that money is the number one reason to kill someone and so it seems obvious that you'd suspect me. The others may not be particularly flush with cash, but, as far as I know, there are no bailiffs or former prep-school chums ringing for their money each day."

"Are things that bad?"

His arms collapsing to his sides, he looked exhausted. "They were until yesterday. Dad's death could be my saving grace. So is it really that difficult to understand why I've been terrified since you got here?"

His tone of voice was plain and honest in a way that I hadn't heard from any of his siblings. He was appealing to me for clemency and compassion and I'd like to have believed him, but something held me back.

Sure, I had sympathy for the guy. If anything happened to him, it was his wife and kids who would suffer most. But then, at the end of his little speech, as he looked down at the floor despondently, he shot an infinitesimal glance up at me and I knew it was all an act.

"Fine, if you don't want me to tell the police tomorrow that you're the most likely culprit, help me work out who else it could have been. I know about Edmund's temper and Beatrix's sour relationship with your father. I know that he made Daisy break off her engagement and that Audrey never forgave him for what he did to your mum. What else is there to find out?"

He sat up again in his chair as if he was trying on another personality. "To be honest, I don't know who could have killed him. I mean, we're all capable of it but I don't know what one thing could have pushed them over the edge.

"We loved our father, but we didn't like him. Whenever we spent time here together, he was cold and critical. He'd have us competing against one another for his entertainment. Audrey was always the paragon for him of course; the golden example we all had to live up to. But within one hour of being here, we'd all be fawning over him – boasting of petty achievements in the hope he might approve. It was pathetic."

He was easy to read. I could tell that a lot of what he was saying was true. The hurt that his father had caused was real and wouldn't go away with his passing. There was so much more he was choosing to hold back though, so I decided to nudge him on.

"Are you glad he's dead?"

He looked up at me again but didn't answer the question. "On my eighteenth birthday, he promised that, once I finished university, I'd be put in charge of his investments. It was possibly the proudest day of my life. You see, that's where the money is. His company does well and the estate turns a profit through the vineyard and some smaller interests, but it was what my father did with his money that created our fortune. What I didn't know was that he'd made that same promise to Audrey."

He ran his hands across his face, like he was just waking up. "It was always going to be my sister who got the big job. When I set up my company, he allowed me to invest the profits from P&P but that was just a consolation prize. Audrey is the genius. She's phenomenally talented at researching the businesses we've made our money from and has an uncanny instinct for market trends. I was stupid to believe he had chosen me. I should have known that Dad's greatest thrill in life was messing with us. We weren't his children, we were science experiments."

I asked him again, "Are you glad your father's dead?"

"Yes, I am." There was no lie there. His eyes were clear and wide. "He made me and he destroyed me. My only regret is that I didn't help stick the knife in."

"So who do you think did?"

"Edmund." He took a deep, dramatic breath. "I think it was Edmund. Daisy told me how she found Dad, strung up on the wall like that and I immediately knew that it would take rage. It would take pure hatred to do something so extreme. Beatrix can shout and scream and curse us all to hell and Daisy can cry all day long, but they don't have the animal aggression that I've seen in Edmund a thousand times.

"We've lived with the open secret of his savagery for too long. When we were kids, I once saw him take a knife from his wall and go out into the fields past the vineyard. We waited by a rabbit hole and, when one came out, he grabbed it and slit its throat. He couldn't have been more than seven at the time, but the joy he clearly felt in extinguishing that poor creature's life was inhuman."

He was the first of the siblings to pick a single suspect and I couldn't tell if he was doing it out of self-preservation or genuine belief. Beatrix and Edmund wore their faults with pride but Cameron was all sheen, all surface. The glimpse I'd caught of what lay beneath wasn't pretty.

"Come on," I said, standing up from the player's bench. "I reckon we've got time for a game before dinner." I picked out his ball from the machine and handed it over to him. "We can start again from scratch. No hustling this time."

Over the next twenty minutes, I didn't learn much more about the Porter family or who could have killed their father, but I did manage to beat him by fifty points.

Chapter Seventeen

Cook helpfully informed me that we'd be eating in the grand salon and that the family always dressed for dinner. Considering that Mr Porter himself had come from a working-class background, I found all these airs and graces confusing. He'd told me that he hadn't spoilt his children but made them work for their money. Still, he could hardly say he'd kept their feet on the ground.

I decided to do something about my outfit before we ate. My smiley t-shirt already looked out of place walking Vomeris' ancient halls. I could only imagine it alongside those five elegant beauties, all dressed up to the tens. Luckily, I'd come more prepared for a formal evening than anything else really. I had a long, graceful ball gown that would do just perfectly. Sadly, the only footwear I had were flip-flops, a pair of old trainers or my black Doc Martens. I clomped downstairs to dinner, trying to hide the boots by wrapping the high-slit skirt of my dress around me as much as possible.

"That is a bloody cool outfit, Izzy," Beatrix surprised me by saying when I arrived back in the salon. "It's sophisticated, but still totally you. I respect that."

"Oh, thanks." I definitely turned redder than a post box right then.

"She looks like a punk got halfway through a makeover and gave up." Edmund had obviously never heard the expression *charm offensive.*

"Sorry, I didn't bring any formal shoes. To be honest I'm not great at packing for holidays."

They were all there waiting for me, each standing behind a chair spaced out around the extremely long dining table.

Daisy pointed me to the only free space and smiled shyly. "I like it as well, Izzy. We're too stuffy in this house. It's about time we changed things up a bit."

"Oh, things are going to change." Cameron sat down at the far end of the table so the rest of us followed suit.

"What's that supposed to mean?" Beatrix fired her words across at him.

"There's no point keeping this place for a start. We never needed this ridiculous house and, as far as I'm concerned, the sooner we sell it, the better."

"What on earth are you-" Edmund began, but the eldest in the family interrupted him and all other voices fell silent.

"I really don't think it's necessary to be carving up the estate when our father's corpse is still only a few rooms away." As Audrey spoke, Gladwell arrived with a trolley carrying drinks and the first course. "And besides, until we find out which of us killed Dad, we won't know who's entitled to the inheritance."

I hadn't really thought about this before. It made sense that the murderer would not only end up in jail but cut out of any dividends from their wicked deed. I wondered if it was an automatic process or the others would have to contest the will.

Gladwell distributed large plates with tiny purple and orange creations on them. I wasn't sure what they were or how to eat them, but they were very pretty. For a moment I questioned whether they were appetisers or table decorations. Finally, my hosts picked them up and popped them in their mouths so I did the same.

Gnyaaarrrrr! Eating that is like falling through the clouds into a swimming pool filled with foie-gras custard!

"An amuse-bouche of caramelised beetroot with mandarin crispbread and aroma of lamb," Gladwell explained.

Food is the one area on which my brain and I tend to be in agreement; it was a taste explosion. My bouche was very amused.

"How's it going anyway, Izzy?" Why did lovely Audrey have to pick that moment to talk to me? I was still gurning from the appetiser and failed to make anything more than a seedy grunting noise. "Have you made any progress?"

"I'm sure it won't be long before she comes to the right conclusion." Cameron glanced down the table at me knowingly.

"And what's that meant to mean?" Edmund was immediately agitated by his brother's words.

"Just, own up, E. We all know you did it." Tiny purple crumbs sailed from Cameron's mouth. "You're wasting everyone's time with this charade."

"Calm down, Cameron," Audrey put in.

"Yeah, Cam. Listen to big sis." Edmund slammed his fist down on the table so that his cutlery jangled together. "Unless you want Izzy to hear your dark little secret."

Cameron's arrogance once more disappeared. His emotions had been pinging back and forth all evening and I wondered whether he'd started drinking before dinner.

It was Beatrix's turn to stir the pot. "I'd certainly like to hear what Cameron has been up to."

"And I'd like you to shut your mouth from time to time." Cameron was a lion once more. I'd only seen a hint of his dark side in the bowling alley, but, now that it was out, it would not be re-caged.

"You know what?" Edmund rolled his cotton napkin up into a ball and tossed it into the centre of the table. "If you all think that I killed Dad, perhaps we should go through the evidence."

It's about time someone else pulled their weight.

Shhh, I'm listening.

"Fine, I argued with him on the night he was killed, but it was in everyone's interests. If the old miser had shared his wealth around, he probably wouldn't have ended up dead."

Gladwell was serving white wine to go with the next course and as soon as Cameron's glass was full he grabbed it and knocked it back. "You hear that, everybody? Edmund practically admitted he's guilty."

The youngest Porter child was about to hit back at his brother but checked himself at the last moment. "That isn't what I said and you know it. I'm saying there's no reason to suspect me above anyone else."

"I'm afraid that's not entirely true." Audrey spoke in her usual open manner but it was tempered with concern for her brother. "You're our little soldier, E. You've always been quick to anger. If Dad upset you and you took it too far, we'd understand. We just want everything to be sorted out quietly."

"Is that what you think then, Audrey? You think that I did it?" He looked vulnerable as he stared across at his sister in the chair opposite. When she failed to reply he continued speaking. "That's all right. Two votes against me. Let's see whether I can win anyone round."

If he really was innocent, I could only imagine what he was going through. Having your close family explain why they think you're a murderer can't be a pleasant experience.

"I'm no soldier. The weapons, the army stuff; that was all Dad. I went along with it because I wanted to make him happy. You say I have a temper, but I got that from him too. It's there in each of us. Even Daisy emits a shriek of pure fury once in a while."

His silent sister flinched in her chair and turned her eyes away.

"Exactly," Cameron cut in. "We all have that rage in us, but you're the one who lets it show."

"No. The difference between me and the rest of you is that I say what I'm thinking. I don't pussyfoot around important issues and hope for the best. I don't coat my poison with candy floss the way you do. I tell the truth, which is why you've never been able to handle me."

Gladwell had left and reappeared with the second course. It was quite impressive how he stuck to his professional duties without mind for what was being said right in front of him. I didn't pay him much attention though as I was watching the family psycho-drama unfold.

Edmund turned to his closest ally. "B, do you think that I did it?"

"No, I don't." Beatrix shook her head confidently. "I don't know for sure who killed Dad but I'm certain it wasn't you."

"Okay. Two to one." He attempted a smile. "What about you D?"

Daisy looked shocked just to be addressed. She slowly turned her head to meet her brother's gaze. "I…" For ten seconds, that was all she managed to get out but finally her words came. "I have no idea. I'm not sure I even want to know who killed him."

"Fine, you abstain." Edmund cast his eyes down the table towards me. "It looks like you have the deciding vote, Izzy. Do you believe I killed my father?"

What do you reckon? He's put on a pretty good show.

Just like his siblings, Edmund was conflicted. He was not one thing or another. Though he had shown a sensitive underbelly, he was still the arrogant, aggressive chancer I'd taken him to be when we first met. A plea for trust wasn't enough to rule him out of the investigation, so I decided not to answer.

"I'll let you know tomorrow, right before we call the police."

He smiled and nodded his head in a rather old-fashioned manner. After that, something broke in the atmosphere and the all-out warfare we were building towards turned cold.

Gladwell chose his moment well. "A starter of spiced citrus bean soup with parmesan croutons."

The serious eating got underway and cordiality returned to place a cosy blanket over the hostilities. Voices were lowered, big talk became small talk and the evening sunlight, shining in through the antique glass windows, gave everything a warm, peaceful hue.

When dinner had concluded-

Noooooo! You forgot the chocolate mousse. You have to talk about the chocolate mousse.

Oh, fine. Cook's chocolate mousse was so good that, if she'd been the chef in a nunnery, I'd have donned a habit just to have a taste. It was so good that, if you could buy it in the supermarket, I'd go online and have a whole truckful delivered to my house each week. It was so good that I scoffed it down in about four seconds flat.

And, when dinner had concluded, Gladwell came in to bang a gong. "Ladies and gentlemen, if you'd like to retire to the ballroom, drinks will be served."

As he got busy clearing our plates and glasses onto his trolley, we filed out of the room. It was all so staid and formal that I felt as if I was a passenger on the Porter family cruise ship. I needed to get a focus on everything that had happened, but instead I was carried along by the glamour of it all.

I shouldn't have worried. Things were about to get crazy again.

Daisy was the first to enter the ballroom and her scream immediately travelled back to me. "The face…" was all she managed to get out before, in a rather graceful swoon, she collapsed to the floor.

I tried to make sense of the scene before us. The ballroom was sparklingly beautiful. Its floor-to-ceiling windows were adorned with red velvet curtains to contrast with the polished, pine dance floor. The only problem was that one wall appeared to have been attacked by an animal-rights group. That's not what happened, but it certainly looked that way.

At the other end of the room, someone had placed a creepy mask on the mantelpiece. Just above it on the wall, they'd painted five lurid words in what I had to assume was blood.

"The sins of the father," Cameron read out with a tone of disgust. "Who the hell would do something like this?"

I walked a few steps closer and came to understand why Daisy had fainted. "The face" she'd seen was no mask. Looking like the mounted skulls on the library wall, Geoffrey the Pig's head had been propped up for us to find.

I watched the reactions of the four Porter children who remained conscious. Cameron's mouth was hanging open in shock, Beatrix was lingering in the doorway, as if afraid to fully enter the room and Audrey had gone to attend to their youngest sister on the floor. Only Edmund looked unfazed by this unexpected event. But then, maybe it wasn't such a surprise to him.

"Have any of you been in this room today?" I asked, breaking the stunned silence.

"I saw Cameron in here." Beatrix was happy to jump on this fact. "I was out on the lawn and I saw him through the window. He was standing right there." She pointed to the fireplace.

"Yes, but that was ages ago. And I was only in here to make a phone call. The reception is better down here and I needed quiet."

I studied Cameron's face, trying to work out if his initial shock was an act. Audrey had got her sister up to sitting and Edmund brought a chair from the side of the room. Daisy looked unsteady but pulled herself up before trying to speak.

"Is that…?" she began. "Is that Geoffrey?"

I'm pretty sure she was more attached to the family pig than she'd been to her father and it was hard to for me to break the news. "Yes. Gladwell found him in his pen. I didn't tell anyone about it because I couldn't be sure why he'd been killed."

"The barbarity." Cameron turned to look at his brother. "Is this your idea of a joke?"

Edmund had a wry smile on his face. "Oh, come off it. Why would I kill a pig? All this theatrical, over-the-top nonsense is hardly my style."

"Edmund, did you do it?" Audrey looked stern and fixed her little brother with her impenetrable gaze.

His voice rose higher and his smirk disappeared. "I just told you, it wasn't me. We're not kids anymore, you know? You can't always blame me because I'm the youngest. What would I even gain from splashing pig blood around?"

142

It was a good question. What would any of them gain from this grisly act?

"I think this was for my benefit," I told them. "One of you is trying to scare me off. First the vase, now this."

"If that's true, then enough is enough." Back on her feet, Audrey came to stand beside me in solidarity. "Izzy is here to do a job and we have no right to intimidate her. Whoever did this has to stop."

"It might as well stop, because whatever you do, it's not going to work." I didn't look at them but stared at the dripping letters on the sumptuous wallpaper. I very much doubted they'd be getting that stain out. "I promise you right now that, by this time tomorrow, one of you will be in police custody."

Go, Izzy. You're a tiger!

Silence returned to the ballroom. The suspects glanced about at one another moodily before the tension broke.

"Okay… then perhaps we should enjoy our final night together?" That mischievous grin was back on Edmund's face. He walked over to the corner of the room where a cabinet built into the wall concealed a large hi-fi. Plugging his phone into a dock, he pressed various buttons and loud music burst out of speakers that were hidden all over the room. "In the face of such uncertainty, isn't it best we dance?"

He ran to Beatrix and pulled her onto the floor. She didn't want to join in at first but Edmund held a strong pose and wouldn't let her escape. The music was a very modern sort of tango and it was clear that the duo knew what they were doing. Beatrix flicked her elegant heels up and around her brother in time with the melody and, at the end of the first phrase of music, Edmund tipped his partner low to the floor, then swung her back up to standing.

"Show offs," Cameron shouted. "How are we supposed to join in with that?"

Just then, Gladwell pushed his clinking trolley into the room. It held a huge selection of spirits on its upper shelf and glasses, ice and mixers underneath. Taking in the scene, he came to a sudden stop. He looked like he was about to shout at us but swallowed the words, spun on his heel and immediately walked back out.

I couldn't blame him. He'd treated poor Geoffrey like a pet for years and here were his employers, dancing about beneath the beast's severed head. They were a seriously weird bunch, he'd got that much right.

Edmund directed Beatrix out onto the patio, so I pushed the drinks cart after them and, once everyone was there, began to make up gin and tonics.

In vino veritas. In gin-o muchas veritas.

Daisy seemed to have got over her shock and even dipped back inside the room to crank the volume up and change the music. The Beatles informed us that it had been a hard day's night and Cameron grabbed hold of his returning sister to join in with the dancing. Though perhaps they weren't up to Beatrix and Edmund's standard, Daisy and Cameron had clearly had dance lessons in their youth and performed a convincing jive complete with lifts and drops.

The sun was just setting behind the trees at the end of the lawn and the world was awash with yellows, reds and every shade in between. I offered Audrey a drink and we stood watching the two pairs compete.

There was an awkwardness to the silence between us that was completely at odds with the freak, joyful moment playing out. It told me something about the relationship she shared with her siblings. It wasn't just that she was the eldest, she'd been held up by their father as an example and was the obvious successor to take over the family business now that he was gone. But more than that, she was the designated adult in the family. The mum ever since their real mum had been sent away.

Far from making her happy, this responsibility appeared to hang heavily upon her.

"Don't you dance?" I tried to sound chirpy but I don't think I managed it.

She let out a sigh. "Oh, they normally make me, but it's not really my thing."

"Does this happen a lot then?"

She looked at me side on. "Far more than it should at our age." With her authority and self-control, it was hard to imagine her ever being young. "It was something that Mum started after big dinners when we were kids and, somehow, we've never grown out of it. Even with Dad dead in the library and Geoffrey in the ballroom, we Porters love having a ball."

144

Edmund swung near us just then and had obviously caught a bit of the conversation. "Which means it's time you cut in." He sent Beatrix off in a spin and snatched up Audrey.

Perhaps inevitably, she was a better dancer than any of her brothers and sisters. Dressed in a short, monochrome satin dress, her skirt flared out as her brother launched her up in the air then brought her back down to make two tiny stops on either side of her. They hopped off across the patio and I felt a buzzing on my wrist so I accepted the call without anyone noticing.

"Sorry, Izzy." It was Dad. "I didn't mean to press the button. Everyone here is having a great time." I could hear them in the background making a racket. "I had no idea that Greg was such a good dancer! He's leading Emilia around the office with the most phenomenal rock 'n' roll moves. Your mother and Ramesh are really going for it too."

"You should be here, Iz," Ramesh told me, his voice distant and out of breath. "We had pizza delivered from Don Carlo's and Fernando has gone to get booze! Dean's off on his date, but I'm pretty sure that I've prepared him for it. I-"

I clicked the call off. They were so noisy that I was sure someone would hear. The song finished and, laughing and out of breath, the dancers on this side of London came to a stop. The quieter Sam Cooke song that replaced it gave everyone the chance to catch their breath. Even Audrey was smiling now and the communal feeling made me forget for a while what I was there to do.

Three minutes later, they set their glasses down to jump about to Chubby Checker. Daisy grabbed hold of me and pulled me into the circle where everyone was doing the appropriate steps as the singer called them out. I was surprised how good a twist the boys managed, working down very low, while still shimmying to the beat, before popping back up again.

"I like you, Izzy," Beatrix told me as we whirled around one another. "I wish it was under different circumstances, but I'm glad you're here."

I don't know if it was the music or the heat or perhaps just the alcohol, but euphoria had invaded my body. My head was light, my muscles loose and for a moment I wanted to believe that I was as good a dancer as any of them.

"I like you too," I screamed back over the music which blared out from the ballroom and across the estate.

I jumped in the air, swished my around and forgot all about dead bodies, incarcerated boyfriends and my limited career prospects. I looked into the eyes of my companions to share the joy they were feeling and, for the duration of that three-minute pop song, I knew what it felt like to be part of a big family.

Chapter Eighteen

At some point, I remembered Mr Porter, hooked in place by antlers and skulls, and I felt a bit guilty. Not for him so much as his kids. *The sins of the father* had taken their toll and whoever had killed him would suffer the consequences. As I ducked, shimmied and spun around with those five beautiful humans, that seemed like a terrible thing.

The gin bottle drained down, the music got louder and the Porter children kept on dancing. My buzz of self-belief would not last long though and I soon returned to the patio to watch them. A few lively songs later, Daisy joined me. We sat beside one another without saying anything but I got the definite feeling that she wanted to talk.

"Shall we go for a walk?" I asked and she nodded and stood up.

The grounds of Vomeris Hall were illuminated like every day was a wedding. Neatly strung fairy lights led us to the path across the lawn and, in silence, we followed it to a part of the estate that I hadn't visited before. A large stone semicircle, supported by towering pillars housed a statue of some previously adored goddess. I suppose it had been built as a sort of temple but reminded me of a Greek amphitheatre.

We sat on the steps at the base of the figure. From there we could just about see the others still enjoying themselves. The imposing form of the house was picked out behind them in shades of fiery orange by huge upright lamps that were concealed beneath the ground.

"It's beautiful here," I said and hoped that Daisy would join in.

"Yes, we're very lucky to have this place." She didn't sound as if she believed it and cast her gaze to the floor.

When she didn't say anything more, I figured it was time I blathered on about something. "You know, I've always thought my family were weird. My mum is the most enthusiastic person on earth and everything we do ends up in a ridiculous anecdote that we get to enjoy over and over for years after. On every holiday – every school trip and summer picnic from my youth – you could be sure that something completely absurd would happen. There must be people in the world who live their lives without the slightest incident, but not us."

I watched her as I spoke but she showed so little response that

I wondered if she hadn't heard me. "Anyway, I thought we were eccentric but I've never had a dance party under the watchful gaze of a murdered pig before."

Daisy laughed in the same way she did everything else – vague and prettily. "I know what you mean. The occupants of Vomeris Hall are hardly normal, everyday folk. Our Mum knew how to have fun though. She used to try to get Dad to loosen up but it had the opposite effect. He wasn't always so cold and shut off from the world. I like to believe that he was a loving man in his own way, even if he did have trouble showing it."

The sound of the dancers died down again and I knew what I had to ask her. "I'm an only child and, ever since I arrived here, I've been wondering something." I paused to study her perfectly symmetrical face in the dim light. "Everything you guys have told me suggests that one of you killed your father because of the way he treated you. But you had four siblings and a mother too, wasn't that enough to cancel him out?"

She looked back over at her family. "I don't know if you've realised this, but we really do love one another. We have our fallings out, like any family, but we've always been close. Perhaps that's what I've found so difficult this week; the idea that one of them has been hatching plans without the rest of us knowing."

She breathed in and held it for a moment like she was trying to get over the pain. "I love my brothers and sisters and I know I always will. More than I loved my father and mother and more than any boyfriend I can imagine. It feels like I'm only a person in combination with them; one piece in a five-piece puzzle that's useless on its own."

She excelled at imprecision but I needed to pin her down to hard, cold facts. "I heard that you broke up with your fiancé. Is there any hope you'll get back together?" It wasn't very subtle.

She laughed a tragic laugh. "I don't think so. It wasn't just that Daddy made me break up with Peter, or that he threatened to cut me out of his will. He spent weeks trying to convince me that the man I'd fallen in love with wasn't worthy of me. I was starting to wonder if Daddy wanted to keep me away from men altogether. Either way, it worked and I'm not sure Peter would want me back after what I did."

"What was it that your dad objected to about him?"

She frowned like a moody teenager. "Everything. They'd only met a few times at public occasions but Dad was convinced that the man I'd chosen to marry was a gold-digging, womanising, future wife-beater. Perhaps his greatest sin though was that he was poor."

I picked up a tiny pebble from the floor and sent it skipping towards the house. "I thought your father was a self-made man. Didn't he come from a working-class background and build himself up?"

She made a little humming sound before replying. "That's right, but if you'd spent as much time around rich people as I have, you'd know that people like my dad are often the most snobbish of the lot."

"It's funny." I took a sip of my vodka and lemonade, which I certainly hadn't left behind on the patio and was enjoying a great deal, thank you very much. "My mum would be happy if I married the bloke from Sainsbury's who collects trolleys and sells a bit of weed on the side. And I don't mean that metaphorically, she literally tried to set me up with him once."

I'd made Daisy laugh again, but it didn't last long. "He didn't just do it to me, you know. Audrey was all set to marry her boyfriend straight out of uni. They'd planned the whole wedding – booked the honeymoon even – when Daddy changed his mind and said it couldn't happen. I think that's why Beatrix has never come close. She flits between men, the less reliable the better, because she always knew that our father would get the final say."

"He let Cameron get married though."

She shifted her weight on the hard, stone step. "Yes, well no one ever accused my father of being an enlightened man."

A warm breeze suddenly picked up and caressed her glossy brown hair like she was standing on a New York subway grate. She stretched her arms out to enjoy it and I could tell that we both experienced the same tingling buzz as the air kissed our skin. When the wind died down again, her joy faded away and the magic died.

I didn't let myself get distracted. "Did none of you think of rebelling? I mean, it's only money. Wouldn't it have been worth losing it to get away from him?"

"It's easy to say things like, 'It's only money,' when you don't have any." She sounded just like her father then and I was taken aback by the sudden change. "I'm so sorry. That came out wrong. I'm not saying you wouldn't understand, I'm saying that the upbringing we had changed us. We were taught that wealth was oxygen, it's very hard to give that up."

What she was saying made sense. For all the rage and rebellion among her siblings, they were still there. Still part of the Porter clan and presumably still listed in the will. She'd opened up to me and I could sense it was time to ask her the questions that I really needed to know.

"Can you tell me about Thursday night?"

"Oh dear. I knew this was coming." She let out a short, sharp breath. "I don't think there's much to say. We ate, we drank, we danced. Edmund made a scene like always and Beatrix helped calm him down."

"What kind of a mood was your father in?"

"Not a great one. He was upset about Audrey going away. God knows she deserved a holiday but he thought otherwise and they'd parted on bad terms. Over the last couple of years, he's become simultaneously clingier and more cantankerous. We've all suffered because of it, Audrey more than anyone. I thought we were coming together on Thursday to celebrate my new job, but it was really an excuse for Dad to have a rant. You can imagine how he felt about the rest of us when even his golden girl had let him down."

"Did anyone lose their temper except Edmund?"

Sitting on the step above mine, she glanced down at me curiously. "Didn't the others tell you? I felt sure they'd have said. To be honest, I've been scared this whole time that they'd dropped me in it."

I looked back at her, my face blank, so she continued. "I threw a strop. I don't know why, but it all seemed like too much effort that night. Cameron and Edmund were trying to get one up on each other and Beatrix was her usual catty self. It was supposed to be my moment, my celebration, but I felt like they barely noticed me, so I shut my mouth and didn't say a word throughout dinner."

She looked up at Athena or Aphrodite or whoever we were bowed before. "Of course, the wine was flowing and, without really wanting them to, all my thoughts came bursting out. I expected B and my brothers to stop me but, instead, they joined in. For probably the first time in our whole lives, the four of us were screaming at Dad.

"For Cameron and Edmund, it was about money. For Beatrix and me, all we've ever wanted was freedom. But there in the ballroom, between the main course and dessert, we unloaded on him and he just smiled. He didn't even answer back. When we ran out of steam, he called for Gladwell, had a martini and offered to dance with Beatrix. I swear he enjoyed the whole thing."

"I keep asking what went on that night and always get a different answer." I allowed a hint of irritation to creep into my voice.

"Well that's hardly surprising." She had a knowing expression on her face as she replied. "We're phenomenally selfish people, Izzy. They probably only remember their own part in what went on."

I'd had to work hard for this small revelation. Neither Edmund, Cameron nor Beatrix had told me about the argument with their father. But hiding the truth didn't make them killers. Perhaps they were protecting their little sis.

"I have one more question," I announced when my thoughts had run their course. "Edmund told me that Beatrix was cruel enough to have killed your father and Cameron was desperate enough. He didn't give me much more to go on than that, so what do you think he meant?"

She hesitated and I saw the Porter family loyalty kick in once more. "I don't want to get either of them in trouble. I have no idea who killed Daddy so please don't think I'm trying to sway you one way or another by saying this but…" Another pause. "Cameron has massive debts. We're not supposed to know about them of course, but I heard him talking to Edmund a couple of months back when we were here for Audrey's birthday.

"Edmund knows some people that Daddy would never have let into Vomeris Hall. Less than legitimate contacts, if you see what I mean. And, well… Cameron was keen to make use of them."

"Loan sharks, that sort of thing?"

"Yes. Or at least that's what I imagine they were."

"He told me he owed money to his prep-school chums. I guess he didn't want me knowing how bad the situation really is." Daisy swallowed hard, like she was uncomfortable addressing such issues so I moved the conversation on. "And Beatrix? Why would Edmund say she was cruel enough to kill?"

She looked straight at me and I knew she'd answer the question. "I

151

sometimes think that B is the toughest of us all. She's the one who's come closest to leaving Vomeris for good. There were long periods when she skipped these family weekends because she'd found someone more fun to spend time with. Eventually Dad would get sick of it and threaten to cut her off and she'd run back here like the rest of us. But, each time it happened, she'd be gone for a little longer and I really thought that, one day, she'd leave and we'd never see her again."

I shifted again to get comfortable. "But how does that make her cruel?"

Daisy smiled and her eyes traced out a spiralling pattern on the ground. "Because all the people she hangs out with are just toys. Even in the family, it can feel as if we're props for her to play with. The men she dates are her key to a good time, her friends are a ladder to climb and we are the safety net she can fall back on. I know that she loves us, but she's not good at expressing it and, for Edmund and me in particular, that's hard to accept."

There was something very fragile about Daisy. Even with the gin running through her and her tongue loose, she was hazy and imprecise. Instead of an interview, it felt like I'd spent the last twenty minutes reading an abstract poem. Silence consumed the space between us and, for a little while, I thought her final verse had come to an end.

The music in the distance had changed to upbeat jazz and, like toddlers at playschool who'd been told to express themselves, the dancers' moves had become larger and more pronounced. Their clearly defined, formal steps had been replaced by wildly thrown shapes with accompanying howls and yelps. I could tell that it wasn't just the alcohol that made them act like that, it was the end of an era and this was their chance to mark the occasion.

"Why did I have to be called Daisy?" Her words came out of nowhere and I wish I could have known the exact chain of thought that had preceded them. "I sound like a children's character. Names have power and I swear mine made me weak."

That was all she said. She offered no further explanation and I didn't ask for one. We returned to our pensive silence and I realised that this was the only window I would be allowed into her world. When the night was over, she would go back to being her usual distant self – like a woman in a coma given some short reprieve.

152

Chapter Nineteen

For the hour or so afterwards, I can only remember strange, divergent images. I was sitting on a sofa in a room with red-curtains covering every wall. Seated alongside me, Mum, Agatha Christie and my teacher from nursery school were chanting something loud and aggressive, and for some reason my clothes were covered in milk. I was just about to work out what it all meant when a painful sensation travelled up my arm like a lightning bolt and I woke, still on the steps of the Greek temple, entirely alone.

Looking back towards the house, I could see that the Porters had retired for the evening and, as I struggled to make sense of the fading dream and that strange buzzing that was still pulsing through me, I realised that Dean was calling.

"Izzy, quick, there's someone in your room!"

I jumped to my feet, immediately discovered what a bad idea this was and had to sit back down again. I was experiencing that odd half-awake fuzziness you get when you wake up unexpectedly.

"Who's in my room?" I managed to ask. The world in front of me was still out of focus.

"I can't see who it is, it's too dark."

"Dean!" I said very urgently but then didn't know where to go from there. "How was the date?"

"There's no time for that. Get up and run. Now."

I did as instructed and the warm wind rushing over me made me feel human. By the time I got to the patio, I was almost back to normal – though I hadn't run so far or fast since an ill-fated sports day when, aged seventeen, I managed to both win the Year Thirteen four-hundred-metre sprint and get a detention for vomiting on my P.E. teacher Mr Bath.

I was just about able to keep my dinner down and zipped into the house through an open doorway. The lights clicked on in the corridor as I rushed along it, but there was no other sign of life. Stopping only momentarily to recover from a stitch, I bombed it all the way to the west wing and up the grand staircase to my room.

Now that I'd arrived, I realised I was perfectly clueless about what I was supposed to do next. I looked about for a weapon but the landing was dark and the only items small enough to carry were a silver picture frame with a photo of a horse or a standard lamp. It was a tough choice.

"Dean, what if it's the murderer in there and they've come to kill me?"

"Don't worry, Izzy. Just turn the light on and we'll catch him on the camera as he leaves."

"Urmmm… Well, that's reassuring." I put my hand on the doorknob and prepared to do something stupid. "Dean, tell my folks that I love them!"

With the standard lamp held aloft like a spear, I dashed into the room, screaming out a war cry as I went. Once inside, I had to hunt around for the light switch. It was pitch black, just as Dean had said. This slow, fumbling process removed the element of surprise I'd been relying on for my protection. It wasn't too much of a problem though as the only other person in the room was naked, asleep and almost definitely drunk.

My kind of man!

Shhh! You've got a filthy mind.

No, actually you've got a filthy mind.

Touché.

Edmund was face down on my bed with only a small cushion to protect his modesty. I tried not to notice how firm and muscly he was but, as we've already established, I have a filthy mind.

"What are you doing in here?" I placed my trusty lamp down and he began to stir.

"Go away, Izzy," he said into the covers. "I'm not going to have rumpy pumpy with you and that's final."

"Then why are you in my room stark-bottom naked?"

"Oh, fine. We can have sex. But don't blame me if I fall asleep. It's been a very long day." I had to piece together most of this sentence from the grunts and sighs he made.

"I don't want to have sex with you, Edmund. I want you to get out of my bed and put some clothes on. Preferably not in that order."

He snored in reply and, walking over to the bed, I could see he was fast asleep once more.

Room for a little one?

Oh, be quiet. Where are we supposed to sleep now?

I found a blanket and curled up on an armchair that was far too small for me. At least I wasn't cold, but I didn't sleep well that night as Edmund was a phenomenally noisy roommate.

When the day dawned and I woke up with my neck cramped, my limbs all knotted together and my shoes still on, Edmund was gone. I got into bed and slept for a while longer and when I woke up for good, I was not at my best. I didn't have the energy to get up and deal with my spoilt hosts, or investigate a murder even, so I just lay there under the quilted covers in the four-poster bed that I wished was mine. My mind wandered between recent and distant memories. Instead of working through evidence or narrowing down my list of suspects, I found myself back in Castleton Square Manor aged eleven.

I'd managed to steer clear of Tedwin and Noémi for the remainder of my first day there, but, on Saturday morning, our mothers despatched us off into the grounds to play. Ever since the incident in the library, my cousins had been looking at me like they wanted to cook and eat me. As we crossed the lawn to the secret den they promised to show me, I wished myself back to the treasure trove of detective fiction I had stumbled across.

Their secret hideout was actually a stone grotto with an ornamental water feature bubbling away over a pile of rocks. It was surrounded by high walls made from roughly hued stone. They'd been sculpted to look like a natural outcrop, incongruously rising up in the middle of a neatly groomed, English garden. I could tell immediately that what my demonic cousins liked best about it was its distance from the prying eyes of parents and staff.

"We don't want you here," Tedwin told me as he sat down beside the fountain.

"You're poor and you should leave." Noémi spoke as if this was the way of things and that, by intruding upon their summer holiday, I was disturbing some natural order.

I was tired of feeling out of place and answered straight back. "Well, I'd rather be anywhere else on earth but I'm here until Monday so you'll have to put up with me."

"No, we don't." Noémi's voice was cold and adult. She sounded like a driving instructor in the way she calmly laid out her plan of action. "We're going to get rid of you before then. We're going to make it so that nobody here likes you and they send you away. You should have been nicer to us."

Tedwin joined in with her assessment. "You should have cried, then maybe we wouldn't have to do this."

"You kids are crazy. I thought I was the unlucky one – growing up in a house the size of your bathroom – but you're entirely mad."

"You should have cried," Noémi repeated and walked calmly over to her brother.

Without standing up, Tedwin rolled back his sleeve and held his arm out to his sister. They were like automatons, programmed to carry out their creepy plan for revenge. With their eyes fixed on me, Noémi put both hands on her brother's arm and, with all her strength, twisted in opposing directions. Even as his skin turned red and tears came to his eyes, Tedwin didn't call out.

"What are you doing?" I screamed but the hell-girl wouldn't let go.

She smiled her evil smile and that's when I ran at her. I didn't care if Tedwin was a willing participant, I couldn't bear to see anyone suffer like that. I knocked into Noémi just hard enough to make her let go. She fell gently to the floor, and the worst you could say was that I had crumpled her pretty white skirt.

She responded with a, "Thank you, Isobel," and got carefully to her feet. "Come along, Tedwin. Time to go."

They put their hands together and left me behind in the grotto. I sat down to make sense of what had happened and the injustice of a world that would allow two such monsters so many advantages in life. I watched as they walked away with their usual eerie calm. They got about halfway across the lawn before Tedwin screamed for their mother and they both started to run.

"She attacked us, Mummy." I heard him shout for my benefit, as they were still far from the house. How could I have been so stupid? I should have known exactly what they were about to do.

I was older, taller and faster than them but they had a massive head start. I knew they'd be able to get their side of the story across before I found whichever parlour or sitting room our mothers were taking tea in. I broke into a sprint all the same and caught up with them in a downstairs salon where everything was painted duck egg blue.

Just as I got there, Noémi burst out crying. "It was horrible, mummy. She's a beast."

"We only wanted to be friends," Tedwin joined in. "I don't know why she was so cruel."

"Is this true, Isobel?" their mother asked in a tone that suggested she already knew the answer.

"I didn't touch them."

My Mum was looking at me in horror. "Tedwin has a nasty burn on his arm, Izzy. Are you saying you didn't cause it?"

I could sense the ground being pulled from underneath me. I suddenly knew how it felt to be one of The Central Park Five, The Birmingham Six or Dr Richard Kimble from "The Fugitive".

"It was Noémi, she did it to get me in trouble." I knew there was no point arguing but I couldn't give up.

"Oh yeah?" The devil girl turned her gaze on me. "So how did my favourite dress get torn?" She spun round to display an immense split, running up the rear of her skirt. That little witch must have done it herself as soon as she got in the house.

I turned to the adults to plead my innocence. "I'm telling the truth." They'd done a great job of stitching me up and even I realised how unlikely this sounded. "They told me they were going to get rid of me right before they did it. I promise, I-"

"Enough!" Mum's cousin Elizabeth rose up to her full height to peer at me. She rang a pretentious little bell that was placed on her tea tray and, a moment later, a maid appeared. "Martha, take this child away from me and see she is suitably punished."

I looked at Mum, desperate to believe that she would finally stand up for me.

"I didn't do anything. I'm telling the truth."

"Quiet," Elizabeth answered for her. "Feral children like you only learn in two ways, with the cane or the back of the hand!"

Martha the maid grabbed my arm to pull me from the room. I'll never forget the look on my mother's face as I went. She was speechless, trapped between the need to protect her daughter and please her overbearing cousin. And though she has apologised a hundred times since for not speaking up, it still hurts to think about that moment. I saw Mum's helplessness and the two little monsters' diabolical grins and something inside me broke.

"We'll soon have you behaving right," Martha announced as she tugged me along after her.

She was a small, wiry woman with a strong grip and a loud voice. She didn't stop yanking or huffing until we'd made it to the kitchen, at which point she sat me down at the table and gave me a great big smile.

"Now, what can I get for you? There's fresh jam tarts made or there's some fruit cake in the pantry if you prefer."

I had just been through one of the most traumatic moments in my life. My cheeks were red, puffy and streaked with tears, my heart was broken and I had no idea if the false promise of cake was the first part of my punishment.

"Aren't you going to beat me?" My eyes go as big as side plates when I cry.

Carrying boxes of veg from the garden, a couple of kitchen hands had arrived to laugh at me.

Martha joined in. "Course I'm not. I heard what you said in there and I know what those little brats get up to. Even if you'd given them a hiding, I wouldn't punish you for it. The lady of the house might think we're her personal slaves, but there's a limit to everything." She came over and, with a gentle hand removed my long, sodden fringe from my eyes. "So what will it be, cake or tart?"

I spent the rest of my time in Castleton Square hanging out with the staff, stuffing myself with delicious food and making my way through their extensive murder-mystery library. I got to see the workings of the house as well. In many ways, the numerous staff were the real inhabitants of the manor. They were the ones who kept the place alive. They were both engine and driver of the great Castleton machine and the rich family who hung around upstairs were merely the passengers.

It was interesting to see what that huge troop of servants could get away with. Though on the surface the maids and butlers were all prim and proper, away from the family, they could do whatever they liked. Unknown to Elizabeth Castleton and her wicked brood, every night was a party in the servants' quarters and, for two short days, I was their guest of honour.

I didn't see my cousins again until we were ready to leave on Monday morning.

"Thank you so much for the lovely weekend," I told them without a hint of sarcasm in my voice as I gave Noémi a kiss on both cheeks. "It was such a thrill to experience a whole different world that I'd only read about in books."

"You're supposed to be sad," Tedwin mumbled as he received his farewell.

"Oh, no. It's been wonderful. But I hope your arm heals up. It looks nasty."

Mum's battered yellow Corsa had been brought round to the front of the house and our bags were inside. I could tell from her voice as she said goodbye to Elizabeth that she was in no hurry to return, which is good because we never did.

I can see that the experience of that weekend left its mark on me. When you catch a glimpse of the wealth that still remains in tiny, isolated pockets of society such as Castleton or Vomeris Hall, it's like being dunked in cold water. Those places couldn't be more different from the Croydon of today with knife crime spiralling and the centre of my town a shadow of what it was twenty years ago.

In reality, neither of those pictures is real though. There's much more to Croydon than stabbings and drugs and Castleton Square Hall was nowhere near as graceful and refined as cousin Elizabeth wished to believe. My investigation at Vomeris Hall was surely coloured by that visit to my Mum's cousin, but whether it was a help or a hindrance remained to be seen.

The sun was peeking in through the curtains and I knew it was time to get up. It was nine o'clock and I only had a few hours left before Audrey would report her father's death to the police.

My idea that just talking to the suspects and observing them at home would be enough to solve the crime hadn't played out as I'd imagined. Each sibling had a complex relationship with their father. He had manipulated and unnerved them throughout their lives to the extent that no assessment they gave could be considered a reliable truth. I had discovered the strange network of guilt, co-dependence and hatred running through the family, but I wasn't sure it had got me any closer to knowing who had done the deed.

What if they're all guilty?

Do you ever make sensible suggestions anymore?

I'm serious. Every one of them has given us contrasting evidence. They love each other but they're happy to point the finger. They loved their father but they all wanted him dead. What if they hatched a plan to make it impossible to work out who was responsible?

It actually wasn't such a stupid idea. It would fit in with the feeling I'd been having that Mr Porter's murder and the clues surrounding it were lifted directly out of a mystery novel. No spoilers, but, *they all did it,* has to be one of the most famous solutions to one of the most famous detective stories of all time.

Not getting any closer to the murderer by staying in bed, I figured I'd get up and ring for some food.

"I'm sorry to be a princess," I said when Gladwell replied through the intercom. "But could you bring me up some breakfast to my bedroom? I've got some thinking to do and I want to be quick about it."

He appeared ten minutes later with coffee and orange juice, along with a selection of cakes, jams, cheeses and cold meats.

I wish we had a butler at home.

Me too.

"I don't think you're a princess just because you make me do my job," the old servant told me. "You've got a busy day ahead and you need all the help you can get."

"Thanks, I think."

A smile lit up his face. "Well, I for one have every faith in you." He poured me some juice and, with a wink of his eye, left the room.

He wasn't the only person I had to call for help. "Dean, did you get anywhere with Cameron's finances?" I sat in bed devouring the pastries as I called. The crumbs went everywhere.

"Oh, so you're alive then?" my mother replied. "Not murdered in your bed by some ruffian."

It hit me that I hadn't reported back to Dean after I'd ventured into my bedroom the previous night. "Sorry, everyone. It was just Edmund in the end. I'm pretty sure he didn't mean me any harm, he was drunk. Dean, how was the date?"

"Went very well, thank you, Izzy." His moany voice sounded

rather pleased with itself. "I was just about to message Samantha for a follow-up."

"Ahhh, that's great news. I'm so happy for you." I tried to sound sincere before rushing things along. "Getting back to the murder enquiry, what have you got for me?"

Dean loudly and rather grossly cleared his throat. "You were right about Cameron. Something fishy has been going on in his bank account. Whenever his mortgage has been due, a large sum has been deposited directly from the Porter & Porter company account. We know his father wouldn't have bailed him out so I reckon it could be dodgy."

"It would fit in with what we caught Cameron and Edmund discussing on that tape you played me yesterday. Edmund was worried about me discovering something. Daisy told me last night that Edmund has all sorts of dodgy contacts. Maybe they were helping to filter money from the company without their father knowing."

"I've been trying to work out who could have planted the pig's head too." I could hear Dean clicking through screens of information as he spoke. "Judging by the camera out in the hall, Gladwell and Edmund were the only ones who went in the ballroom yesterday morning. But what if someone stashed Geoffrey's head in one of the hidden staircases and went into the room without us seeing? On the plan I have here, it looks like there's another one right next door. You'll have to check it out."

"Great. Got anything else for me? Like the name of the murderer perhaps?"

"It was the butler, Izzy!" Mum instantly restated her favoured culprit. "The butler did it. Why won't you believe me?"

Luckily it was Dean who had the microphone. "Well, Audrey was up early this morning talking to Gladwell in her office. Wanna watch?"

My phone buzzed and I accepted the video feed. The screen was too small to make much out but I could just about see the eldest Porter child sitting at a table as her butler served coffee.

"I'm so sorry about Geoffrey." Her voice was smooth and sympathetic. "You finding him like that can't have been nice."

"I have to say, that pig was a truly warm-hearted creature and whoever did him in was a savage."

"It defies belief, it really does." She sighed emotionally. "Surely they could have got a chicken or something from the butcher and it would have had the same effect." She paused to blow on her coffee. "Do you have any idea who did it?"

"Has to be one of the boys, doesn't it? Only Cameron and Edmund could be so heartless." I was surprised how informal Gladwell was with Audrey, but then she did seem to be very fond of him. Perhaps he'd stood in as the father figure that Aldrich Porter had never bothered to be. "You remember the incident with the rabbit when they were kids of course?"

"Sort of. I think I was away at school at the time. Edmund cut one to pieces, right?"

"It was Edmund who killed the poor thing, but Cameron put him up to it. I caught the two of them coming back through the stables and Cameron was all giggles. Called his brother 'a good little killer' as I recall. Sounded like a real future psychopath if you ask me."

Audrey had a grim look on her face. "Yes, but it was Edmund who stuck the knife in and I'm pretty sure the police will want to talk to him about his violent past."

Gladwell corrected his posture so that his back was as straight as a book spine. "What time are you calling them?"

"Around two this afternoon. We mustn't leave it too late. Dad's friend in the police is a patient man, especially after the donation I sent him, but if we take too long we could all be in trouble."

"Well, you know I'm here if you should need any help."

"You are kind, Stephen." She smiled up at him. "What would I do without you?"

Gladwell withdrew the silver tray and the video cut out.

"Interesting, don't you think?" Dean said in my ear. "It shows that Cameron was lying about the rabbit, trying to make his brother look bad."

"It proves something else I've been thinking too," I replied as I pulled on a slightly more suitable outfit than I'd worn the previous morning. "I've noticed that her siblings know nothing about Cook or Gladwell – they really do treat them like slaves. But, to Audrey, they're her equals. It's quite sweet."

"Eyes on the prize, Izzy." Mum muscled in on the call once more.

"Don't get distracted by their personalities; you're there to solve a murder."

"Mum, why are you already at Dean's at nine in the morning?"

My mother let out a sharp *ha!* "I came to bring him some proper breakfast, darling. He's as skinny as a rake."

"Does that mean that Greg had to drive you again?"

"Hi, Izzy!" my stepdad called back. "Don't worry about me, I've got the Sunday crossword to do."

"Bye everyone. Wish me luck!" I ended the call and, dressed in my best work trousers and Che Guevara t-shirt, went forth to solve a murder.

Chapter Twenty

I'm going to be honest now. I was feeling a bit out of my depth.

When I'd investigated Bob's murder, it was all fun and games. There was no pressure to work out who the killer was because nobody thought for a second I'd be able to do it. Well, except Mum, but I think I've already proven that she is not the most impartial reference I can call upon.

With hours remaining to do my job, what did I know for sure? There were a million reasons Mr Porter could have been killed. No one in his family seemed particularly distressed that he was dead and there was no smoking gun to tie anyone to his demise.

It was time to go back to the start and think things through properly. The sun was shining outside and I figured I was brave enough to enter the library again. It turned out I was wrong.

Even as I approached the room, my heart was playing a samba beat. The heavy wooden door didn't help by making a perfectly Transylvanian creak and the room was north-facing so it was much gloomier than I'd imagined. But none of that was nearly as creepy as the fact that Mr Porter was no longer suspended from the stags' heads on the wall.

My first thought was, *Ahhhhhhhhhhhhhhhhhhhh, zombie!* But then I calmed down a bit and remembered what it said in the only book on forensics I'd bothered reading since my first investigation. Rigor mortis sets in shortly after death but disappears about thirty-six hours later, at which point the body becomes limp and would give in to gravity. It was only natural that Porter had fallen to the floor, it would have been scarier if he hadn't.

This basic fact, which I should have thought about much earlier, led me to another revelation. When Porter was murdered, his body would have been too floppy to sustain itself shoved in on the wall between the skulls. Whoever had killed him must have returned to the library to put finishing touches to the scene.

Oh my goodness. That means… Wait what does that mean?

Nope. I haven't a clue.

164

I went further into the room to make sure he was behind the desk and someone hadn't moved him. He was and they hadn't, but there were still discoveries to be made. A slit in the curtains allowed a sliver of daylight to land right on the spot where he now lay. Mr Porter was starting to smell bad. He was face down on the carpet, his arms and legs awkwardly arranged beneath him and the wounds on his back quite clear. I could see at least ten small holes where the knife had cut his shirt and the sky-blue fabric had turned rusty-red.

It made me wonder again why the killer had attacked from behind. Obviously there was the element of surprise to consider, but then Mr Porter would surely have seen them entering. Perhaps it was a question of strength. By stabbing him in the back, the victim couldn't defend himself. This might have been significant if the murderer hadn't subsequently lifted the corpse several feet off the floor to display their brutality to all. The only thing I could think of was that the murderer couldn't bear to look into the victim's eyes as it happened; an interesting conclusion that once again did nothing to narrow our field of suspects.

The more important observation that, I'd completely failed to make until now, was that the murder weapon was nowhere to be found. I'd taken it for granted when I first inspected the scene that it would still be in Porter's back. David had removed the bottle and knife he'd used to kill Bob because they were covered in fingerprints. The big difference between the two murders though was that Porter's had been carefully planned. The murderer was surely wearing gloves and could rely on the fact that they would not have left fingerprints on the weapon. So then, why remove the knife?

I opened the curtains wider and took another look around the body. I'd hoped the daylight might reveal something that I'd missed before but there was not a speck or fibre to be found. Perhaps the police would have more luck later on – not that the mere presence of a suspect's DNA was proof of guilt. With the exception of Cook, everyone had been in the library prior to the murder.

I hadn't thought much about the desk since I'd last been in there so I took another look. The missing family photo was the perfect example of just how intangible the case was. In pretty much any murder mystery I'd read, it could be used as a clear sign that the killer was one of the kids, out for revenge for their father's callous ways. But what if that was exactly what the killer wanted me to think? What if they'd removed the photo in order to throw off suspicion?

I closed the curtains again and dropped the key from the armoury back in the exact spot I'd found it in two nights earlier. I tried to take in more of the space this time. Not just the area around the corpse, but the carpet in front of the door and beside the other bookshelves. Sadly, aside from a thick layer of dust, there was little to be discovered.

Though I hadn't reached any dramatic new conclusion, I felt a hazy sort of understanding starting to take place. It was like the room had a tale to tell and I was finally listening.

I checked the lists in my head off against one another. Suspects, Clues, Hypotheses. Somewhere in there was a path through the three but, until I could find it, I'd have to work through the key scenarios and see what would play out.

Scenario number one, and surely the most likely; Edmund killed his father after they argued about money. It was the popular view among the family and I have to say that nothing I'd discovered ruled out the possibility he was guilty.

Excellent, we've done it. Mystery solved. Now let's go and ask Cook if she can make us another lemon meringue pie.

Ignoring my brain, and my similar desire for sweet treats, I decided to go to the source and sought out Edmund on the patio. He was sitting alone at the white metal table, looking pretty rough from last night's adventure. His normally baby-smooth face was crinkled up and he was wearing the same clothes as at dinner.

"Morning!" I said with an exaggerated smile on my face.

He closed his eyes and his head drooped. I thought he would stay that way but Gladwell popped by at just the right moment with a coffee delivery. The butler disappeared off to one of his myriad duties and I served Edmund his medicine.

"I'm sorry, all right." He opened his eyes and breathed in the powerful aroma, as if just the scent could clear his head. "I don't remember exactly what happened but I know that I woke up in your room and I wasn't wearing much."

"Oh, really? I hadn't realised you were *stark-bottom naked.*" Yet another joke that bore repeating. "What were you looking for in my room?"

"What do you think?" Like a teenage boy, his voice rose unnaturally high.

"I believe the term you used was 'rumpy pumpy'." He winced at my words. "But how do I know that wasn't an excuse? How do I know you weren't there to sift through my possessions or work out what I'd discovered on your father's murder?"

He groaned a little and put his hand to his head. "Let me get this straight. You think that I went to your room to spy on you and, when I heard you coming, took all my clothes off and climbed into your bed?"

"It would be a pretty good cover."

"Yes and a pretty insane plan." He swallowed a mouthful of scalding hot coffee and immediately regretted it. "I was drunk, Izzy."

"Fine. We won't mention it again." I allowed him to stew in awkward silence for a minute before returning to my questioning. "Tell me about the rabbit."

He looked blank. "What bloody rabbit?"

"The rabbit you killed." This came out far too dramatically. I'd have to hold back such theatrical tendencies for the afternoon.

"Oh, for goodness sake." He stirred his coffee angrily. "I knew they'd go on about that. My brother and sisters can be extremely uptight."

"Then tell me what happened."

He rolled his eyes in the direction of the vineyard, huffed and gave in. "I was only about six and it was totally Cameron's idea. He dared me to do it and at first I refused. It was only when he started calling me a wimp that I gave in. He was five years older than me and should have known better, but, ever since then, my family have treated me like the resident psycho."

I felt a bit sorry for him. He no longer seemed like the arrogant playboy I'd taken him for and I could tell that his siblings' low opinion of him was getting him down.

We raced off on different trains of thought and, when he spoke again, he said, "I suppose it's my fault. Dad was really proud after I killed that rabbit and I played up to it. I leaned in to what he wanted me to be, went along with all that army nonsense and tried to make out that I was the tough one in the family. But I swear I've never killed another living thing since that damn rabbit."

The sounds of the estate swirled about us. There were sparrows darting about a honeysuckle bush on the edge of the lawn, a cuckoo called in the woods and that warm summer wind was still with us, rustling the leaves of the trees and flapping at the clean white tablecloth.

"I know how it is," I finally said. "The need to fit in with your family, I mean. After my first stepdad came to live with us, he gave me a makeup set for my birthday and, for about a year, I pretended to be this ultra-feminine little girly to suit the picture he had of me. I changed everything about my personality, the way I dressed and spoke. Then, one day, I realised it didn't make any difference what he thought and went back to being my normal weirdo self."

"Which shows that you're stronger than I ever was." He finished his coffee and put his head back to look up at the sky.

It was a sad moment. Something passed between us and I knew how lost and lonely he was. His girlfriend had left him, he had no job or reliable friends to occupy his time and, no matter what he felt about his father, the man's death could only serve to remind him of their painful past. Killer or otherwise, I knew that vast and complex chains of emotion were running through Edmund right then.

I wanted to say something to comfort him but all that came out was, "I don't suppose you know where there's a vacuum cleaner? I got breakfast crumbs all over the carpet this morning."

When he looked at me next, his eyes had turned pink and glassy. "Sorry, haven't a clue. Just get Gladwell to do it. That's what I'd do." As he spoke, he stabbed his teaspoon repeatedly against the table top.

"Thanks." Another emotional silence passed before I had a good idea. "Hey, what have you got planned for this morning?"

"Nothing much. Enjoying my last hours of freedom before you or my dear family report my murderous ways to the police. Why?"

"Because there's something you could help me with."

As I'd been watching Edmund, it had occurred to me why the killer had removed the knife. Best of all though, I didn't have to do anything to find out whether my theory was correct. I was pretty sure that, if I bided my time, the culprit would come to me.

Chapter Twenty-One

My brain must have been putting in the hours overnight…
You're welcome.
…because suddenly I could make sense of the puzzle before me and I knew what I had to do next. The morning was ticking by, but I was no longer worried about running out of time. I had a plan, a way forward. Although I needed to check some minor details, I was on my way to finding out which of the scenarios on my list was true. I was confident for the first time that, when the afternoon swung by, I would have earned my hundred-grand fee.

I sent Edmund on his way and left the patio. Stalking over to the doors into the ballroom, I was just about to enter when I caught the sound of Cameron ranting down the phone inside.

"I've told you six-hundred times; I'll pay you as soon as I can. I'm not making this up, I'm coming into some serious money and, by the end of the week, I'll be able to get rid of you for good."

There was a pause as he listened for the caller's response.

"Yeah, well I'll be glad to see the back of you too."

Scenario number two said that Cameron was the killer. He was in debt and had stolen from the family business in order to stay afloat. If his dad had found out about it, we had the perfect motive for murder.

Most telling of all though, Cameron had lied. People lie for lots of reasons. I once claimed to be interested in cricket because a bloke I was dating was obsessed with it. I lasted about seven minutes into a five-day test match before the hard truth burst out of me and we broke up. I'd say that pretty much everyone lies – except perhaps the Dalai Lama and odd, saintly humans like Hugh Jackman – but, in my experience, lying to make your brother look like a killer in the middle of a murder enquiry is kind of unforgivable.

Realising that the end of Cameron's call was imminent, I ran from the door, waited twenty seconds then re-approached.

"Ahhh, just the man I was looking for," I said, all chirpy as if I certainly hadn't heard anything he'd said to his scary creditor.

He looked nervous about my arrival, then pretended to be happy.

"How can I help you, Miss Palmer?" To be fair, he might still have been angry that I'd thrashed him at bowling.

Geoffrey's head remained in place on the ballroom mantle and the bloody message was untouched. It was probably good that no one had cleaned up; the police would need to see it, though the poor piggy was looking a little grim.

"I was wondering if you could help me." I used my most innocent voice. "Gladwell told me there were old servant stairs in this part of the house but I can't find them."

He paused like he was trying to make sense of me, but then shook his head as if it really didn't matter anyway. "Yes. They're this way." He led me out of the room onto the patio and then back inside to a narrow passageway. The hidden door wasn't as difficult to spot this time, but a well-placed portrait of an old woman in a flouncy dress meant that I'd never have noticed it if I hadn't been specifically looking.

"That's great, thanks."

He wasn't finished with me. "And may I ask why you wish to see them?"

I made a ditzy little head movement. "Oh, just a silly idea I had. I'm sure it will come to nothing."

He still didn't seem entirely sure what to make of me, but shrugged his shoulders and walked away.

Ha, typical man! Underestimating women for millennia!

Oi, no sexism! You're as bad as him.

My brain can be a surprisingly militant feminist when it suits her.

I was about to go through the door when my trusty assistant walked past, down the corridor, and I decided to call him over.

"Gladwell? Fancy a bit more sleuthing?"

He glanced from side to side conspiratorially then rushed over, looking like a schoolboy on the last day of school – only much older and hobblier. "I thought you'd never ask."

"Now, if I'm not mistaken, this is where Geoffrey the pig's killer hid the severed head. They'd have been able to get into the ballroom without much trouble before dinner last night. As we walk up the staircase, look out for any sign they were here."

The butler nodded and we entered the shadowy space. My clever hypothesis wasn't really so impressive after all as, on opening the door, we immediately discovered a dried red paintbrush and the remainder of a bucket of blood.

"There you go then," Gladwell stated, sounding almost disappointed. "What now?"

"Urmmm, well that was a lot easier than I was expecting, but there's something else I want to check."

With my companion at my heels, I walked up the stairs. "I need to work out if it's possible to get from the ballroom to the east wing unobstructed. Whoever threw the vase and tried their hand at butchery, used these stairs to go unnoticed."

Gladwell couldn't reply because he was concentrating on the climb and seemed quite out of breath from trying to keep up with me. I waited for him on the second landing before making the final ascent. For some reason I'd imagined that the attic would be more or less the same as the rest of the house but with more stuff in. In reality, it was a dark, musty mess of roof beams and killer splinters and, from the moment I entered, I knew it wasn't the place for me.

The ceiling was far too low for a person of my elevated dimensions and I kept banging my head. The entire space was filled with ancient tea chests and artefacts from the Hall's previous owners. There were tall, Indian statues, who looked rather put out to have been forgotten up there, along with several giant African masks and, of course, weapons from all over the world.

"The old lord loved to travel," Gladwell explained as I once more bumped my skull on a beam. "He used to bring souvenirs from wherever he went. Brought back a live zebra once but it didn't survive long."

"Couldn't it handle the British weather?"

"No, it wasn't that. I believe the poor beast was in the garden one day and got knocked over by the baker's wagon." I liked the way that Gladwell's story had this twisted ending but he told it deadly straight. "Look, we can see the stairs up to the old part of the house from here."

He moved ahead, guiding me on a zigzagging path through the detritus of a forgotten family. I wondered why the Sherwin-Nettlehurst clan had left so much stuff behind when they sold the house and where they'd ended up. Perhaps the former inhabitants' descendants were penniless and living in a one-bedroom flat in Peckham, dreaming of their family's past glory. Or perhaps they'd upgraded to a mansion on the Côte d'Azur.

Every thirty metres or so, there were sets of steps joining the various extensions and additions to the original building. There were huge differences in height and, on two occasions, the builders hadn't bothered joining the separate loft sections together and had simply left a hole with a ladder to climb up. It was tough going, and I felt a bit guilty for making Gladwell come with me, but we finally came out on the far side of the house.

The east wing was accessible through another set of backstairs and I was relieved to be escaping from that close, stuffy atmosphere that tasted like tobacco and old wood. With a little effort, our culprit could clearly have traversed the house unseen. I had achieved my objective and was just about to gleefully dance back downstairs when I walked smack-bang into the final bloody roof beam.

"Ouch," was all I could think to say as I collapsed backwards like a beautiful redwood tree, felled by loggers. It wouldn't have been so bad, if I hadn't twisted my ankle as I went down. "Ouch," I said again, as I felt I deserved the sympathy.

Gladwell was quick to react. "Don't move a muscle, Izzy." As he assessed what to do next, he swayed like a martial arts expert about to launch a move. "I've got you."

Swooping down to the floor, the unexpectedly nimble old man scooped me up in his arms and had me downstairs in a flash. If it had been an action movie, slow dramatic music would have been playing as Gladwell fought his aching muscles to save the damsel in distress.

A crumbling septuagenarian; just the type of hero I'd expect us to end up with.

Hey, not so much of the crumbling. This grandad's got muscles!

That would be the tagline of the movie.

He kicked open the door to leave the hidden space and Beatrix and Audrey heard the commotion and came out into the hall.

"My goodness, are you all right, Izzy?" Audrey asked.

Gladwell placed me down on the sofa in Beatrix's dressing room and I tentatively tried to move my ankle. "I think it's fine. It probably looked more dramatic than it was." I smiled at my kindly old saviour.

"Thanks, Stephen. I appreciate it."

"Yeah, good work, Gladwell," Beatrix added with her typical throaty laugh. "Who knew you were such a superhero?"

Audrey looked proudly at her long-serving employee. "Must be all that army training."

"I try to keep in shape." Gladwell was blushing with all the attention he was getting. "Good to know I'm not dead just yet, I suppose."

After a bit of cheesy grinning all round, he and Audrey excused themselves and I was left alone once more with Beatrix.

"What were you doing up in the attic?"

Scenario number three suggested that the sexy vamp in front of me had killed her father for a combination of reasons, the exact configuration of which I'd been struggling to get my head around for the last day.

"I was just poking about really. Doing what Miss Marple impersonators do best."

She looked a bit awkward as she sat down in the armchair beside me. "Oh dear, is that what I called you when you arrived?" Her tone was almost conciliatory.

"No, but Edmund did."

She let the words hang there for a moment. "That sounds about right. I'm sure he didn't mean anything by it."

"Oh, I know. In fact I saw a whole other side to him yesterday."

Ha, backside. Good one, Izzy.

I could see her relaxing into the conversation, her bare feet scrunching happily together on the carpet. "Edmund's bark is loud and his teeth look sharp, but what he doesn't realise is that he's a pussycat with a personality crisis."

"Cameron and Audrey wouldn't say the same." I waited to see if she'd take the bait. "Why is it that you always stand up for him?"

She looked at the ceiling of her sunny bedroom as if she hoped to find the answer there. "I suppose because he's the baby and I've always felt bad when the others pick on him. Audrey's the oldest and it's been her life's work to set him on the right path. Cameron's in the middle but that didn't stop him bossing poor Edmund around. I just think the odds were stacked against little E and so I tried to put that right."

"What did your dad think of him?"

She let out a long, tired breath. "It's hard to say what the great Aldrich Porter really thought of anything – except Audrey maybe. He adored Audrey. He once said to us that she was the single thing he'd got right in his life, which you can imagine was music to my ears."

She glanced once more at my ankle but was clearly thinking of other things. "You see, Dad talked a lot without saying anything. He instructed and corrected but I don't remember him telling me a single personal anecdote. I have no idea what his childhood was like or why he fell in love with my mother. He was a robot with limited functions. And, as we get older, I can't help thinking that we're starting to act the same way."

"Do you really think you're anything like him?" I pulled my ankle towards me to massage it. Despite the drama, it wasn't in a particularly bad state. If anything it was my head that was sore. "I get the impression that you're the one who rebelled most of the five of you. Daisy told me as much last night."

She smirked at that and I remembered that this was the same hot-headed person who'd raged against her murdered father less than twenty-four hours before. "Oh yeah? What else did she say?"

Easy does it. You don't want to spook her.

"She said that you use people. She told me about the men you've lived with who were nothing more than an escape from this place." I decided to ignore my own best advice and hit her with the truth. "You're the one who showed your father that his way of life didn't fit with yours. In fact, if I was going to pick the killer based on who'd have had the least trouble going through with it, you'd be first on my list."

Just as I was hoping, she enjoyed my outburst and, instead of screaming back or walking away, she smiled as she replied. "You're probably right. We decided long ago which of us are the hunters and which are prey. Audrey is too clean and organised to let a spurt of blood come near her, Cameron was too busy trying to be Dad to have time to kill anyone and Daisy is strangely… well, bloodless I suppose."

Her voice was suddenly weak and hollowed out. "But I'm the hussy, the trollop, the scarlet woman, so my low morals are surely to blame. That's the kind of thing I've had to put up with for the last twenty years, why would anything change now?"

A streak of Edmund's hard-done-by attitude ran through her words. I'd learnt not to be put off by such tactics and continued prodding her. "You all have your roles in the family. If you're the tramp, Edmund is the hothead, Daisy is the waif, I suppose Cameron is the also-ran and Audrey is the mum. But instead of offering any evidence to show you weren't the killer, you've provided me with another reason for why you wanted your dad dead."

Though I'd maintained my stern tone, she smiled again and I could tell she enjoyed having me as an adversary. "And what's that?"

"Aldrich Porter was never overflowing with love for his children but he seems to have accepted their flaws. He didn't expect much from Cameron, fostered Edmund's bad temper and left Daisy to her aimless ways. If Audrey's the only one he celebrated, then you're the only one he judged. He didn't just break up your relationships and deem your boyfriends unsuitable, he condemned you for your behaviour, isn't that right?"

It was a stab in the dark but something about her manner told me I was on the right track.

Her response only confirmed it. "I think I'd rather talk about something else."

A testy silence fell and I let my eyes wander to her horse-riding wall where a young girl looked full of optimism for the future, as she celebrated various achievements. "Who's that with you in the photo?" I pointed to a plump, rosy-cheeked woman who appeared in a few of the shots with her arm around Beatrix.

"That's my mother, Izzy. I'm not surprised you don't recognise her, it's probably the only photo we have left of her in the house. I made sure she lived on, despite my father's best efforts to erase her memory."

"But I saw a photo of her with Daisy as a baby and she looked completely different. Did she really change so much?" I remembered what Audrey said about their father falling out of love with their chubby, middle-aged mother.

A look of horror crossed her face and I knew I'd said the wrong thing. "I'm feeling a bit tired, but it's been lovely chatting." Getting to her feet, her expression had changed entirely. She was suddenly cold, hard and calculating. "I'd hate to monopolise your time. You're going to be busy if you want to identify the killer before this afternoon."

I held her gaze as I swung my legs from the sofa and tested the weight on my bad ankle. "Who's to say I don't already know who it is?" If I hadn't had to slowly limp from the room, like a footballer faking an injury, that'd have been a pretty badass closing line.

Sadly, it took me so long to walk out that, by the time I got to the door, I'd remembered something else I wanted to ask her. "I don't suppose you know where the vacuum cleaner is kept? I got my breakfast everywhere this morning."

She looked at me like I was insane and I wished I hadn't said anything.

Chapter Twenty-Two

It was a waiting game now. I was convinced that the guilty party still had one final act to carry out but, until they did, I was at a bit of a loose end. I still had to find a vacuum – I was determined to clean up after myself and not leave it to Gladwell to do everything – but aside from that, I didn't have tons left to do before I could call everyone together, scare the hell out of them and then reveal the murderer.

I figured I'd go and have a chat with Audrey as it would probably be my last chance. At the very least, I could verify a few of the other stories I'd heard and find out which of my suspects were telling the truth. I poked my head into her bedroom in case she was at home. Her dressing room wall was covered in certificates and diplomas. It was not just her various business accolades on display, but every commendation, dating back to her school days, for science, maths, ecology projects and jobs fairs. It was like someone had taken her permanent record and based a decoration scheme around it.

She wasn't there so I turned on my direct line to my futuristic assistant as I hobbled downstairs. "Dean, have you seen Audrey anywhere?"

"He's not here, Izzy." It was Mum's hairdresser, Fernando. "He's gone for a coffee with Samantha. Things are getting serious there."

"What about Mum?"

"She and Greg are doing their tai chi on the roof, I could fetch them down if you like?"

"No, it's okay." I paused to think. "Is Ramesh there?"

My friend's voice came back to me but it was distant and grumpy. "I am, Izzy. And I'm still not talking to you."

"Fine." So much for my crack-squad of helpers. "Okay, Fernando, have you spotted Audrey on the cameras anywhere?"

"She's in her little study, Izzy. She went there after getting changed. Cameron has been pacing about all morning in a foul mood. Edmund is reading in the smoking parlour and Daisy hasn't come downstairs yet."

I was impressed at how succinct and efficient he was. "Thanks very much. As soon as Mum and Greg come down, or Dean's employees appear, I want you watching those screens like your lives depend upon it. Something is going to go down this morning and I need you guys."

"I'm on it, Izzy. You can count on me."

Next time, we'll just bring Fernando along and leave the others behind.

Sounds like a plan.

I tapped to end the call and continued on my slow journey. My ankle wasn't hurting, but I couldn't remember how to walk normally for some reason.

"Ahh, Izzy," Audrey said as I entered her office on the ground floor. She had a way of making me feel very privileged that she was even saying my name. "I was hoping to talk to you. Do you think you're any closer to finding the killer? I'll have to call the police at two o'clock, so there's not much time left."

She motioned for me to sit down in the free chair in front of her desk which was covered in important-looking papers. The comparatively small room, with its wooden panels and richly patterned wallpaper all in warm shades was homely and inviting.

"I'll have the name for you before lunch." I spoke very confidently, though I was still relying on external forces for this to be true.

She looked at me archly then and the next scenario rose to the front of my mind. Audrey had been in Bangkok, there was no doubt about it. Dean's crew had found her records on the Thai airport systems and there was security-camera footage of her passing through passport control. Short of her finding someone who looked like her, putting them in a wig and sending them abroad – which might have worked in Christie's day, but wouldn't in the modern era of facial recognition, e-passports and retina scanning – there was no way she could be the killer. Scenario number four said that she was working with someone else and so just as guilty.

I wouldn't be much of a detective if I didn't give it any consideration, but there were a few good arguments against this possibility. On the surface at least, she didn't have much reason to want her father dead. She was financially independent through her work on his investment portfolio – and it was widely known just how successful she had been. Her father had held her up as a bright shining symbol of excellence to the rest of the family. He was proud of her, loved her more openly than the others and it was hard to see why she would have had him killed. Add that to the fact that she was the one who called me in the first place and it was difficult to imagine her being involved.

"Have you enjoyed your stay with us?" I could see she was teasing me, but it was still nice to be asked.

"Oh, yes. I've always wanted to go on a murder mystery weekend."

She laughed her perfect laugh and smoothed her skirt over her knees like she'd just done something naughty. "Would you like me to call for some tea?"

"No, I'm fine, thanks. But I wanted to ask you something that has been playing on my mind. Gladwell told me yesterday that he'd caught Edmund with you in the games room once and that he…" I paused, unsure how to phrase such an accusation against her brother. "Well, I heard that Edmund almost struck you."

Her fingers curled around the spiralling wooden armrests on her chair. "Oh that… Yes, it happened but it was a couple of years ago now."

"Do you mind me asking what Edmund was so upset about?"

She glanced to the door as if afraid he might walk in. "Money, of course. With Edmund it's always money." She sighed a weary sigh. "I'd given him some in the past, in fact I've tried to be generous with all of them. I never agreed with Dad's idea of keeping us hungry. We'd grown up with far too much luxury for it to make any sense. But Edmund had become dependent upon me and, when I told him I was cutting him off, he didn't take it well."

"Do you think he would have hit you if Gladwell hadn't come in?"

She must have been waiting for this question. I could hear the click in her dry throat before she spoke. "I don't judge Edmund. He had as hard a time as anyone with our father. He's the youngest and I'm the oldest so we suffered in different ways but I've always had a lot of sympathy for him." I didn't think she would answer the question, but then she adjusted her position in her chair and her eyes landed on mine again. "I believe he was upset and frustrated by the situation and, yes, I think he would have hit me."

"And is the violence you experienced that day the reason why you originally thought Edmund had killed your father?" I kept my voice steady and free of any judgement.

"Yes. That day and all the others when he ended up screaming and shouting and throwing things across the room." There was a teacherly tone to her voice. I could tell that her role in the family had lent her such tendencies.

"Thank you, Audrey." I took a moment to process what she'd just told me. "I was afraid you'd say that. I can't imagine it's very nice to have to talk about your brother in such a way."

"He's not the only one who could have done it, but I still think it's possible." She smiled and her beauty and youthful looks were enhanced by that deeply maternal manner which sometimes emerged. "I knew when we first met that you'd be able to do this. There's something special in you that my father failed to identify. He told me on the day you came to see him, that he couldn't understand how he'd underestimated you so greatly. He thought he could read people, but he was wrong about you and Bob and it riled him no end."

"I like to confound expectations." I have no doubt I was blushing like an idiot.

"I mean it, Izzy. Thank you for trusting me to come here. I know it must have seemed like a strange request but I still think it was the right thing to do."

"I just hope the police agree." We shared a quiet grin before I left her to her paperwork.

The morning was almost gone and the killer still hadn't made their move. I figured I'd tick off the final clan member and went in search of Daisy.

Fernando had spotted her heading out into the garden and I found her on the grass reading a summery romance beneath a broad oak tree. It was another stunningly hot day. The sky was the colour of a baby boy's bedroom and the sun beat down on me as I walked across to that shady oasis.

Daisy looked perfectly at home, sprawled out on the lawn. She was the wildest, most organic of the five siblings; a wispy thing of nature, floating through life on the wind as much as her own desire. It was easy to imagine that she had grown up in that spot, just as her name suggested.

"Good book?" I asked as I sat down beside her.

She looked up at me and I knew that my presence there was less than welcome.

Leave her alone, she's reading!

Scenario number five was the hardest to fathom. If it existed at all, it would require Daisy's whole ethereal wood-nymph persona to be an act.

No chance.

If that were true though, it was a good act to play. Not one single person had seriously put her forward as a suspect. Audrey had insisted that all of her siblings were capable of murder, but, in reality, nobody had seriously considered Daisy's involvement. The fact remained that she was the one who'd found her father's dead body and so she could easily explain away any forensic evidence.

Someone had to find him.

Daisy had just as much reason to want her father gone as the others. She was hardly a grand success. Considering the opportunities and education she'd benefitted from, starting a low-level job in a gallery, aged thirty, wasn't much of an improvement on my recent form. Her father's death would provide her with unlimited wealth and she'd never have to work again.

Ridiculous.

Add all that to her father calling off her engagement and her mood on the night of the murder, when an evening in honour of her achievements was railroaded by his bad temper, and I think you've got an interesting case to consider.

Not a chance.

Well, fine. Can you do any better?

Hell yeah, I can.

Scenario number six, Cook and Aldrich Porter were secret lovers and he divorced his wife to be with her. When the time came to tell his children, he couldn't bring himself to reveal the truth and the relationship remained a secret. When Cook realised that her long-time amour would never admit to their love, she confronted Porter, stabbed him in the back and hung him from the skulls on his wall.

Hmmm, I don't think that's quite it. But thank you for your input.

When she finally spoke, Daisy seemed resigned to my company. "I like fluffy, silly books. They help me escape all my troubles."

"Do you have so much to worry about?"

She thought about her answer. "Not anymore maybe. I have no

illusions that my father ever loved me, but in some ways, I got off lightly." The way she spoke made it hard to imagine having a nice casual conversation about our favourite movies or what had been happening on Britain's Got Talent. "I was the only one who didn't play the game. I never tried to win the impossible prize of our father's love and so I never picked up any battle scars. And besides, I'm rich and free now, just like everyone dreams."

I didn't know where to go from that strange confession so I changed the topic. "What's the book about then?"

"Love. They're always about love." She frowned like this was a bad thing. "Romances aren't so different from mysteries really. They follow a simple formula. I get what I want from the story and, when it's over, I forget all about it and move on to the next one."

I smiled back at her and was about to ask whether she knew where I could find a vacuum cleaner when a scream rose up from the house and someone shouted my name.

Cameron stuck his head out of the ballroom. "Izzy, get over here now."

We jumped to our feet and sprinted back across the lawn. I dashed through the doorway to find Beatrix turned to stone as she once more took in the hideous scene above the mantelpiece.

Right on cue, the murder weapon had reappeared.

Chapter Twenty-Three

A long, golden dagger, which looked as old as any other artefact the house over, was sticking out of the top of Geoffrey's forehead. As if the poor creature hadn't been abused enough, his killer had designed one final indignity.

"We were on our way to see you on the lawn when we spotted it," Cameron explained.

"Who would do these things?" Beatrix's voice was frail but at least she hadn't fainted like her sister.

I approached the fireplace to take a closer look. The ornamental dagger's handle was bound with fine gold wire and a large red stone caught the light on its hilt. Unlike the weapons I'd seen in the armoury, it was clean and bright and I imagined that someone had gone to a great deal of trouble to polish it up before use.

I spoke without turning back round to them. "I believe that's the weapon your father was murdered with."

"This was Edmund's doing." That well-pronounced hatred was back in Cameron's voice.

"You can't say that, C," Beatrix insisted. "We don't know he had anything to do with it."

"Well, I do." The words stayed with us as we awaited his evidence. "There was no sign of the knife when I was in here earlier and, since then, I saw him skulking about. He practically had a heart attack when I caught him in the hall. You mark my words, Edmund put it there, because Edmund murdered Dad."

I tried to calm him down to get the precise information I needed. "Getting worked up like this isn't helping." I paused and waited for him to stop pacing. "Tell me exactly when you saw Edmund."

"Less than an hour ago. I'd say around twelve o'clock."

Daisy had been silent this whole time but went over to comfort Beatrix. Presumably alerted by Cameron's shouting, their older sister appeared in the room. I watched for Audrey's reaction but she was her usual calm self as her brother once more lost his cool.

"You'll notice, of course, that he's the only one not here right now."

Like a two-year-old having a tantrum, Cameron threw his arms about as he spoke. "He'll probably turn up in a minute, asking what all the fuss is about."

"Calm down, Cameron." Audrey put both hands in front of her to pacify him but it had no effect.

"No, I will not. Edmund's not going to get away with it this time. I'll see to that."

I decided to get a hold of things before Cameron beat his brother to a pulp. "Did anyone else see Edmund in the ballroom?"

Beatrix swung her gaze round to me, her eyes wide and frightened. "He was in here first thing this morning. But that was before breakfast even. It doesn't mean anything."

I came to stand beside her. "What was he doing?"

She hesitated before replying, looking round at her siblings as if searching for help. "We were on the way to breakfast and he ran in from the corridor to look whether Geoffrey was still…" The words got stuck in her throat before she came to her brother's defence. "That doesn't prove anything. He was just curious whether Gladwell had cleared everything up or not."

I walked to the middle of the room to address them. "As you can imagine, my investigation is coming to an end. I'd like you to go to the kitchens to find Cook and Gladwell and then meet me outside the library in half an hour." I tried not to give too much away with my voice but I knew what they were thinking. "Please stay together and don't let anyone out of your sight until I return."

I took a moment to study their reactions. The room held its silence as I turned round and quickly walked away. I had all the pieces now, all the clues I was going to find, but I still needed time to think. Mr Porter's killer was screaming out to me; I couldn't let it drown out the quieter voices. Just because something made perfect sense, that didn't mean it was the right solution.

I ducked into the petit salon on my way to confront Edmund. Ten minutes was all I would have to get my thoughts clear in my head. I stood in the middle of that elegant parlour and, as the morning sunlight bounced from mirror to mirror, I looked at myself properly for the first time since I'd arrived. I was completely out of place; an outsider, a novelty, a freak. With my ridiculous t-shirts, inappropriate footwear and long, flyaway hair that hadn't seen the inside of a salon in months, I didn't fit in there. And that's why I would solve the case.

The initial charm and wonder of the Porter family and their ancient palace had worn off and I'd got to see the reality that lay underneath. I looked at myself in one of those elegant, mirrors with its intricate, gilded frame, and I no longer saw a girl out of her depth, I saw a detective. All that was left to do was prove that my chosen theory was the right one.

I sat down in the chair I had occupied on my first night at Vomeris Hall and closed my eyes. In an instant, I was back home in West Wickham. I could picture myself, sat cross-legged on our rather worn living room carpet with three flip charts on easels in front of me. There were no expensive paintings on the wall, no rare antiques or luxury furnishings but I had something better. I had the truth.

I'd spent the last two days working through the Suspect list and it hadn't got me far enough. By their own admission, practically anyone in that house could have killed the fallen patriarch. It was the evidence I should have paid more attention to, starting with the crime scene itself.

The key, the domino and the bottle were the things that had jumped out at me. Anything else there – the missing photo, the displaced ball, and the position of the body – could be read in too many different ways. But the trail of clues that went from the desk over to the bookshelf told me everything I needed to know about the crime scene. The key which led me to the source of the murder weapon, the blood-spattered domino from the games room and the antique glass bottle with its bitter scent that I'd at first taken to be cyanide but was most likely almond essence, pilfered from Cook's pantry.

And what about the events that had unfolded since then? The thrown vase, the murdered pig and the message in blood had succeeded in their primary aim. I had been distracted from the murder itself and started chasing about the house in search of a ghost. I hadn't been scared away though, I hadn't given up, so whoever had directed this sideshow was only partially successful. Far from throwing off my investigation, this pattern of threats and gaudy violence had helped me to understand the Porter family better. Now, with the reappearance of the murder weapon, I had a good idea who was behind it.

So, Suspects, Clues and Hypotheses. I could have made a separate list for everything I'd learnt about Mr Porter, though not one word upon it would be complimentary. I had no doubt that his own acts were behind his demise. Whether it was the way he treated his ex-wife, his merciless business practices or his clinical manipulation of his own children that had finally done him in, I would get to the truth in time.

I felt so close to understanding what had happened on Thursday night but there was something still not quite right. I felt too alone to be able go any further. I missed having Ramesh and Mum and all the gang around. As much as I liked to believe in my own personal genius, solving Bob's murder had been a group effort and there was one person more than any other who had supported me. David knew just what to say to give me the confidence I needed. So, for a brief moment, as I sat in that grand, mirror-lined space, imagining myself to a smaller, slightly messier one, I pictured my boyfriend there beside me and I knew what I had to do next.

I opened my eyes and clicked my watch on. "Dean? Did you work out who put the pig's head or the dagger in the ballroom?"

"We're still going through the feeds, Izzy. I had to pop out so I'm a bit behind but I'll try to eliminate everyone I can. For the moment I can tell you that it wasn't Beatrix or Audrey. I'll get back to you as soon as I have anything more." He made this weird sort of choking noise and I knew he was about to criticise me. "It's a shame you didn't put a camera in there. That would have been handy."

"If only I'd known." I felt a bit defensive. "Who would have thought a ballroom would get so much use?"

"The butler did it, Izzy!" My mother interrupted. "He knows this house better than anyone and could have planted the murder weapon there without being seen."

"No way." Greg sounded comparatively animated. "It's Daisy. How else can you explain why she's so withdrawn all the time?"

Fernando from Penge was next up with his theory. "Cameron's your man, Iz. You're on the right track."

A voice I hadn't heard for a long time came down the line. "Izzy, this is Danny. I flew back from South Africa because I realised that I can't live without you." My heart beat faster. "I love you, Izzy. I always have."

Come here, lover boy!

I tried not to get distracted. "Danny, I don't want to sound insensitive but I'm right in the middle of something."

"Is it because of this Edmund that your mum's told me about?" He suddenly sounded furious. "What's he got that I haven't?"

"Right at this moment, about a one-in-seven chance of being a murderer."

He managed to get a little angrier. "So that's what you go for, is it? Bad boys?"

"I'm sorry, Danny. I don't have time to get into it right now. I've got a murder to solve." I stood up and made my way to the door. "Dean, where's Edmund?"

"He's in the smoking parlour." The tech-genius breathed down the line. "Do you think it's him then? Was Cameron telling the truth?"

I didn't answer. I was out in the hallway, headed to one final encounter before I wrapped up the case for good. Energy surged through me and my gentle stroll down the corridor turned into a sprint. When I finally reached the smoking parlour, I smashed the door open, half terrifying Edmund who was sitting in an armchair with a copy of Christie's *And Then There Were None* open on his lap.

"Hey. You know, this is pretty good."

It really annoys me how people don't expect Agatha Christie to be a great writer when she is clearly a legend. Sadly we don't have time to talk about that right now. Remind me to come back to the issue at some point in the future – I swear I could write a book about it.

"Don't try to distract me by talking about my favourite topic. Cameron says that you were the one who planted the murder weapon in the ballroom. It's time you told me the truth."

Chapter Twenty-Four

When we got to the library, everyone was there waiting for us. Cook held her hands in the air. She had presumably been handling food and didn't want to get anything messy but it looked like she was surrendering to the police.

"Here he is," Cameron said, as he caught sight of his brother. "We ought to make a citizen's arrest so he doesn't escape."

Edmund barely reacted, even as his oldest sister came to his defence.

"That won't be necessary." Audrey sent a glare in Cameron's direction. "Let's hear what Izzy has to say before we do anything rash."

"It's great to see you all here." I always know just the wrong thing to say. "I've brought you to the library because I want you to take a look at the crime scene before the police close it off. If you can avoid touching anything as we enter I would appreciate it."

"Oh, Izzy. I do love a bit of drama." Beatrix displayed her typically wicked grin.

I put my gloves on and carefully pushed open the heavy wooden door. Cameron entered the room first, with Beatrix, Daisy, Edmund and their employees following after. Audrey hesitated again before entering, but finally stepped through and I joined them all inside.

The suspects stood in a row at the back of the library, as if waiting for a police line-up. Before starting in on what we'd assembled for, I watched them one last time. Gladwell was as upright and professional as ever, Cook hadn't put her hands down and the surviving members of the Porter family wore a range of expressions, all the way from nonchalant to terrified.

I steadied my nerves and began. "I wanted you to see exactly what Aldrich Porter's death entailed." I pointed to the space which his body had previously occupied. "He was stabbed from behind, held upright as he bled out, then left on the floor, face down, where he remained for some time. Notice the channel of blood on the wall between the two stags' heads where he was hoisted up. There's another stain on the carpet, near where he now lies. Whoever killed him did not provide the luxury of a quiet resting place. Some hours after the murder, his killer returned, picked up the body and wedged him in amongst the skulls on the wall."

Beatrix looked confused. "How do you know what happened after he died?"

"For his body to stay in that position, rigor mortis would have had to set in. That doesn't happen for several hours after death. He was stiff when I arrived here, and remained like that for a couple of days before he slumped down to the carpet once more."

"And?" Cameron retained his typical impatient look. "What does that prove?"

I took a step back, resting my weight on my heel. "It proves the killer was painting a picture. Ever since I got here, I've felt like a character in a golden-age mystery. Not just because of the incredible old building we are standing in, but because that's what one of you wanted me to believe."

I walked a few steps along the line until I was looking dead in the eyes of the youngest son. "I'm pretty sure you wrote me off as a stupid little girl from Croydon who thinks she can solve mysteries just because she's read a bunch of detective novels."

"I'm not going to deny it." Edmund folded his arms with glee. "I genuinely thought you were stupid."

"Thanks for your honesty." I dropped his gaze and walked on. "I'm pleased to tell you that you were wrong. I don't just *think* I know how to solve mysteries, I do know how. The fact that Mr Porter's killer left me a trail to follow told me far more than the trail itself. You see, when I first entered this room on Friday night I discovered three significant items which you might just be able to spy over in the corner beside the bookcase. I found a domino, a key, and a small glass bottle with the distinctive smell of bitter almonds."

"Such items would look perfectly at home on the cover of a classic crime novel. But, tell me this; who goes to the trouble of providing a spotless murder scene then leaves a trail of breadcrumbs for me to trace after them?"

I allowed my words to sink in before explaining my thinking. "I spent my first day here trying to work out what each item could tell me.

189

The key led me to the original home of the murder weapon, but no closer to the truth. The almond smell would make anyone who reads detective fiction think of cyanide, yet Mr Porter was stabbed to death. And the domino appears to be a straight-up red herring. These three artefacts looked the part and kept me busy but told me nothing."

"The key led me on a hunt for something that wasn't there, the domino made me focus on a room that had no connection to the killing and all the fake cyanide furnished me with was the recipe for Cook's famous cherry tarts."

Cook gave me a conspiratorial wink, which, I concluded, had more to do with her homemade desserts than the murder.

"The gruesome reality was that Aldrich Porter was stabbed repeatedly with a long-bladed dagger." I grabbed Cameron from the line, spun him around and plunged an imaginary weapon ten times into his back. "From the amount of blood on the wall, I'd say that the knife punctured his lungs and perhaps his heart. Though the attacker would have held him from behind, like this, it seems inevitable that Porter would have already known who was in the room with him, or at least caught a glance as the killer waited for him to bleed out."

There was some hushed murmuring so, like an attentive tour guide, I decided to move the party along. With a wave of my hand, we were back out in the corridor. I was tired of running a one-woman show and decided it was time for a bit of audience participation.

"Cook, how long have you been working here?" We came to a stop in a particularly gloomy stretch of hallway.

"Since the 1980s, can you believe it?" She let out a chuckle, her mucky hands finally at her side.

"More than half your life in fact – most of which has been spent serving the Porter family." I turned to her employers. "Cameron, I don't suppose you know the name of the woman whose food you grew up eating?"

He looked flustered and pulled absentmindedly at the cuff of one sleeve. "We've always referred to her as Cook."

"What about you, Beatrix? Could you hazard a guess?"

"Oh, fun. Hmmm… Dolores?" She didn't seem concerned by her ignorance. "I think she looks like a Dolores."

I set her straight. "No, her name is Brenda. And she did not kill your father."

"Hey, why does Brenda get off so lightly?" Edmund was being a brat again.

"Because she had no motive, no interest, and no time to kill anyone as she was too busy slaving in the kitchen. She and Gladwell are the only ones here who stand to lose out from the death and I'm certain she's not the killer."

He rolled his eyes and made a begrudging sigh of acceptance.

I turned back to the trusty domestic. "Actually, Cook, you can go if you prefer."

"Oh? Is that okay?" She looked surprised. "Only I've got a pie I have to pop in the oven. Otherwise there'll be nothing for lunch."

"Go for it." I stepped aside to let her pass.

"Thanks, dearie." A smile shaped her round cheeks. "Don't forget to tell me *who done it.*"

We watched as she toddled off towards the kitchen, her hands once more raised.

"You can go as well if you want, Gladwell, though I'm guessing you'd like to stick around till the finale."

I gave my assistant a cheerful nudge and turned my attention once more to the Porter children. "Unlike the cook, the butler and all of you, I haven't lived in this house for decades." I pointed down the corridor which seemed to stretch into infinity like a black hole. "I had to learn the layout to be able to get a sense of this strange labyrinthine estate. I had to memorise the floor plan and explore all the hidden corners."

I started walking as I spoke, headed after Cook towards the kitchen. "Audrey told me you all have secrets to keep, but your house conceals even more. In fact, it's two houses in one. There's the Vomeris Hall that visitors get to see and a network of hidden corridors and forgotten rooms which would once have been used by a multitude of workers from footmen to scullery maids. The staff have almost all gone but those unseen spaces remain."

We arrived at the first servants' staircase I had explored and I flung the door open to reveal the dusty cubby hole. "One of you has been making use of these stairways in order to put me off my task. The same person who launched a vase at me on my first day here, murdered poor

Geoffrey the pig and removed his head in order to scare me."

"Savages!" Gladwell still hadn't got over his porcine companion's death. "Geoff was a gentle-hearted innocent."

Audrey put her hand on her retainer's shoulder to comfort him. "Izzy, is this leading somewhere?"

"Yes. It's leading us to the stables." Cutting across the back patio, we soon made it out to the scene of Geoffrey's slaughter. "I've brought you here to show you that actions have consequences."

"It's only a bloody pig." Since I'd started the tour, Cameron had been even more uptight and aggressive than normal.

"Yes, that's exactly what it is." They were standing in a horseshoe formation as I continued with the sorry tale. "A dead pig covered in blood because of one of you. This is not a game we are playing. First your father then Geoffrey were murdered. Punishment is the only inevitable outcome."

This dramatic proclamation just sat there and I knew I'd made them think long and hard about the reality of the situation. I was feeling pretty proud of myself, until Edmund started laughing and ruined all the tension I'd worked so hard to build.

"Sorry Izzy. But that was way over the top." His flippant remark didn't faze me and I immediately started back towards the house.

Just like a group of tourists, certain members of the party lagged behind and I had to keep stopping to wave them on. Gladwell's sprightly energy had apparently deserted him and he was once more hobbling with Audrey's arm for support. It took a lifetime to get back to the ballroom and I was beginning to think that my attempt at injecting some drama into the proceedings was more trouble than it was worth.

Tut tut, Izzy. Poirot never has such problems.

Once inside, I stopped in front of Geoffrey's slowly festering head and turned to address them. "When I was a teenager, I played a game where you had to decide upon the murderer from a list of suspects. There were all sorts of clues at the scene of the crime but each one applied to various people. A fish hook, when a bunch of them were fishermen, a slice of bread, though several were gluten intolerant. By working through the clues, you could slowly rule out suspects until there was only one left.

192

"This weekend has felt like I was playing that game. I wasn't investigating a murder, so much as somebody's idea of one. But, as I read the clues and considered the motives, the process of elimination led me no closer to the truth."

I turned my focus to the four siblings who were present on the night of the crime. "This is a case filled with contradictions for a truly contradictory family. You all claim to love your father, but you couldn't wait to get away from him. You wanted to rebel and yet you were desperate for his love. You were his disciples and his victims. His fans and his foes. I thought that I could come here and charm, trick and steal what I needed to know from you, but he raised you to be so duplicitous that I very much doubt you can tell the truth from a lie anymore."

"Come on, Izzy." Edmund really wasn't doing me any favours. "Just get to the part where you tell us who killed him, would you?"

I paused, studied each one of them and started in on the task of tying the disparate threads of my enquiry together. "People always think the butler did it, but I'm afraid it's not so simple in this case." Sitting at the side of the room on a velvet-covered chair, Gladwell gave me a knowing look before I continued. "Let's go through some of the limited facts that I know for absolute certain. First, Audrey really was in Thailand at the time of the murder. I'm sorry that I felt the need to check, especially as you'd been the one to hire me, but it could have been a cover story to hide your guilt."

She was her normal, generous self. "That's all right, Izzy. I appreciate how thorough you've been."

"Second, just like Cook, Gladwell would gain very little from his master's death and, as far as I can tell, has always served your family devotedly. And third, there's one person that nobody seriously put forward as the killer, which, to my mind, makes her the perfect suspect. After all, it's hard to imagine Daisy raising her voice in anger, let alone a dagger."

"I didn't kill him," she protested, her tone as fragile as ever. "I already told you, I could never have hurt our father like that."

"That's right Daisy. You couldn't be the murderer because you loved him." I allowed my tone to grow more insistent, the volume to spike higher. "You loved him despite the fact that he dismissed you as weak. You loved him though he controlled your life right down to which men you date. You loved him, even though he divided you at birth from your real mother!"

Daisy's eyes darted to her brother and sisters, as if trying to work out who had spilled her secret. She looked more nervous than she had all weekend and I knew that my theory was correct.

"I'm right, aren't I? Your biological mother was a woman who worked at P&P. An intern or secretary, I imagine. Someone your father could impress, seduce and throw away like she was nothing. But you, he kept hold of."

"We all know this," Audrey came to stand in front of her sister, like she wanted to shield her from me. "You can't possibly consider it proof that Daisy is the killer."

"I don't," I snapped back. "I'm saying it's proof that you've been protecting her. Your father was unfaithful and brought home a baby which he told your mother to raise as her own. You've provided me with a long list of Aldrich Porter's sins but none of you thought to mention that?"

I directed my accusations at each member of the family in turn and not a sound came back. "Daisy was the one who found the body so you sought to shelter her. On the night he died, she'd finally had enough of being ignored and overlooked. She lost her temper in front of everyone and again you kept me in the dark. Dear little Daisy had every reason to kill her father which is why you systematically hid the evidence from me."

"But… I didn't even…" She was so distressed by the allegation, she couldn't finish her sentence.

Leave her alone. First you stopped her reading her book, now you're accusing her of murder when you know she didn't do it. Have a heart.

"Are you seriously saying you think Daisy is the murderer?" Beatrix was still unable to entertain the idea.

"No. I'm saying that my job hasn't been easy when even the best among you is implicated and every scrap of information you've fed me has been contradicted elsewhere."

I took a quick glance at the weekend's second corpse. "Daisy may be innocent, but Mr Porter is lying dead in the library so somebody must have killed him. Just like somebody murdered your pet pig, somebody cut his head off and placed it right here and somebody removed the dagger which killed your father and buried it in Geoffrey's skull."

I took two steps closer to them. "You've all lied, but only one of you was so desperate to hide your crimes that you fabricated a complex plot to keep the truth hidden." I swallowed hard and took a breath before finishing. "And now I know who it was."

Chapter Twenty-Five

Nobody spoke. Even Edmund's self-satisfied grin had disappeared. *We're almost there. Get 'em!*

In the hush that had fallen, I decided to take them back outside. There was only so much walking around I could put them through and I figured that the harsh afternoon sun might help me cast some light on the secrets that were about to be spilled. I sent Dean a quick text through my watch, then sat down at the head of the white, metal patio table.

My six remaining witnesses spaced themselves out on the matching chairs and waited for me to begin. I took in the scene, knowing that it would be my last opportunity. The roses growing at regular intervals up the façade of the house smelt particularly sweet that day and, on the wide lawn in front of me, someone had set up a game of croquet that would never be played.

"Like the rest of you, I never bought into the idea of Daisy as the culprit." I glanced at her and felt sorry for the girl who, on the surface at least, suffered her father's callous predisposition most deeply. "The worst thing I can say is that, even now, you are unable to throw off the shackles your dad placed upon you. If you still love your ex-fiancé, my advice would be to marry him as fast as you can. Otherwise you'll spend your life trying to live up to the ideals of a dead man who never gave a damn about you in the first place."

She seemed to relax for the first time that weekend, her shoulders sinking down casually into the chair. To be honest, it was a bit of a disappointment. Daisy as savage killer is just about the best twist I could have come up with, but it was not to be. Her older brother was sitting across the table from her so I turned to him next.

"And what about you, Cameron? A man of business; a man born to walk in the great Mr Porter's footsteps. It's a poorly kept secret that you are up to your neatly pressed collar in debt. Even your employees know it and you confirmed as much when I beat you by several scores in the bowling alley." I knew that would annoy him and enjoyed the snarling lip he sent my way in response.

"Hang on a second." It was Edmund interrupting once again. "Cameron is only the fifth of the seven suspects you're going through so he obviously isn't guilty. Why don't you skip ahead to reveal who the killer really is?"

"Why don't you be quiet?" I felt like punching him.

Go on, Izzy! Punch him!

I ignored Edmund – and my darker instincts – and returned to grilling Cameron. "As I so quickly learnt, you do not like to lose, but, with your father alive, no other outcome was possible. He saw you as a washout, a failure, a flop. And though you present yourself as the respectable brother, that couldn't be further from the truth, could it?"

"I have nothing to hide." He crossed his arms and turned away as if to prove the falseness of his statement.

"Oh, really? You've told me countless times of your brother's barbarity, of how only Edmund could have murdered your father, but you neglected to explain that you were the one who spurred him on to violence as a child. You were the one who convinced an innocent six-year-old to murder a defenceless creature for your entertainment. So why did you lie about it?"

His eyes jumped back to me. "That was just one moment. E has been a beast his whole life."

"Thanks very much, big brother."

"Edmund, be quiet." He kept breaking my rhythm with these petty comments. "What about you, Cameron? Are you really so free of blame? The way I hear it, Edmund's not the only one with a temper. You wish to be admired and yet the only power you possess is through fear and intimidation." I watched each word that I delivered ripple across him. "You're a thug, with none of your father's sophistication. You never lived up to his example which is why you never won his affection."

Cameron cast his gaze around the other members of the household. "Are we paying her to insult us? Where's the evidence? Where's the proof? Anyone can throw accusations around."

"How about covering up the fact that you were stealing from your father's company? How's that for a motive?" There was a sharp intake of breath from his little sister, but the others stayed silent as I kept on. "Your debts had got so bad that you resorted to theft. You present yourself as a whiter than white, upstanding member of the family but you're the one who has sunk the lowest." I screwed one hand into a ball and smashed it down on the table. It hurt. "You knew it wouldn't be long before your father found out. So, in your desperation, you could see no other option than to get rid of him for good."

"This is ridiculous." He turned from me to stare across the lawn.

"You said yourself that you were the last to speak to him on the night he was murdered. Admit it, the two of you argued over money and you went off in search of a weapon. Once everyone had retired for the night, you returned to the library, determined to punish your father for everything he'd put you through."

"Of course I didn't."

"You killed him because he wouldn't help you out of the hole you'd dug."

"No! It's not true." He was suddenly breathless. His eyes widened as he looked at me once more. "There's a world of difference between scrambling for money to provide for my family and murdering my own father."

My pulse was racing now, my nerves on fire.

I love this bit. Finish him off.

"So you admit that you stole from his company?"

"Fine, yes. But it was my money. If the old fool hadn't been such a scrooge I wouldn't have had to."

"You stole from your family then killed your dad to cover it up."

"I said, no!" As his denial echoed across the Vomeris estate, a flock of crows took to the sky. To the surprise of everyone there, the emotion got too much for Cameron and he started to cry. Huge teardrops formed in his eyes and he bowed his head over the table.

I had no sympathy for him and pressed on. "How many criminals are there in this family? Your father did nothing to stop a savage rapist, your brother has been defrauding the company and one of you is a murderer. But Cameron says he didn't do it. It wasn't Daisy and Audrey was a million miles away. Which means only Edmund and Beatrix remain."

I paused to look at them at the far end of the table. "The popular theory among you is that Edmund killed your father. Ever since I arrived here I've been told of his famous temper, but if anyone has shown true rage towards the man lying dead in his study it's you, Beatrix."

"Finally," she said taking great pleasure in her moment. "I've been looking forward to this."

"You should probably rein in that excitement. But then, you've always been the rebel of the family. You were the first to leave your father's protective umbrella; to detach yourself from your childhood home. And, when we talked of your upbringing, you were the one who showed your pain most deeply."

I took a deep breath before laying out the rest of the evidence. "You tried to convince me that the reservoir of hate you possessed for him was due to the way he dispatched your poor mother from the family. In reality, just like Cameron, you see your father's greatest sin as not sharing his cash around. You told me you were so desperate that you'd even imagined marrying one of the wealthy suitors he would have picked for you."

I could tell I wasn't getting through to her. The evidence I'd worked so hard to accumulate was just white noise to Beatrix, so I went on the attack. "But what if there was a simpler way to maintain your luxurious lifestyle without having to put up with some old fogey?"

I paused to let her respond but then thought better of it. "You used to be a showjumper and we all know what they do with horses that get too old to ride. You couldn't put your dad out to pasture so you figured the abattoir was the best place for him."

She did not seem troubled by my suggestion. "If only I'd thought of that ten years ago. It would have made all our lives so much sweeter. Even if they'd caught me, I'd be out of jail by now. I'm sure I could convince any judge that our cruel father drove me to it."

I smiled at her response. "You may still have to. After all, you're the only one in the family with a flair for the dramatic?"

I'd touched a nerve and her whole body stiffened. "What's that supposed to mean?"

"It wasn't just horse riding you excelled at as a child. You had a love of the stage too."

She was clearly no longer comfortable with my line of questioning. "What's that got to do with anything?"

"Oh, just a feeling I had. I saw the photo of you in a play on the wall of my room and the headshots you had done. It made me wonder what could have been."

"What have my afterschool activities got to do with any of this?" Having felt that I'd won her over in the last couple of days, the superior tone was back in her voice and she looked at me like I was dirt.

"You tell me." I held her icy stare. "You dreamed of having your name in lights, didn't you? As a failed actress you'll surely have noticed the theatricality to everything that has gone on? Not just in the way your father was murdered – nor the scene of the crime, scattered with classic crime-fiction paraphernalia. Think about what's been happening over the last 48 hours. The message written in blood, the inexplicably reappearing murder weapon and poor Geoffrey's head mounted on the ballroom mantelpiece. They're hardly everyday occurrences."

I scraped back my chair from the table and the metal legs made a teeth-jangling screech. "Since I arrived at Vomeris, I've felt like an extra in an episode of Poirot. Or at least, that's what the killer wanted me to think." I stood up from my seat and, one careful step at a time, made my way over to her. "Audrey is all business, Cameron is more of a military history man, Daisy is into romances and I very much doubt that Edmund has finished a book in his life."

Edmund caught my eye, but it wasn't his turn. I was standing right beside my prey, for once happy that my height allowed me to tower over someone. She squirmed in her seat, and I wondered if she knew exactly what I was about to say. "And yet you, Beatrix, 'love a good murder.'" I lobbed her words back at her like a hand grenade. "Whoever organised this dramatic extravaganza has done their homework. They knew the tropes of a good country house mystery and delivered them in spades – all to distract from a simple fact."

She screwed her fists together tighter. "I don't know what you're talking about."

I didn't let up. "Beatrix the wild child, the vamp, the drama queen. I was warned about you before I came here but even I was taken in by the magnitude of your personality. Sadly for you, the one person who mattered most never fell for your charm."

There was a free chair beside her so I sat down to look her in the eyes. "Was that why you killed your father? Because he couldn't give you the love you so desperately needed?" I paused to put my thoughts together. "No. I don't think so. It was nothing so complicated, was it, Beatrix? The reason Aldrich Porter became a body in the library is because he had the money and he wouldn't give you any."

The sounds of the garden suddenly came into focus. The starlings chattering in the distance and the leaves of the willow rustling in the breeze had previously been melded together as background noise but now emerged as individual sounds. I thought that Beatrix would break through it all to deny my accusation but instead she reached into the pocket of her jeans and pulled out a box of cigarettes. Without taking her eyes off me, she lit one and inhaled deeply. She was clever and wouldn't say a word to incriminate herself.

"Okay. Now I'm the one lying." I cracked the quiet that had fallen and every last one of them could breathe again. "A passion for detective fiction does not make you a killer – as I hope I prove. But everything else I said was true.

"Somebody staged this weekend for my benefit, except it wasn't Beatrix. Even before Mr Porter was murdered, the killer had planned exactly what would unfold and how the killing should be presented. Which means they knew I would be sent for and that I couldn't resist coming to investigate. So whose idea was it to call me?"

The five siblings glanced around at one another. They were no longer a team and their familial bond suddenly seemed irrelevant.

Presumably happy to be in the clear, Daisy was the first to reply. "It was Audrey."

And I was quick to correct her. "No, Audrey had my number and called me, but who gave her the idea in the first place?"

We turned to the eldest daughter and, with a heavy heart, she opened her mouth to speak. "I... I don't think this proves anything, but Edmund was the one who originally suggested calling."

Edmund threw his hands in the air and shook his head. It was the classic defence of a hard-done-by youngest son. "I meant it as a joke and you all took it seriously."

I turned to face him. "You were the one who brought about my coming here and it only makes sense that you planned much more. You told me how you'd seen the article about me in the Croydon Advertiser."

He was uncowed and jutted his jaw out in response. "I thought it was the Herald?"

"You're no great fan of crime fiction, but everyone has watched murder mysteries on the telly. It wasn't hard to plant a few props at the scene of the crime, or return to the body to sculpt the tableau which you made sure poor Daisy discovered the next morning."

"Oh, yeah, that's exactly what happened." His sarcasm reached new heights of disdain.

"We know you argued with your dad on the night of the murder. You wanted me to believe that it was for Cameron's sake you were trying to free up your inheritance and that you didn't mind one bit that your girlfriend had left you or that your swanky flat in Kensington would have new tenants. Sorry to be a cynic, but I don't take you for the altruistic type."

He jumped to his feet, but Cameron was too quick. The older brother grabbed Edmund by the arms to hold him in place. I couldn't resist the urge to walk round the table and look at him face-to-face one last time.

"You tried to charm and befriend me – to win me round. You even came to my room in the middle of the night to see if that would do any good, no doubt taking the opportunity to rifle through my possessions in case I'd found anything that could implicate you."

"You're wrong, Izzy." He struggled to pull free but Cameron was taller, heavier and evidently stronger than him. "You said it yourself, I'm the black sheep of the family, the obvious culprit, why would I have killed Dad if I knew everyone would suspect me?"

I'd thought about this a lot and had my answer prepared. "It's the perfect double bluff. You're so obvious no one would ever believe you'd done it."

"That's insane!"

I'm kind of with him on that one, Iz.

"What's insane is that you'd think you could get away with it. You have a history of violence, you-"

He didn't let me finish and was wriggling like a sardine to be free. "History of violence? I killed one rabbit!"

I was getting under his skin and knew it wouldn't take much to provoke the reaction I needed. "You threatened members of your family."

"What are you on about? I've never laid a hand on anyone in my life."

"Nice try." I didn't dare blink for fear of missing the right moment. "Audrey told me what happened when she cut off the money she'd been giving you."

His gaze flew to his sister like a dart and she pulled her chair back from him instinctively. "What have you been saying, Audrey? Tell them I didn't touch you."

"Why would anyone believe you?" Cameron put in. "I knew it was you from the beginning."

Beatrix was up from her chair, perhaps still hoping she could protect her favourite sibling. Daisy was the only one who didn't react. She sat perfectly still, as if bracing herself for an explosion.

I still had evidence to lay out. "You killed your father and tried to confuse the picture by redesigning the murder scene in the style of an old mystery. When it was clear that I was getting close to the truth, you tried to scare me off. I'm not easily frightened though and when your games and threats came to nothing you made a fatal mistake. Cameron saw you leave the murder weapon in the ballroom."

"Izzy, it's not true." His voice was broken, his face twisted in horror. "You have to believe me, I'm being set up."

I took a step closer. "So you're saying that Cameron was lying? You're saying you didn't plant the dagger that killed your father in the ballroom?"

"That's exactly what I'm saying."

I smiled mockingly. "So, Cameron was lying and you were, what? Reading a mystery novel in the smoking parlour all morning?"

He turned to look at his brother, the act over, the terror on his face wiped clean. "Yes, I was reading an excellent Agatha Christie novel in the smoking parlour with a video camera trained on me at the exact moment that Cameron says he saw me in the ballroom."

All eyes turned to Cameron. "You can't have… That's not fair."

A momentary silence followed but, this time, they knew it was no act.

"How dare you try to shift the blame on to one of us?" Beatrix looked like she wanted to murder him herself. "You rat."

I had more to say and kept my focus on Cameron. "If it hadn't been for the bizarre series of distractions you'd planned, I might never have suspected you."

Cameron released his grip on his brother. He peered around the faces of his loved ones but found no sympathy there. "You've got it wrong… I…" His eyes landed on his older sister as if she, more than anyone, could save him.

Audrey opened her mouth to speak but no words came.

I decided to give him one more opportunity to confess. "I suppose you were desperate but that's the problem with plotting the murder of a man who never left his own home, it's hard to make it look like an accident. All the dead pigs and red herrings in the world can't cover up what you've done."

"No…" was all he managed and I knew that he wouldn't give in.

Oddly, it was Gladwell who broke the impasse. Without a trace of his previous unsteadiness, he got up from his seat and walked over to the oldest son of the Porter family – the man who centuries before would have inherited all the wealth and grandeur he was about to be dispatched from.

"How could you have done that to Geoffrey?" Happy to at last claim justice for his piggy friend, Gladwell seized Cameron by the arm. "And your father too, for that matter."

Dean had called the police on my order and I could hear faint sirens on the far side of the house.

"Is it true, Cam?" Daisy asked, coming back to life.

"I've got nothing to say until I speak to a solicitor." Cameron had found his voice but lost all his fight. He barely looked like he had the energy to remain on his feet, as his no longer faithful servant pulled him towards the ballroom door.

The swindling, self-interested murderer peered back at us one last time, but there was nothing left to say. He hunched his shoulders, bowed his head and allowed himself to be taken away.

Chapter Twenty-Six

There was a lot of explaining to do.

As I finished going through the evidence to the remaining Porter children, fifteen police officers stormed the house. I will never forget the contrast between that moment and the light-hearted scenes we'd enjoyed in that exact spot the night before. When the wave of boys and girls in blue arrived on the patio, my hosts were sitting in stunned silence. None of them seemed sad to be losing Cameron to a lengthy prison sentence, no matter what they might have claimed.

Inevitably, Audrey was the first to engage with the two Detective Inspectors who were running the case. But, soon after she started her account of the weekend, a rather distinguished senior officer appeared in her smart black uniform with shiny silver buttons.

"Izzy Palmer?" she asked when she spotted the person who looked most out of place there. "My name's Chief Superintendent Riley, I was a friend of Mr Porter's. I'd like a word somewhere quiet."

Without waiting for my reply, she turned back to the house and, accompanied by one of the uniformed constables, led the way inside. I suddenly knew how Cameron had felt when I'd put him to the sword. My heart was thundering, my hands all sweaty and I wasn't sure I'd be able to speak. I could only conclude they were about to cart me off to the station for interfering with a crime scene, tampering with evidence or impersonating someone who knew what she was doing.

Don't worry, Iz. If they send you down, I'll go with you!

But, when we arrived in the breakfast room, she didn't clap me in handcuffs as I'd imagined. With a sympathetic smile on her face she said, "You'd better explain what's been going on from the beginning."

She had a down-to-earth manner that made me want to tell her exactly what she needed to know and the whole story came pouring out of me.

"That's crazy," she concluded once I'd finished. "That is literally crazy."

The other officer looked similarly mind-blown as he took me back to my employers on the patio. Despite the gang of new visitors, the house suddenly felt grim and hollow. Beatrix and Daisy consoled one another and admonished Edmund for going along with the ruse I'd planned. I can't say that I hadn't enjoyed it and, in all honesty, he'd been a willing accomplice.

I'd had a sense for some time that he was being setup. While Edmund had never spilt the beans on his brother's misdeeds, Cameron had taken every opportunity that arose to incriminate him. Short of it being an overly elaborate double bluff, I realised that I could only get to the truth by trusting Edmund.

It's understandable that Cameron didn't cough up to it. It always strikes me as weird that, in practically every murder mystery, the killer admits their guilt as soon as the evidence is presented to them. Still, I had no doubt that, with the facts I'd already uncovered and the methods the police were yet to employ, it wouldn't take much to send him down for his crimes.

The one thing that surprised me was that Cameron had accepted his fate so meekly. Perhaps the pressure of hiding his guilt all that time had got too much for him; perhaps he was glad to be caught. There were no expectations left to fulfil, he could finally be the absolute failure that his father had marked him out as.

Audrey didn't let her emotion show but I caught hints of her relief bubbling beneath the surface as she rushed about, helping the police make sense of everything. For her, the most important thing was that her father's killer had been brought to justice and she was free from the shadow that his death had cast.

When the inspectors were finished with her, I asked if we could have a chat and snuck off to her office. The walk there reminded me of my first night at Vomeris Hall, when I'd traipsed behind her through the dark house, my mum's purple suitcase in tow. It amused me that there were still so many rooms I hadn't been in.

"There's something I never got round to asking you." I picked up a plate with a Thai sunset on it that was resting in front of a selection of business manuals. There was a small fiction collection near the bottom of the bookshelf, but only a few murder mysteries. "Why did your father name you alphabetically?"

She sat down at her desk and paused before answering. "One of daddy's little jokes I suppose." She peered out through the window.

"His middle name was Zachary. Aldrich Zachary Porter. Mum used to call him the A to Z man and he claimed he wanted to have a child for every letter of the alphabet. Audrey, Beatrix, Cameron, Daisy and Edmund but there would be no Fred or Francesca. He saw it as yet another failing on my mother's part."

"You guys make my family look normal."

She laughed and motioned for me to sit down in the chair in front of her. "The one positive thing you can say about my father's behaviour was that he never treated Daisy any differently from the rest of us. He gave her the same opportunities and it was the only time I remember him showing any regret for his actions. She wasn't the product of some long affair, but a drunken fumble after an office Christmas party."

I've said it before and I'll say it again: office Christmas parties are dangerous and should be banned.

Something changed in Audrey then and I could tell she was tired of talking about her father's mistakes. "I'm so glad it's all sorted." She sounded as if she was discussing a minor clerical error or a misdirected letter. "I set up your payment to go through automatically so it should be in your account by now."

"That's great." I got comfy in the high-backed leather chair. "Actually, I was meaning to talk to you about that. You see, I'm going to have to double my fee."

She was still smiling when she replied. "How do you mean?"

"We both know that Cameron didn't kill your father." I paused to make the moment last a little longer. "If you don't want me to tell the police who was really responsible, you're going to have to pay up."

"I've honestly got no idea what you're talking about." The way she was nervously scratching the edge of the desk suggested otherwise.

"Do you really expect me to go through all the evidence?" I was exhausted by this point, but let out a sigh and began. "There were so many things that told me you were involved, I just didn't want to believe them. You see, I like you Audrey. Even now, I think there's a lot of good in you."

Her warmth had suddenly disappeared and she busied herself tidying stray papers into a pile on her desk. "Perhaps you should leave."

"I told you earlier, whoever killed your father did their homework.

There was something perfect and methodical about the initial kill; clean even. And you were the only one in the family capable of planning something like that."

"I thought you said you had evidence, not mild hunches." Her voice was back to the business-like tone she had used with the police.

I ignored her response. "The first mistake that you made was to divert from the plan. I'm guessing that it all changed the night that I arrived. Edmund made a scene, shouting and complaining about my presence here, and you figured it was too good an opportunity to waste. Pinning the blame on your shiftless younger brother was a perfect fit."

She looked confused. "Well now you're contradicting yourself. Cameron is the one who's been taken away in a police car."

"Yes, Cameron is a thief, a liar and he needlessly murdered a perfectly friendly pig. He deserves to be where he is, but he didn't kill your father. You worked very hard to prove to me that Edmund was responsible and, perhaps, if you hadn't pushed Cameron to go to such lengths, I would have fallen for it."

"I have no time for this."

"You've spent your whole life trying to make your father happy but nothing was good enough for him." I studied her face for any brief microexpression that would give her away. "You were the only one who didn't leave him. You ran his business better than he could. You cared for him and this house and he called you his golden child, even had a photo of you right in the middle on his desk. But what good did that do when he wouldn't let you make decisions for yourself or be with the man you loved?"

She sat back in her chair, regarding me curiously as she had when we'd first met. I thought she was going to contradict me but she remained silent.

"Your father was not a good man. He said he never spoilt his children but there's more than one meaning to that word. He turned you against your mother and forced you to compete for his love. He controlled your lives from the moment you were born; the others rebelled, but not you. You studied the degree he chose for you, worked at the businesses he picked and went into the job he deemed to provide you with."

I didn't take a breath put pushed right through, carefully building the case against her. "I've no doubt that, as the years went by, you regretted your decision. Cooped up together, even in a palatial house, was poisonous and you came to despise him. You must know every sin he committed. Not just against your family but his employees too. Against David and Will and an intern called Pippa who came to the house one day to sell her silence. Did he make you his accomplice? Were you the one who sent the payment to keep her quiet?"

She offered no answers. She just shook her head, so I continued.

"The only way to put an end to his control – for you to be the head of the family that you'd acted as for so long – was to get rid of him entirely. He could have lived for another thirty years and you didn't want him telling you how to live your life for a single day longer. But how can you get away with killing a man who never took a step outdoors?"

"This is all very interesting." She spoke like she really meant it and I realised what a capable actress she was. "But, in case you've forgotten, I was in Thailand on the night of the murder."

I took my time before replying, looking around the cosy little room with its fireplace and thick curtains. "You're very good at getting people to do what you want, aren't you, Audrey? When you discovered that Cameron was stealing from the family, you thought that you could use it against him. Did he know you were behind the murder or did you convince him it was Edmund? He'd have done anything to hide his own crimes and probably didn't think twice about what you'd been up to."

"I was in Thailand," she repeated with a sudden snarl in her voice.

I took a pen from her desk and slowly began to dismantle it. "You're very good at winning people over, getting them on side. Ever since we met, I felt an intense connection to you. Like we could be best friends if you only had the time. Is that how you got Gladwell to murder him?"

"Oh, right. The butler did it?" She struggled to get the words out. "I thought you said I was good at this. Why would I have come up with such a clichéd plot?"

"That's just the thing! It's such a cliché that it rarely occurs in crime fiction. But you're the great Audrey Porter – expert researcher, world-class administrator – and with a tiny bit of effort, you would have known just that. You realised that I would never land on such a hackneyed solution which is why you called me here."

I could see her brain ticking over. A list of considerations was scrolling in her head; potential escape route, how to deal with the police, what excuse might persuade me I'd made a mistake.

I wouldn't let up. "You had the country house, so why not stage a murder? You thought you'd create a story that was so contradictory and confusing that there was no possible way it would lead back to you. At the very least, a couple of days of me poking around and muddying the forensics couldn't do you any harm, right?"

I cleared my throat loudly before continuing and followed it up with a rather unrealistic cough. "When I was a kid, I stayed at a grand house with my mother and saw how places like this really work. The staff can do what they like without anyone noticing and I think you banked on that with Gladwell. He had no motive to murder your father, had been a loyal servant for decades and would gain nothing from the death. You were the only person here who showed him any affection and he was putty in your hands.

"Just like you children with your father, Gladwell needed love and attention. He would have done anything for you, so you manipulated him. I bet you told him your secrets, detailing all of the terrible ways that the wicked Aldrich Porter had mistreated you. And before long he hated the odious man just as much as you did. But Gladwell wasn't the killer, he was the murder weapon."

"That's enough." Her words were severe and resolute. They extinguished all other sound in the room and shut down my argument. "You're right, I made him do it. I convinced him it was the only solution and he went through with it because he loves me. Leave Stephen out of this and you'll get your money."

Oops, too late.

I'd got one thing wrong about her. I'd imagined her as a heartless manipulator, but, in truth, she cared about Gladwell. I'd seen it that morning and failed to add it all up. He'd become the father that her real father never tried to be.

"You said it yourself," Her voice had become hoarse and I thought it might finally break. "Daddy was an evil man, so I got rid of him. He picked me as his favourite but that didn't mean he loved me. I was just his bargaining chip. From the time I was sixteen, he sent me out to charm clients like a cheap escort and he knew exactly what he was doing. That's why he cancelled my wedding. I was worth more to him single and available than married and happy."

She tugged at her perfect, glossy hair as she spoke. "The only reason he had my photo on his desk was because he saw me as the culmination of *his* achievements. He put down my success to his scheming rather than my talent. He was a monster and the world is a better place without him."

"You're only telling half the story," I shouted back at her. "By making it look like Edmund was the killer, you were just as judgemental and cruel-minded as your dad had been. You didn't care in the slightest that your idle, little brother would be collateral damage in your scheme. Or was that your plan from the beginning? To throw the blame onto him?"

"No, you're wrong." Her words were definite once more, like she'd taken her time to sculpt exactly how they should sound. "I never wanted to involve Edmund. It was Cameron's doing. He was desperate and came to me for help. I admit that I thought he would lead the police even further from me, but I didn't want any of my siblings to go to jail."

Her fear showing, her pace increased. "Trust Cameron to stuff everything up. I should have known not to involve him. I only suggested that he do something to divert attention from his theft but he went rogue. Killing Geoffrey and taking the murder weapon was all him."

Every word she spoke incriminated her more. "You're lying; you've been lying since I got here. Gladwell fed me information on Edmund at your request. You both said that Edmund was violent towards you, except it's not true. Edmund is a lot of things but, to my great surprise, he's no liar. He's loyal. He could have told me about the money Cameron stole or the truth about Daisy's mother but he kept everyone's secrets."

I could see her brain working at a thousand miles an hour to find an explanation and, when that failed, she shouted, "Half a million!"

Yes! Take the money! We really could go on the Orient Express with that much.

"Sorry, Audrey." I took my time, standing up from the desk before delivering my final judgement. "It's over."

On cue, she caught sight of something through the window and her composure crumbled entirely. "No, this isn't right." Panic racked her voice as officers pushed Gladwell into a police car in full view of where we were sitting – just as I'd asked them to. "Stephen doesn't deserve this. He's a good man. I'll admit what I did, just tell them you were wrong about him."

She must have known that what she was saying didn't make sense and collapsed back into her seat.

"You said it yourself, you were in Thailand, Audrey." I cleared my throat for a second time. "You couldn't have killed him on your own."

"Fine, I'll say that Cameron did it. God knows there's enough evidence."

The door swung open and Chief Inspector Riley entered. "I think it's a bit late for that," she said and pointed up at the corner of the room where a small black camera was just about visible on the top of the bookshelf.

Audrey was enraged. Her muscles flinched and her head twitched about wildly, but she wasn't giving up. "This is entrapment. None of this will hold up in court."

"No one forced you to kill your dad," I told her, dismissing another of her arguments.

"I didn't know that I was being filmed. It's inadmissible."

"Common misconception, I'm afraid," Riley explained as she took out a pair of handcuffs and pulled her up to standing. "Audrey Porter, You are under arrest on suspicion of conspiracy to murder."

As the Chief read the suspect her rights, I was hoping to think up a pithy comment to mark the moment, only nothing came to mind. Audrey's eyes flicked about the room desperately. But, just like her brother an hour before, she sensed that the game was over and the energy drained out of her.

Without a trace of resistance, she was escorted from her study, along the corridor and out of the main entrance to a waiting car. It was a sad sight to see such a brilliant person throwing everything away. She was a killer but I understood her desperation. Aldrich Porter had shaped every detail of her life and was as much to blame for the murder as she was. A quote I'd learned at university popped into my head.

"The sins of the father are to be laid upon the children" - *Shakespeare, fancy.*

I stood silently in the front garden with the Chief Inspector and watched the car drive away.

Ooh. Why don't you say, 'There'll be no butlers where she's going'?

Nah, the moment's passed. And besides, there will be a butler where she's going. They're both off to jail.

Chapter Twenty-Seven

The neon lights were blinding but I pressed on with my explanation. "The big thing was that Cameron and Gladwell had both told lies about you and I knew that the only person who could be pulling their strings was Audrey. I thought that someone was doing all that stuff just to scare me off but, when I realised the murder weapon was missing, it was clear that they'd taken it to shift the guilt. As soon as it reappeared I knew who was being implicated and who was lying."

We were at the 'Vomeris Hall Murder' wrap party that Dean had organised and I was the guest of honour. To be honest it was the last place I wanted to be. I'd much rather have stayed at home with a jug full of margarita mix and 'World's Stupidest Parking Attendants' on TV.

Everyone was there. Not just the tech squad and our gang of amateur sleuths but Danny, Ramesh, Will, two of my dads and, perhaps most surprisingly, Edmund Porter. "Sorry, Izzy, but I still don't understand how you worked it out. I mean, what told you for sure that it was Gladwell?"

We were in Fridaze Lounge Bar in South Croydon but the DJ had turned the music down so that everyone could hear me. It was not my natural milieu.

"Urmmm." I was trying to remember. "The vacuum cleaner was probably what did it."

Edmund stared back confused. Everyone else stayed quiet, hoping to glean some insight into my brilliant mind. "How do you mean?"

"Well, the area around the body was spotless, there weren't even any breakfast crumbs, but the rest of the room had a clear layer of dust all over the surface. And if someone had cleaned up the murder scene, why were there clues strewn about?"

"But how did that tell you who the killer was?"

I hesitated before answering. I didn't want to make him look like a total idiot in front of everyone. "Because no one else in the house knew where the vacuum cleaners were kept, let alone how to use one. The murder weapon was really shiny too. Sorry, but you Porters weren't bred for domestic duties."

I got a laugh from Fernando and a couple of Dean's geeks at that. His assistant Emilia was a few drinks in and bawdily declared, "I'll come round and vacuum your carpets, Edmund. If you know what I mean."

I continued to lay out the case. "There were other things too. Gladwell was wearing crisp new clothes when I arrived for the weekend. I knew he could have had multiple uniforms but everything about it was immaculate and it made me wonder whether he'd got rid of his regular one. The tea in Mr Porter's cup hadn't been drunk which suggested he was killed shortly after it arrived and something about the way he was murdered never sat right with me. I was pretty sure that, if one of his kids had done it, they'd have wanted to look him in the eyes as the blade went in."

"Personally, I never thought Gladwell had it in him." Ramesh still wasn't happy with me but couldn't resist a party.

"I did," my mother was quick to shout out. "I said it from the beginning. I just knew the butler did it."

She would never let me forget this, so I ignored her. "Gladwell played the part of the frail, old duffer but, as I proved when I faked my injury in the loft, he's as strong as anyone. He'd been in the army and clearly worked hard to maintain his fitness. His stiff leg didn't stop him picking up Porter's body and suspending it from the wall.

"It was only when I realised that Audrey was involved that Gladwell's role in the murder was confirmed. Though her siblings were fond of their big sister, none of them were exactly close to her. The only person who she'd trust to plot a murder with was the man who'd been there for her through thick and thin. No one else paid any attention to the staff at Vomeris, but, to Audrey, they were part of the family."

I was warming to my role as party entertainer. "When Cameron gave himself away, and I knew that he was the one who had plotted all those amateurish distractions, there were only two explanations. Either he was the killer or someone had put him up to it to throw me off the trail. Well, Audrey was the one with power over both Cameron and Gladwell, so the pieces clicked together. I took a gamble outing Cameron as the killer, but it was the only way I could think of getting Audrey to let her guard down."

"What about the subterfuge with the police at the end? Where did that come from?" Dean was a different person. Smiling brightly, the only nerves he showed were the regular glances at his phone to see whether Samantha had messaged him. He was very much looking forward to introducing me to his girlfriend.

My adoring audience beamed up at me – did I mention that I was standing in the DJ booth, speaking into a microphone?

"I knew Audrey would never confess outright, so I helped her along. I hadn't imagined that Gladwell's freedom would hold such sway over her though. I thought she'd have agreed to pay my inflated salary and that would have been enough to convict her. I was surprised that the Chief Inspector went along with my scheme, but I promised her a confession and she trusted me."

There were some coos of appreciation as I came to the end of my presentation. Both Danny and Edmund were looking at me like I was the hottest thing on two legs since sliced bread was fused onto Jenifer Lopez's perfect body (which never actually happened.)

My dream boy Danny held his hand out to help me down from the pedestal I was on, as DJ Coolpants cued up 'Lady in Red'.

"Listen, Izzy. I really need to talk to you." There was something almost shy about the way he spoke to me then and I realised that the last few months were the longest time we'd gone without speaking to one another since we were kids. In his tight, black V-neck t-shirt, he looked like a chocolate that I wanted to unwrap. "I should never have blamed you for what happened. It was childish of me and I have to tell you that-"

"Izzy Palmer, get back up here!" I had never imagined seeing Dean Shipman from Bromley on a stage at a party addressing the crowd - unless it was to tell everyone he'd planted a bomb. "I've planned an extra little surprise." He grabbed me by the arm and pulled me away from Danny, up the steps and onto the platform. "Look over there."

I turned around to see a video projection on the far wall. Two men and a woman were grinning back at me from a bare, white room. No doubt one of Dean's micro cameras was capturing the party for their entertainment.

"Hello, Izzy," the woman on the left of the image said. It was my old buddy D.I. Irons of the metropolitan police. I hadn't seen her since I'd solved Bob's murder. "Your friend Dean called to tell me what you've accomplished. So fixing up a phone call was the least we could do."

"That's right, Miss Palmer." Her partner, D.I. Brabazon was unusually cheerful. "We're terribly grateful for all the help you've given us."

"We'd never have caught this fella if it weren't for you and now you've solved another murder!" The three of them chortled at D.I. Irons' comment before the remaining member of the trio took his turn.

"Hi, Iz." My boyfriend David was there on the wall for all to see. "I just wanted to tell you how proud I am. It sounds like you've done an incredible job."

"It's Izzy's boyfriend, everybody," Mum explained to the audience. "Coming to us directly from Her Majesty's Prison High Down where he's awaiting trial for murder."

"Mum!" I screwed my face in her direction.

"I *am* sorry, darling." She looked guilty and quickly followed it up with, "Izzy was the one who cracked the case and helped put him inside."

Ramesh joined me on the stage to grab the mic from Dean. "Iz, don't you have anything you'd like to say?"

All eyes were on me as I struggled to think how a person is supposed to respond in such circumstances. "Urmmm... It's lovely to see you, David."

Not bad. I'd have gone with, 'Say hello to Gladwell for me.'

"I just hope I'll be back with you very soon to celebrate your success." David smiled his perfect smile and my stomach lurched the tiniest bit from missing him.

"You'll be lucky," Irons quipped and all three of them fell about in hysterics. "His court date has been set for the first of October!"

As their laughter continued, the revelation hit me right in the gut. I'd known that David's case would have to come up before long, but finding out with everyone there was torture. It made me want to jump from the stage and bolt for the exit.

"I've got an announcement to make too," Dean said, then unsentimentally cut the video feed. "Since I met Izzy, my life has changed for the better. If it weren't for her I wouldn't be here tonight, about to introduce you all to my girlfriend... If she ever turns up that is."

Dean's posse of tech-nerds let out a coordinated, "Woo woo woo!"

"But, seriously, we're here to celebrate this brilliant person standing next to me. So raise a glass – drinks are on me until eleven – to my mate Izzy."

"To Izzy!" my friends, loved ones and assorted acquaintances shouted back and I knew I had to get out of there.

I stepped off the stage hoping to be swallowed up by the crowd but I was a head taller than most people and stuck out even worse. I didn't want to be celebrated or toasted. A party was the last thing I needed so I made a beeline for the door.

Danny gently caught hold of my arm. "Izzy, I really need to finish our conversation."

"Sorry, Danny," I told him, suddenly fighting for breath. "I honestly want to talk to you but I can't right now." I searched for an explanation but nothing came. "I just can't."

I hated seeing him look so hurt but it was all too much. I pushed my way out to the street and allowed the marginally fresher air of South End Village to fill my lungs. The heatwave was almost over, the clouds were that unique shade of grey that I'm pretty sure only exists in the UK and I could feel a storm coming on. All around me, the neon lights of vaping shops, dog-grooming parlours and nail bars fought for my attention with takeaway chicken and kebab signs. I thought for a moment that it'd be a nice idea to faint.

"Are you all right, Izzy?" I hadn't heard Edmund come out after me but there he was, just as handsome as ever, even in the dim glow of South Croydon.

"Yeah, I'm ticketyboo."

He laughed and moved closer. "I think people were expecting you to make a speech or something. You disappeared."

"Oh, whoops."

He retained the more mature, reflective persona that I'd caught glimpses of on our last day together. "Hey, it's your party, you can cry if you want to, but I want to say thank you in person."

"Thank you for sending half of your family to jail?"

"No. Thank you for making sure I didn't end up there." His smug grin was nowhere to be seen and he looked uncharacteristically serious. "I underestimated you, we all did."

"Yeah," I said. "People do that a lot."

There was a brief silence between us as a red double-decker bus growled towards the centre of Croydon and we looked straight at one another.

"Listen, Iz." The road cleared and the moment passed. "I've got to meet some friends up in town." If he'd invited me then, I'd probably have said yes. "But you should call me sometime. I have a feeling we could have a lot of fun together."

I was short on words again. "Yeah. That sounds... fun."

He winked at me and walked out to the road for a sleek black Audi to come to a gliding halt like he'd cast a spell over it. He opened the rear door and vanished behind its tinted window. The car drove off and I was alone – for about seven seconds.

"Izzy!" I could tell that something was wrong even before Dean made it out to me. "It's over, Izzy. It's all over." He was back to his usual adenoidal tone of voice.

"Dean, calm down." It made me feel better to be dealing with someone else's problems instead of my own. "Just breathe and tell me what the matter is."

"It's Samantha." I'd kind of guessed this much. "We were so happy together. I don't understand what went wrong."

Tears were hurtling from his eyes to a splashy fate on the pavement. I put a hand on his shoulder to comfort him. "Whatever's happened, Dean, it's going to be all right."

"She's left me, Izzy. Gone back to her ex who works in a Texaco garage on the A217. She said I was out of her league and we could never be together."

I made some sympathetic noises and then asked, "Wait, you're out of *her* league? Are you sure she knows what that expression means."

He was really sobbing now. "She said that she always feels inferior to me because I'm so chirpy and positive about everything. With Nigel – that's the bloke from the garage – she says at least she's not the loser in the relationship."

I was struggling to get my head round this. "Oh, that's terrible."

"You and Ramesh did too good a job. I've priced myself out of the market." He put his head on my shoulder – well, more like lower chest as he's pretty short – and had a good cry.

I managed to console him and after a chat, another brief sob and the consumption of half a packet of tissues, his tears finally dried. I was about to take him back to the party when I noticed through the window that my mum was leading Danny, Will, DJ Coolpants and our neighbour from West Wickham in a conga line and I knew it wasn't the place for me.

"Actually, Dean. Do you mind if I don't go back in?" I braved a glance through the cracked open door. "It's just that, I think Mum deserves a night to let her hair down and I'd probably only dampen the mood."

He paused with his hand on the door and looked up at me. "You do you, Izzy." He breathed in and back out again heroically. "You do you." He gave me one last conflicted smile and headed into the bar.

I started walking to the bus stop and, before I even got there, Ramesh had texted me.

Classy move skipping out of your own party, Iz. Re-spect.

Thanks, Ra.

I've decided that I can forgive you for leaving me behind at P&P on one condition.

What's that?

You have to promise to take me on your next adventure.

Done. Anything else?

Nothing.

Unless you fancy trying the new German place in Purley this weekend. I have a hankering for currywurst.

Goodnight, Ramesh.

My phone disappeared back into my bag just as the 312 pulled up. I tapped my card, mumbled to the driver and climbed to the top deck of the bus. As soon as I sat down, all the confusion that had been swimming around my head ten minutes earlier returned. I didn't know who I was or what I was going to do with my life. The man I loved was in prison, the man who loved me would most likely be living in our spare bedroom for the foreseeable future and I felt like I hadn't slept in about six centuries.

Calm down, Izzy. We've just made a cool hundred grand. Let's blow it on hookers and hot chocolate.

No.

Then why not use it to set up a business. Personally, I thought that 'The Clever Dick Detective Agency' was a brilliant name.

Hmmm, maybe.

Thumping music danced through one window and out the other as the bus shuttled past The Swan and Sugarloaf. I couldn't deny that "Private Detective Izzy Palmer" had a nice ring to it. And it wasn't as if I had any other great career prospects lined up, but there was still something holding me back. As much as I'd got a kick out of the cases I'd investigated and still dreamed of treading the path that my literary heroes had beaten, something about the idea didn't feel quite right.

Is it because, if we go along with Mum's plan, she'll take all the credit and we'll never hear the end of it?

That's it! Got it in one!

Get your **Free** Izzy Palmer Novellas...

If you'd like to hear about forthcoming releases and download my free novellas, sign up to the Izzy Palmer readers' club via my website. I'll never spam you or inundate you with stuff you're not interested in, but I'd love to keep in contact. There will be one free novella for every novel I release, so sign up at...

www.benedictbrown.net

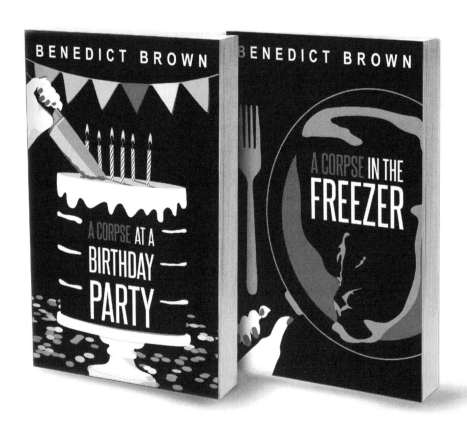

Get the next **Izzy Palmer Mystery**
from June 28th at **amazon**

**Pristine beaches, Spanish sunshine
and murder by the bucketful.**

About This Book

When I started this series, I knew that Izzy would head to the country before long. I wanted to write this book as a homage to the country house mysteries which I grew up reading, but also as a thank you to Karen Baugh Menuhin, the bestselling writer who put me onto the power of indie publishing. If you like period mysteries in a Christie-esque style, you must search out her books.

Vomeris Hall isn't a real place but was inspired by many houses I've visited. Mum took us to a million stately homes when I was a kid and it's become a tradition to visit one with my wife on our wedding anniversary. Last year we stayed in the Royal Berkshire Hotel near Ascot then drove through the picturesque villages of Surrey in southern England. This is where the seeds of **"A Corpse in the Country"** came from and, in particular, I used Wotton House in Dorking as inspiration for the grand estate which Izzy gets to explore.

Her next adventure, **"A Corpse on the Beach"**, will be out in time for summer. Hopefully we will all be free from confinement by then, as, so far, the book has been written in lockdown. It has been a strange period for my family and the future can look rather scary. It has always been my dream to work as a full-time writer and – through these unexpected circumstances – that is now my situation. So, I hope you'll stick with me and my books to find out what happens next. Make sure you sign up to the **readers' club** on my website where you'll be able to access the free novellas and stay up to date with new releases.

Acknowledgements

Before I go, I should probably say sorry and thank you. Hmmm, who should I apologise to? Let's go with, the British upper classes for Ramesh's comment that you dabble in the occult to maintain your wealth. I have seen no evidence to back up such claims and I hope there are no hard feelings. Oh, and youngest children, sorry to all of you. I am one and I know how hard it can be – poor Edmund!

Thank you as always to my wife and daughter for your constant love and support, and for designing my beautiful covers, to my wider family for reading my books and my crack team of experts – the Hoggs and the Donovans (**fiction**), Paul Bickley (**policing**), Karen and Jonathan Baugh (**marketing**) and Mar Pérez (**dead people**) for knowing lots of stuff when I don't.

I will never stop being grateful to my friend Lucy Middlemass. We spent years talking about our writing and reading each other's work. It got to a stage where every funny thing I wrote was to make my friend laugh. I like to think there's a lot of Lucy in my detective and wish every day that she was still here to enjoy Izzy's ridiculous tales.

The biggest thank you though, has to go to my readers who have been incredible since **"A Corpse Called Bob"** was released. I have received so many wonderful comments and spoken to lovely people from all over the world. If you have the time, **please write a review** on Amazon. Most books get one review per thousand readers so I would be infinitely appreciative if you could help me out.

About Me

Writing has always been my passion. It was my favourite half-an-hour a week at primary school, and I started on my first, truly abysmal book as a teenager. So it wasn't a difficult decision to study literature at university which led to a masters in Creative Writing.

I'm a Welsh-Irish-Englishman originally from **South London** but now living with my French-Spanish wife and presumably quite confused infant daughter in **Burgos**, a beautiful medieval city in the north of Spain. I write overlooking the Castilian countryside, trying not to be distracted by the vultures, hawks and red kites that fly past my window each day.

I previously spent years focussing on kids' books and wrote everything from fairy tales to environmental dystopian fantasies right through to issue-based teen fiction. My book "**The Princess and The Peach**" was long-listed for the Chicken House prize in The Times and an American producer even talked about adapting it into a film. I'll be slowly publishing those books over the next year on Amazon.

"**A Corpse in the Country**" is my second full length novel for adults in what I'm confident will be a long series. If you feel like telling me what you think about Izzy, my writing or the world at large, I'd love to hear from you, so feel free to get in touch via...

www.benedictbrown.net

Printed in Great Britain
by Amazon

79774305R00130